From the Undertime to Paratime, All Heard the Trumpets of the Temporal Guard.

It was our first indoctrination lecture. We were addressed by a small man in the black singlesuit of the Guard.

"First and foremost, the Guard relies on voluntary subjection to absolute discipline. It's a small organization with a big job. We don't have the personnel to coddle discipline problems. Minor offenses merit special work assignments or dismissal. Major offenses normally result in a sentence to Hell and dismissal. High Crimes lead to a sentence on Hell and a chronobotomy."

I understood everything but the last term. Most of us must have worn the same puzzled expression because he stopped and explained.

"Chronobotomy . . . that's a condensation of a medical term. Means surgical removal of all time-diving abilities. Sometimes limited planet-sliding talent remains, but that depends on the individual."

At that point the room seemed a lot colder.

L.E. Modesitt Jr.

THE FIRES
OF PARATIME

A TIMESCAPE BOOK
PUBLISHED BY POCKET BOOKS NEW YORK

This novel is a work of fiction. Names, characters, places and incidents are either the product of the author's imagination or are used fictitiously. Any resemblance to actual events or locales or persons, living or dead, is entirely coincidental.

Another *Original* publication of TIMESCAPE BOOKS

A Timescape Book published by
POCKET BOOKS, a Simon & Schuster division of
GULF & WESTERN CORPORATION
1230 Avenue of the Americas, New York, N.Y. 10020

ISBN: 0-671-45033-6

First Timescape Books printing November, 1982

10 9 8 7 6 5 4 3 2 1

POCKET and colophon are registered trademarks
of Simon & Schuster.

Use of the trademark TIMESCAPE is by exclusive license
from Gregory Benford, the trademark owner.

Printed in the U.S.A.

*For Christina,
in time and in fire*

THE FIRES
OF PARATIME

I

Picture a man, or, if you will, a woman, standing in an empty room, a plain hall lit by slow-glass panels and green glowstone floors.

The person standing there wears a black jumpsuit with a four-pointed star on the left collar and wide silvered wristbands. The bands contain microcircuitry.

Suddenly, the man, or, if you will, woman, is gone.

The slow-glass panels still light the hall.

Some time later—a few units, a few days, rarely longer —the traveler reappears in the same spot and walks out of the hall.

That is all there is to it, the base action of the Temporal Guard at Quest, the single city of the Immortals of Query, that hidden planet circling a very ordinary yellow sun in a very ordinary galaxy.

There's no such thing as a race of time-divers, you say, Immortals who ride the paths of time a million years or more, who manipulate cultures in their corner of the galaxy?

Let us lay that question aside for a time.

III

Call me Loki. It's as good a name as any, better than most, and besides, that's what my parents named me.

What better name for the grandson of Ragnorak, for the child of fallen heroes, fumbler in the complex intrigues of the Immortals, sometime god, time-diver, and idiot savant par excellence?

The dominoes of time have toppled, shoved into new patterns by the winds of change, those chill winds that howl down the corridors of time, those black rays of time-path tossed carelessly out by each sun and vaulted and trod by the time-divers of Query in their ceaseless efforts to maintain their precarious position on the top of time's totem pole.

A too-florid description, perhaps, but accurate for all the verbosity.

I am serious. Queryans are Immortal, but nature balanced it nicely since the genetic interlock required for fertilization and the time-diving ability kept births low— less than one per couple per millennium. And accidents did happen, time-diving ability or not.

Queryan time-divers ranged through time, and since time is space, so to speak, through space as well. As a precaution, all children were locator-tagged at birth, although the talent didn't usually develop until later, nor fully until puberty.

Only a few of us had innate navigational senses, and most Queryans never went far from Query. Back-timing on Query itself is out. The Laws of Time are inflexible. If you dive at all on Query, you dive planet-clear.

It all starts with the Test.

The Test, that trial that determines whether a Queryan gets advanced training, membership in the Temporal Guard, or whether he or she stays a planet-slider for a long, long life—that was my first turning point. . . .

On that morning that may never have been, the sky of Query was blue, with overtones of green that made the hills circling the city of Quest and the peaks behind those hills stand out in even sharper relief than the clearest holo could project.

The morning was cloudless, as so many mornings in Quest are. I had place-slid to the park surrounding the Square, breaking out of the undertime with the thought-chill that always ends a planet-slide or time-dive.

The Tower of Immortals stands in the center of the Square, surrounded solely by grass and the low fireflowers that flicker scarlet under the golden sun. The glowstone walks leading to the Tower are edged by the fireflowers.

Although four portals open from the Tower, Queryans not belonging to the Temporal Guard enter only through the South Portal.

The Tower soars from its rectangular base into a dome which climbs to a spire. The Tower is out-of-time phase, and the spire flares with the fires of a thousand suns captured in the timeless and untouchable depths of the faceted slow-glass facing.

The oldest holos of the Tower from the Archives show no change, even though the mountains in the distance are a shade sharper and the hills a trace harsher. While Quest has altered in little particulars, the Tower of Immortals has not.

As I stared at the Tower on that morning that may not have been, none of this crossed my mind. Too young to note the changes in the vegetation in the park from century to century, and filled with the elation of becoming a Guard, I studied the Tower as a present I was about to receive.

If you see a good holo of the Tower, you can see how the edges blur. That's because the walls of the Tower proper, except for the rectangular wings, are partly out-of-time phase, which renders it indestructible, as well as unchangeable. That's unless the Temporal Guard were to pull it down stone by stone.

I stood and stared, convincing myself that, red hair and

all, I would be the first of my family in eons, that is, since my grandfather, to pass the Test and join the Temporal Guard.

Wishing would not make it so, and clutching my illusions, I began to walk up the glowstones to the south portal. I could have slid right up to the entrance, but ceremony means much to all Queryans, particularly when a youngster elects to take the Test.

The portals were dark, but the interior of the Tower was bright with slow-glass panels, glittering and lit with the light of not only golden suns, but red suns, blue suns, orange suns, and white suns. Yet for all the light, as I entered the Tower, I felt a sense of coolness, quiet, and peace.

Not that I hadn't been there before. With my parents, tutors, and friends, I had walked all the public corridors, the meeting halls, and the Hall of Justice.

Before I realized it, I was at the archway to the Testing Hall in the west wing of the Tower.

A tall woman, with white-blond hair and deep black eyes, waited.

I had heard all the Guard participated in routine functions, and I concealed my surprise with a curt nod and a simple statement.

"Counselor Freyda."

Query made no distinction between civil and military, between compulsory and voluntary. The Tests determined who could join the Guard, and the Guard was the government. Ability determined position in the Guard, and the Counselors directed the Guards to implement the policies laid down by the Tribunes.

So I was surprised that Counselor Freyda, rumored to have been a close friend of my departed and possibly late grandfather, whom many had said I resembled, would be my examiner.

"Loki," she responded.

It was not a lack of warmth, I felt. Rather we are a laconic people, except perhaps for me. That's what comes from living until some accident in a planet-slide or a time fluke does you in.

When you contact the same people over centuries, tight speech and good manners prevail, and the Counselor had always been impeccably correct.

"You need not take the Test." Her eyes smiled, knowing I would.

The formal statement was necessary. Some Queryans never took the Test, used their talents only to travel around Query.

Counselor Freyda had always been an attractive woman, though in my youthful exuberance, I thought all Queryan women were attractive, beauty being a matter of degree.

She rose from the simple straight-backed chair and led the way to the Travel Hall.

The Travel Hall is nothing more than a long, high, slow-glass lit room at the end of the West Wing of the Tower. A series of small equipment rooms flanks the Travel Hall. They open directly onto it through small arches. In practical terms, the Travel Hall is actually outside the main time-protected walls of the Tower. So is the Infirmary. If you think about it, it makes sense.

Most Immortals can't planet-slide or time jump from within the out-of-time phase walls of the main Tower. That's why the Infirmary and the Travel Hall are "outside."

Freyda conducted me into one of the equipment rooms, the Counselors', where the slow-glass wall panels were flanked with heavy gold and black hangings. From the drawers of a carved chest, she took four wristbands, slipped one over each forearm and handed the remaining pair to me.

I put them on, not having the faintest idea what they were for.

"The first part is simple. Go undertime as far as you can, or until I squeeze your arm. When I squeeze, relax, and I'll bring us back. Understand?"

I was all too aware we made a strange pair, she taller and in black, so simple and stark next to my red. If I succeeded, I would wear black. No actual law, but those who serve or have served in the Temporal Guard wear black. My father said it has been so since before his great-grandfather's time.

Realizing I had been daydreaming, I nodded abruptly.

Freyda nodded back and grasped my left wrist. I ducked understream. Instead of latching onto the ground I just concentrated on trying to force myself full back-time, try-

ing to turn the universe bright red like me. I could feel
the redness flashing against the black of the time-paths.

Flashes of blue alternated with the sense of back-time
red I was seeing, and I began to feel like I was dragging
someone. Freyda was signaling. I went limp, blanked my
mind, and let her carry us back to the Travel Hall.

"I doubt we need other tests." Her voice was level, but
with a trace of strain, it seemed to me.

Was there any question? I'd been confident of passing
for as long as I could remember. I'd been practicing fore-
and back-timing on Query at least as long as I could read.
Not that I could actually break out, given the Law of
Non-Interference, but oh, how I had practiced.

Freyda looked carefully away from me toward the far
end of the Hall.

"Custom, however, requires two other phases."

I tensed. What else was necessary?

"Next, slide off Query as you back-time."

"In any direction?"

"How do you determine, Loki?" The question was somewhat pointed, perhaps because custom, again the unspoken,
indicated that I should not have experimented with off-
planet time-slides.

Embarrassed by my gaffe, I tried not to flush, and
stammered, "I'm not sure . . . there must be four. I mean,
red and blue and gold and black, except that you could
call gold and black, cold and hot. Somehow gold ought to
be hot, but it's cold."

"So you've experimented on your own. I might have
guessed. Have you followed a black line out-system and
tried a break-out there?"

Was there a trace of a smile on her face?

"I've followed the lines a little way, but never tried a
break-out."

That was certainly true. The Temporal Guard keeps its
secrets. I wasn't about to break-out somewhere or some-
when that wasn't favorable to my continued existence. I
had followed the black time-paths both blue and red directions just up to break-out on a number of worlds. At that
time I had no way of knowing whether they were cold
asteroids, moons, or planets. I thought I knew, but when
you're experimenting on the edge of the forbidden, you
hold back. At least, I did then.

"All right. We can skip phase two. Follow any black

line back-time, red direction, as far or as near time as you want. Pick a favorable break-out. If it's dangerous and you have trouble, I'll recover you."

I picked the strongest time-path till it branched, took what seemed about a Queryan-sized trail to break-out.

Now, it's easy to say "followed," or "took," but unless you've been a time-diver, the words don't mean much. You can move your body, but the work is all inside your head.

When I first started time-diving, I actually tried to walk through the undertime nothingness. That's a bad habit, like mouthing words when you read. Unless you break the habit you'll never get any distance. You mentally "see" the paths and visualize the shade of red or blue. That's your acceleration back- or fore-time. Most divers can't slide or dive off the planet's surface except along the black force lines, the arrows of the stars.

Some of the older races speculated that the suns throw time rays, as well as other energies. They do, and the black arrows, paths, call them what you will, are what we follow. You have to know when to get off. If you follow the strongest path to the end, you'd wind up in the middle of some star. Not that you'd get that far. The distortion is so great even in the undertime that you'd have to force yourself beyond the mental abilities of all but the strongest Temporal Guards to approach close enough to injure yourself physically.

A knack, that's what it is.

A Guard can feel the "home" sense of the Tower of Immortals if he or she is near Query. Being both in and out of time, it acts like a beacon. Even if you lose your path you can home in on it.

With a quick shiver through the mind I popped out, catching a glimpse of stars in a frozen sky, eyeballs bugging out. Gasping for breath, I ducked back understream, thinking what a dunce I'd been.

That's it. Pick an easy path, stick your nose out without even a question as to whether there's any air out there to breathe.

I fired myself back to Query and the Travel Hall.

Freyda arrived a moment later.

"Like your grandfather. Rash. But stronger. With training, you'll do."

That was my Test.

Sounds simple—but either you can or you can't.

After passing my Test with Counselor Freyda, I slid home to wait the days or seasons before I was called for training.

"I passed! I passed!" I shouted, plunging onto the porch where my parents were eating their midday meal.

"I didn't doubt you would for a moment," said my father, scarcely looking up from his fruit.

"I hope you'll be happy, dear," added my mother.

"But . . . I mean . . . not everyone . . ." I couldn't understand it. They were the ones who had told me the legends of the Guard.

All of them, from the terrible losses of the Frost Giant/ Twilight Wars to the heroic deeds of Odinthor, the Triumvirate, my grandfather Ragnorak—all the sacrifices made by the Guard to restore Query to the glory that had preceded the devastation of the Frost Giants.

I'd gone to sleep so many nights as a child looking up at my father's shining gold hair, listening to him tell about the hardships that his father Ragnorak had endured on mission after mission for the Temporal Guard.

"You don't seem particularly pleased," I charged.

"If that's what you really want, dear," answered my mother, "we're both happy for you." She smiled so faintly it wasn't a smile and turned back to her lunch, a wild salad she'd gathered from the woods behind the house.

Even my father didn't meet my eyes after the first few instants. He picked at his fruit silently.

I thought about sliding out into the mountains to be alone, but what difference did it make? I was apparently alone even at home.

My room was on the second level at the back, overlooking the small gorge which separated the meadow where the house stood from the woods covering the hills. In the distance on a fair day, I could sometimes see the heights of the western Bardwall over the evergreens.

I slumped into the hammock chair on the shady side of my small balcony and stared at the trees.

There was a tap at the door. Doors weren't really necessary, but were there as a matter of custom and courtesy. Once when I was about ten, I guess, my door stayed locked for a month. It didn't seem to matter. That was before I realized my parents could slide around it if they wanted to.

"Come in," I called, knowing from the sharpness of the knock it was Dad.

He opened the door quietly, came out, and sat in the high-backed stool closest to the hammock chair.

"You don't understand, Loki, and you're confused." He waved me to silence and went on. "How could your father, the son of the great Ragnorak, hero and Guard, be so casual about your ability and your decision to join the Guard? I can tell from your face. You're about to say I couldn't make it, didn't pass my Test."

He smiled gently. "That's not quite true. I never even tried to take the Test. Nor did your mother. She's the great-granddaughter of Sammis Olon. I suspect, looking at you, we could have passed. That wasn't the question. My question was: What's the Guard for?"

What was Dad diving at? And why had he chickened out of taking his Test? Who was Sammis Olon?

"To protect us," I answered automatically.

"From what? Nobody's seen a Frost Giant in over a million years." His voice never lifted.

"That doesn't mean there aren't any. And what about the rest of the universe?" He just didn't seem to understand.

"What about it? There's no danger in it, particularly to you."

I couldn't understand him. "Then why did you tell me all those stories about the Guard? They were true, weren't they? *Weren't they?*"

"Yes, Loki, they were true. My father, your grandfather, destroyed promising civilizations, changed history on a dozen planets that were no real threat because of a million-year-old fear. When I told you those stories, I thought you would understand the Guard is a grubby and unnecessary business. I tried to portray the dangers, the horrors, and the arbitrary nature of meddling with Time and the lives of innocents."

"Innocents? What about the time the soldiers of the Anarchate blew off his wrist?" I remembered that one vividly. "Or the time he stopped the Perrsions from using a planet-buster on Kaldir? Or—"

"Everything I told you was true," he interrupted, "or what my father told me. Lying wasn't one of his many vices."

"You were jealous of your own father! That's it!" I was seething.

He backed away from me with a strange look in his eyes.

"That's enough, Loki," he said calmly, almost gently. "I don't think we have much more to talk about. Your mother wanted me to ask about your decision once more. Passing your Test doesn't mean you have to join the Guard, but I can see that your mind is made up."

He held up his hand to stop my objections and continued. "The entire nature of the Guard is subjective. Your mother and I have tried to become as self-sufficient as possible here. We built the house with our own hands, harvest what we can from the lands and the woods. In the Guard you'll find machines to supply everything . . ."

He went on and on and on, telling me over and over, way after way that the Guard was wrong in this, wrong in that. And he'd never been in the Guard. I wondered if he hated his father for being such a hero. Obviously I wasn't going to have that problem.

I listened and didn't try to say a word until he finished.

"Thank you, Dad. Is there anything around here that needs to be done?"

He looked at me as if I'd climbed out from under a rock.

"You really don't understand, do you?" He flexed his forearms, ridged with the muscles developed from his years of manual self-sufficiency, and kept staring.

What was there to understand? For some strange reason, he was giving the Guard a trial and judging it guilty without any firsthand experience.

We sat there for maybe twenty units, neither of us wanting to say anything. An odd picture—a young man and a youth almost a man, yet one was father, one son. On Query you can't tell age by physical appearances.

Finally, Dad slipped off the stool, brushed his longish hair back off his forehead, and walked back into the house.

"You're welcome here as long as you want to stay, son." And damn it, he sounded like he meant it.

I kept watching the trees, as if I could see them grow or something. They didn't. Only thing that grew was their shadows.

The first few days of summer were like that. I couldn't take the sitting. Thought about Dad's comments on the

Guard, the harsh conditions, the struggles, and I got scared. Just a little.

Why should I have been scared? I didn't know, but I started in with the ax and split a winter's worth of wood in a ten-day.

Next came the running. If the Guard wanted toughness, I intended to be ready. I've got heavy thighs and short legs. Do you know what running over sandy hills is like with small feet and short legs?

I tried to chase down flying gophers. Never caught one, but within a ten-day I was getting pretty close before they disappeared into their sand holes.

At first, the temptation to cheat on the running, to slide a bit ahead undertime, was appealing, but I figured that wouldn't help my conditioning much. Besides, I could already slide from rock tip to rock tip without losing my balance.

Once when I was sprinting back across the meadow to the house, I caught a glimpse of Dad watching through the railings. I don't think he knew I saw him and the expression on his face—pride mixed with something else, confusion, sadness, I don't know.

Through all the quiet meals we shared those long ten-days, I knew they didn't understand, couldn't understand.

One morning a Guard trainee in black arrived with a formal invitation from the Tribunes for me to begin training.

Along with the invitation was a short list of what I was to bring with the notation that nothing else was required.

That made packing pretty easy.

Ten of us were ushered into a small Tower room with comfortable stools, a podium, and a wall screen.

Six young women, four young men, girls and boys really, we sat and waited. None of us knew each other, and with the reticence common to Query, no one said anything.

I couldn't stand it.

"I'm Loki." I glared at the tall girl. She had her black hair cut short, and, surprisingly, it suited her.

"Loragerd," she said gravely.

The other women were Halcyon, Aleryl, Shienl, Patrice, and Carrine. The men were Ferrin, Gill, Tyron. I thought women and men, but we were all at that age of being neither youth nor adult.

Like rocks on the beach, waiting, we sat.

Through the open archway marched a small man dressed in the black singlesuit of the Guard. On his left collar was a four-pointed silver star. His hair was so black it was blue, and his dark eyes glittered.

"Good morning, trainees. I'm Gilmesh, and this will be your indoctrination lecture." He settled himself behind the podium, studied each of us for a fraction of a unit, cleared his throat, and went on.

"First and foremost, the Guard relies on voluntary subjection to absolute discipline. The rules are few and absolute. But why do you think we have to do it this way?"

Dead silence. No one was about to volunteer anything, which was just as well because Gilmesh rushed on as if he hadn't expected an answer.

"The Guard is a small organization with a big job. We

don't have the personnel to coddle discipline problems. Minor offenses merit special work-assignments or dismissal. Major offenses normally result in a sentence to Hell and dismissal. High Crimes lead to a sentence to Hell and a chronobotomy."

I understood everything but the last term. Most of us must have worn the same puzzled expression because he stopped and explained.

"Chronobotomy—that's a condensation of a medical term I'm not certain I can remember, let alone pronounce. Means surgical removal of all time-diving abilities."

At that point the room seemed a whole lot colder.

"Well . . . what does the Guard do?" asked Gilmesh, ignoring the chill he had created with his casual revelations. "The Guard is charged with the maintenance of civil order on Query, the elimination of possible threats to Query and other peace-loving races in our sector of the galaxy, and the encouragement of peace. That's it."

Gilmesh surveyed the ten of us.

"Any of you may drop out of the trainee program at any time in the next three years before we get to field training —and probably half of you will. If you decide to leave the Guard after that, you're responsible for two years of administrative duties or an equivalent sentence on Hell. Administrative duties are routine clerical or maintenance functions. In return you'll receive restricted time-diving privileges to a number of systems. Is that clear?"

It was quite clear, even to a group of mixed-age youngsters.

Gilmesh went on outlining more guidelines, rules, regulations, without arousing much interest until the end of his spiel.

"Academic training will take four years roughly, and diving training will start about two years from now. You will not, I repeat, *not,* attempt any time-diving on your own during this period until you are cleared by the Guard. Here's why."

The screen flashed on again, and the narrator began cataloguing the possible dangers of diving by untrained personnel. Impressive—airless planets, planets with poisonous atmospheres, predators, black holes, everything that could possibly go wrong.

It ended with a condensation of the Last Law. "No time manipulation by a member of a species can undo the death

of any other species member from that same base system."
Translated loosely, once a Queryan dies, no amount of time-
fiddling by the Guard can undo that death. If you blow it
and die, you stay dead. Dead is dead.

As I recalled from school, the casualties among the
earliest time-divers had been fantastic . . . well over eighty
percent. I was beginning to see why. You don't think about
it as a child. You slide where you want to on the planet,
and even if you back-time or fore-time on Query itself, you
can't break-out. You feel safe.

Gilmesh ended the indoctrination lecture by giving room
assignments in the West Barracks. He dismissed us after
telling us to locate our rooms, drop off our gear, and report back in one hundred units.

We did and when we returned were directed to Special
Stores for uniform fittings. We each got four black single-
suits and a green four-pointed star to go on the collar.

That was the beginning of the routine.

The classroom work didn't seem all that hard, not to
me, but within weeks Shienl and Gill had left.

I enjoyed the mechanical theory class, taught by a blond
giant of a man called Baldur. Often he was units late or
held us, and his explanations of the importance of mechanics in culture could be long-winded.

Baldur asked questions—lots of them—in a quiet light
voice that penetrated, made you listen.

"Tyron, I know you're not the most mechanically inclined trainee, but you do have the capability to understand
the basic outline of something as simple as a generator."

Tyron flushed and mumbled, "Is it that important?"

Baldur didn't raise his voice, didn't seem flustered, just
asked another question.

"Tyron, most cultures have a ruling class or elite or
power structure. That elite's position is normally based on
its control of the available technology, directly or indirectly, and its ability to direct the use of resources. Control
and direction are maximized when that elite understands
the technology it directs. What happens when an elite loses
its collective ability to understand the basis of the technology it controls?"

"I don't understand. What does that have to do with
generators?"

I didn't understand either, but both Loragerd and Halcyon nodded as if they did, and Ferrin grinned.

"Loragerd?" Baldur asked.

"They begin to lose control. They aren't the elite any-more."

"What about the Guard?" countered Ferrin.

I thought it was a dumb question.

"It's all dumb," protested Patrice. "Ruling classes don't just disappear. And the Guard's no elite."

Baldur never let it go with a simple resolution. "Is the Guard an elite?"

Tyron suppressed a groan, I could tell, but I didn't see why. Sure the Guard was an elite. Pretty obvious.

"Yes," I burst out.

"Why don't you finish the logic for Tyron, then, Loki?"

What logic? I didn't have any, but I decided I'd better bumble through as well as I could.

"If the Guard is an elite," I started slowly, "then it must control some technology. If Guards don't understand tech-nology, then the Guard will lose control." I paused before the immediate objection came to mind. "But the Guard has its powers because Guards can time-dive, and that's not based on technology."

"It's not?" responded Baldur. "How can you power stunners without generators? How can you stay warm and dry in storms without heat or housing, without becoming a rootless society that shifts with the weather? I'll admit the line is harder to draw for Query, but it's still valid."

He stopped, cleared his throat, and continued speaking. "That's something you all ought to think about. In the case of a mid-tech culture like Sertis, the example is clear . . ."

He launched into a description of how the local mon-archs ruled through control of the water supplies—the water empire model, he called it.

We got back to generators before too long, and this time Tyron paid attention. Why the digression would have motivated him I didn't see. That was because I thought generators were more interesting than all that speculative stuff about elites and control.

We had other courses, too, on the administrative law of the Guard, on meteorology, EQ biology, comparative weap-onry—a whole mishmash.

The first year was a sort of crash backgrounder.

In the second year, along with more advanced mechani-cal and technical training, Baldur started us on simple equipment repairs in a side area of the Maintenance Hall.

Patrice protested.

"Why do we have to know how to put all this tangled junk back together? I'm not going to be a mechanic. I'm a diver."

Baldur just smiled. "Do you want an answer, or are you angry because it's difficult?"

Patrice glowered at him. "An answer."

"As a diver, you will be using this equipment, and you'll use it better if you understand it. Understanding only comes when you have a feel for it. Knowing how to repair it gives that feel.

"Incidentally, Patrice," he finished in a milder tone, "no one in the Guard is *just* a time-diver. We all have support jobs as well. If not in Maintenance, then in Linguistics, Medical, Assignments, Research, Archives, or what have you."

I remembered Gilmesh mentioning that, but hearing it and starting in with oily metal and dented wrist gauntlets was something else.

Not that it was all work, by any means. Less than half our day was taken up with academic training those first two years.

Every so often I saw Counselor Freyda. She had me over to her quarters in Quest for dinner two, three times, and told me about my grandfather. I guessed she followed my training because of old Ragnorak.

IV

In the third year the pace stepped up. Not only was the academic load heavier, but we began full-scale physical training. Not just conditioning, but physical flexibility, hand-to-hand combat, weapons familiarization, even life-support equipment training, which included deep space gear.

Carrine resigned a ten-day into the third year, leaving seven of us.

One of the more interesting courses was taught by a Senior Guard called Sammis. "Attitude Adjustment" was the title. That didn't convey half of it.

The day we started, Sammis lined us up in a field on the edge of Quest. We stood in the center of a series of posts of different heights. Each post had a tiny platform just big enough for both feet mounted on top.

Sammis waited in front of us until he had our attention.

"In this course you learn by doing. The first exercise is to slide from the top of one post to the top of the next. Like this."

He winked out and appeared on the platform top of the first post. Like a jagged bolt of black lightning, he slid from post top to post top and reappeared back on the ground in front of us.

"Now you try it." He pointed at Ferrin. "You start."

Ferrin slid undertime to the first post, broke-out with only one foot on the platform, lost his balance, tried to slide, and fell to the grass.

Halcyon giggled. Sammis turned on her.

"Halcyon, you're next."

She made it to the third post before tumbling off.

Eventually it was my turn. I took it carefully, and out-side of wavering on the fourth or fifth post, made it through all fifteen platforms.

Sammis was frowning when I finished.

"Did I do something wrong?"

He shook his head. "No, no. Just . . . nothing."

He left me standing there while he watched Loragerd fall off the platform on the second post.

No one else got past the fifth post that day.

Tyron called it a pointless exercise, but it wasn't. As Sammis explained after watching everyone (but me) fall off the tiny platforms, "This is to get you ready for real diving. In a lot of dives, where you end up could spell the difference between staying in one piece or becoming sev-eral. Some divers"—and he seemed to have someone in mind—"are gifted enough to dive out of the middle of a waterfall while being thrown head over heels. Most of you will find you can't dive except from a relatively stable platform."

Oh, it made sense, all right, and so did all the "attitude adjustments" exercises that Sammis introduced in the weeks that followed.

We each had a different "final"—supposedly based on what Sammis thought we should be able to handle.

Sammis trotted, or slid, me out to a site on the western cliffs.

"Loki, this could be more than you can handle. I want to make it clear. This isn't a test for passing and failing. It was designed to demonstrate what you can and cannot handle. If you get into trouble, just slide clear. Do you understand?"

His face was kindly, almost worried.

I nodded.

"The course is set up in increasing order of difficulty, but it's blind. You won't be able to see your next break-out stage until you reach the stage before. You are not to break-out except next to the locator flags."

"You mean, somehow when I reach the first point, I'll see the second one?"

"Tougher than that. At the first stage flag is a vector direction arrow for the second stage. The same is true for the next, and so on. You may have only a moment to absorb that information before sliding. There are ten landing points. After the last, or when you stop, return here."

I wiped my forehead. The more I heard about this test, the less I liked it.

Sammis pointed to a flag fluttering below the top of a cliff overhanging the beach.

I nodded and slid, but I didn't break-out immediately. Even though it's difficult, you can get some idea of what a landing point involves from the undertime, like looking up from beneath the water at twilight.

The ledge was narrow. Something white fluttered from the rock. I oriented myself undertime to break-out facing the white object.

The ledge was even narrower than I'd anticipated, and the wind gusted around me. The permaflex vector arrow attached to the flagstaff indicated a point on the rocks offshore. Even from the cliff tops I could see the surf crashing over them. In between the waves, I could see another banner. Belatedly recalling Sammis's injunction not to hang around, I slid again.

From the understream I watched the breakers and tried to locate the vector directions before I broke-out on the rocks. I'd never tried delaying a slide consciously before, but it seemed to work. The vector arrow was attached to the flagstaff.

I appeared on the wet and very slippery rocks right after a substantial wave, hoping the area would be water-free for at least a unit or so, and concentrated on the vector. The arrow pointed back to the cliffs further down the coast. The course pattern was apparently a zigzag along the coast line in order to conceal the next point from the previous point.

From the undertime, point three was on a thin spike of rock jutting out from the cliffs. The spike wavered as the flag fluttered in the wind. Was the rock wavering, or was it my undertime perspective? I decided to see if I could flash by it.

I'd never done a slide that way before either, but I didn't like that flag placement.

I actually put a little weight on the stone for an instant and felt it give before I ducked back undertime. The vector arrow pointed to the base of the cliff below.

Sammis be damned. This course had been set up for keeps. But I was going to finish it and find out why.

Point four was established on the rocks protruding into the surf, a fragmented peninsula. From the undertime I could see the white flag and the vague form of the vector arrow, but not much else.

What was the catch here?

Was there a tidal blow-hole? A rock-sucker flattened out under the flag waiting for me to step down? Physical reactions are an illusion in the understream, but I felt I shuddered as I hung there, thinking about the acid touch of a giant rock-sucker snapping up around me.

How about coming out next to the flag at a slight angle in order not to be where the course designer planned for me to arrive? I was supposed to touch each point. How close?

Finally, and the moments hung like icicles while I decided, I skipped through. My second guess had been correct. One of the largest rock-suckers I'd ever seen was draped flat over the rugged rocks, with a tentacle loosely circling the white flagstaff.

I was back undertime virtually instantaneously, but even so, the rock-sucker's sting-arms whipped through the space where I'd been fast enough for me to sense a sudden rush of air as I slid undertime.

The fifth flag was not at sea, nor high in the cliffs, but straight along the beach line to a level space on the sand.

I studied the flat circle around the flag from the undertime, but couldn't see anything out of order. I jumped onto the sand as close to the flagstaff as I could manage, focused on the vector arrow, and tried to locate point six.

I didn't get that far before I was tossed head over heels into the air by a blast of wind. I felt strangely light.

I'd managed to memorize the directions, although I hadn't seen the flag for the next point. I slid undertime from my midair tumbling and reoriented myself.

The farther along I got, the less happy I was about this test. The air blast generator or whatever wasn't a test. Deliberately designed to see if I could slide undertime after I'd been bushwhacked.

I put it behind me and slid half-blind in the direction the arrow had pointed. Seemed longer, but since it's all subjective in the undertime, the unseen examiners couldn't tell my fumbing so long as I located the seventh point.

The obstacle for point seven was clear. They, whoever "they" were, had lowered the flag from an overhanging cliff, letting it float in midair, a good fifty feet above a loose talus pile. No way in the world I could obtain momentary footing, let alone a firm stance. I hovered there, though that's not precisely how it works, in the undertime, trying to figure out how to get a look at the vector arrow.

I could give up, but somehow, someway, I'd be damned if the unknown "they" were going to get the best of me.

Well if I could hang in midair while undertime, why not in real time? Not exactly the same, but it was worth a try. Maybe I could leave my heels sort of undertime as an anchor.

I tried it . . . and damned if it didn't work. I wasted no time and studied the locator diagram, glanced along the vector path, saw the glimmer of white and jumped back undertime.

As I slid on a low angle back down to the surf line, I wondered what was next. The white flag was there, all right, and I reached it before I thought I would.

Again—for some reason—I hesitated on break-out. Dimly from the undertime I could see the flag whipped by the spray and wind, located as it seemed to be in the middle of an overactive surf line. If I broke-out there, I'd be pounded by the surf and tossed onto the rocky shore. But was that the test?

I wanted to kick myself when it penetrated. No small white rectangle where the vector arrow should have been. A phony point eight, short of where the real point eight was.

The actual point eight was in the middle of the waves farther out, the tall flag anchored from beneath the water with no place to break-out. I did the split-entry trick a second time, leaving my heels locked in the undertime, and studied the vector arrow pointing to the ninth flag as quickly as possible. It pointed up the coast and right into the middle of the lava cliffs.

Right in the middle of the cliffs was an understatement. The break-out point was a small cubical room hollowed from the solid rock without any windows or doors. I could tell as I circled the space in the undertime that it was surrounded with machinery of some sort.

Beginning to feel more than normally nervous about the last stages of the damned test, I became more convinced than before it wasn't any ordinary test.

From the undertime I could sense the power of the machines buried in the walls of the rock chamber. Even though I couldn't determine anything, I was betting they would be focused on me the minute I appeared.

They were bending the rules, and so would I. I slid back undertime to the beach below. I didn't exactly break-out, but I did manage to get a good chunk of rock, shuttled back undertime to point nine, and studied the chamber.

By wandering around the limp flag and straining to pierce the uncertainty that separates the "now" from the undertime, I could see a vector arrow sheet attached to the rock wall behind the staff.

Still skeptical, I pitched the rock into the chamber. For a long moment, nothing happened. A greenish light filled the other side of time, the "now," pervading the space in the rock.

Gas! If it were a test of capabilities, nothing fatal would be employed, only something painful or humiliating.

While the gas swirled around and clouded the chamber, I decided, perhaps foolishly, to flash-slide by the vector arrow and get a peek at the directions.

I made one pass, less than a unit in real time, and managed to absorb the direction and approximate distance. The almost instantaneous slide still left my face stinging.

That's a disadvantage of time-diving. You're left suspended with whatever hurts until you break-out. True of pleasure as well, which leads to some interesting permutations, I'd been told, but that was lockerroom gossip.

Point ten took awhile to pin down, subjectively, that is. The directions were confusing, and damned if I was going back for a second look and more gas burns.

The last point, once found, was simple enough. Location was what took the time. The vector arrow had indicated an incredibly long, virtually vertical direction. If the scale was correct, and I had no reason to disbelieve it, my last point had to be well above Query's surface.

In the dark above Query, I located an orbiting structure. Through the silver haze that divided the undertime from the objective "now," I could sense that the space station, if that was what it was, had been there for eons, if not longer.

The outer spokes of the wheel were gouged and pitted, and one of the arms was holed through.

Groping around half-blind in both the space darkness and the hazed undertime, the subjective time dragged out before I pinned down the elusive tenth flag in a small compartment with heavy metal doors at each end.

I hesitated. Every other spot had been trapped. By then, of course, the gas burns were getting to me. Subjective feelings, because the intensity was constant. I just wanted to get the test over with.

I knew whoever set the course was playing on my impatience, and I was tempted to sit up there in orbit for what seemed subjective hours until I figured out the latest catch. I snooped around as well as I could, discerned no equipment, could sense no energy concentrations.

Finally, I decided it had to be the location and the airlessness which were the tests. I made a flash-through appearance in the chamber, long enough to register if anyone had left any device to record my presence, and slid back down to the beach where it had all started.

Sammis was waiting, sitting on the sand with his head in his hands and his knees drawn up, a morose look on his elvish face.

Some of my pent-up anger lessened on seeing him in the unguarded position, strengthening my suspicion that he had not been the sole architect of the test course.

"Sammis," I said, my resolve to keep my mouth shut evaporating rapidly, "who the Hell designed your little course?"

He scrambled to his feet. I had the feeling I wasn't supposed to be back yet.

"Are you all right? How far did you get?"

"All ten. At least, if that airless hulk of a space station was number ten, I got through all of them."

He made me recite all of them, and I did, rather impatiently.

"Look," I snapped as I finished responding to his grilling, "if I said I did all ten, I did all ten. I'm not about to lie to anyone about it. Damned if I'll lower myself by lying."

"What?" he asked. He paled slightly, I think.

Abruptly, I realized I was still a trainee, and fairly junior at that.

"I'm sorry. I'm a little keyed up."

"I can understand that, Loki."

He still hadn't answered my question. Tried once more. "Sammis, who designed that course?"

"The final responsibility for evaluating the attitude adjustment skills of his trainees rests with the instructor."

That, or some variation, was all he said. I knew someone else was involved.

I just didn't know who.

V

There's a Hell of a lot to Temporal Guard training. Advanced training is practically always on a one-on-one basis. It has to be. Abilities vary so greatly from individual Guard to individual Guard that a standardized program would fail.

Freyda stayed on as my field diving instructor. She wasn't as good as I was even then, but she was well-acquainted with the impetuousness I displayed, acted as a brake on my lack of caution. Freyda was nothing if not cautious.

She was so cautious I was stunned to find out through casual gossip that she'd spent a short contract with my grandfather Ragnorak before he had disappeared on a long-line, back-time dive.

Later, it made a bit more sense, when other trainees hinted that the Counselor was cautious in all areas but one.

On Guard matters, however, she was all business and didn't hesitate in using whatever or whoever was best for the Guard.

"You're going to Sinopol with Baldur. Procurement. Requires a complete cosmetic," Freyda announced one morning as I entered the Training Rooms.

"Sinopol?" I'd never heard of the place.

"Hunters of Faffnir, high-tech, a million back. Get a briefing from Assignment and a full language implant. I mean *full*, with complete fluency. Then report to cosmetics. You two leave tomorrow."

I got the picture. I was the porter for the heavy technological gadgets. Could be interesting even for a coolie. I

buttoned my lip and marched over to Assignments, where
Heimdall motioned me to an end-console with a single
abrupt gesture.

After I had the briefing tapes firmly in mind, Heimdall
shoved me out the archway toward Linguistics. There was
I laid out under the Gubserian language tank to absorb a
complete dosage of Faffnirian.

The language tank is an experience in itself. When I
tottered to my feet after an afternoon of high-speed implantation, I muttered my thanks in gibberish—gibberish to
anyone in the Tower. It would have meant "thank you . . .
I think" to a Hunter of Faffnir.

Recalling the elaborate code duello of the Hunters, I
belatedly noted that the doubt in my voice would have
earned an immediate challenge from any full-fledged
Hunter in Sinopol, but the young Guard tech, Ordonna,
just smiled. She was used to the disorientation.

It was late by the time I reached Cosmetics, and I
hoped everyone had disappeared. No such luck. Two
Guards were waiting. They popped me into a conditioner,
pulled me out thirty units later, and shoved me in front of
a mirror. I had dark brown skin.

After covering my hair with gunk, they stuffed my head
under some sort of electronic gadgetry. I came out with
hair so black it was that incredible tinge of blue.

I trudged to the east portal of the Tower and slid straight
to my rooms in the West Barracks. I collapsed on my
couch, barely remembering to set the wake-up for the
next morning.

Baldur was waiting for me at the Travel Hall.

"What did they tell you?"

"Standard briefing."

Baldur shook his head. "How's your hand-to-hand? Any
good with a knife?"

"Nix on the knife. All right on the hand-to-hand."

I was being modest. I was good on the hand-to-hand,
partly because I cheat. I can't explain it, but I used my
diving/sliding ability to speed up my reactions and motions. Never met another diver who could do it the way
I can. Sammis could anticipate, and he was the best I
knew.

"I hope you're better than that. The odds are a hundred
percent you'll have to fight at least once on this trip."

"I'll do all right."

He pulled me over into a corner.

"Loki, I've heard you're the hottest Guard since Odinthor or before. I've also heard that you forget to listen. Listen, please, and save us both some trouble . . ."

He was off and running about the fantastic technology of the Hunters of Faffnir, their ultra-courteous social structure, and their nasty habit of challenging each other to fights on the slightest pretext. I tuned it out because I'd already gotten it from the briefing tapes.

Baldur meant well, but he went on and on.

"Loki, I give up. You know it all. I hope you don't have to pay for it like Mimris did. You ready?"

"Sure." Who was Mimris? I wanted to know, but after that sermon I wasn't about to ask.

"We're sliding to the objective 'now' site of Sinopol before diving straight back. I'll need a breather in between. As it is, I can barely reach High Sinopol. That's one of the reasons for the trip and your presence." Baldur grimaced and brushed his long blue-black hair out of his eyes. Usually it was white-blond.

I knew I was diving along as a glorified porter, but why the rush? Heimdall and Freyda hadn't said a word, just pushed the buttons and sent me off. Baldur was bluntly admitting this dive was almost beyond him.

I looked at Baldur again, as if he were a different man.

"Beginning to wonder, aren't you?" He smiled wryly. "I should have started with our politics. Remember, we're a totally parasitic society. We're moving into a time phase where the average diver can't reach many high-tech cultures. The Guard is reluctant to meddle and create artificially spurred high-tech systems. In the meantime, Terra and possibly Wieren may develop into high-tech cultures. Predicting is chancy, especially when our own lights could go out if we're wrong."

"What lights?" Baldur's words made sense, but not too much.

"Loki, can you build a generator, make a glowbulb, even forge a knife?"

"No, can you?"

"As a matter of fact, I can. But I spent four years on Ydris learning how before old thunderbolt Odinthor decided to undo the place. As far as I know, I'm the only one on Query who can build anything from scratch, and that's the point. We beg, borrow, and steal."

"But we have the copier."

"We stole that, too." Baldur cut off the philosophy with
a smile. "I'd rather not have to go to Sinopol. It's at the
fringe of my ability. We need a certain compact generator,
and you're the only one who can lug that much metal a
million years. So we're going. Please keep your lip sealed
and act insignificant."

I nodded. What else could I do? Baldur was overdrama-
tizing, but who was I to dispute it? He'd convinced the
Counselors and the Tribunes. Besides, I liked the thought
of being indispensable.

"We'll break-out in a small room I rented on a long
contract. We'll round up enough stellars to pay for the
generator, pick it up, and return to the Travel Hall. Hopefully, you'll return to regular training better equipped to
understand than before."

I nodded politely again.

We walked over to the Travel Hall and suited up with
outfits Baldur had obviously brought back on a previous
dive.

I dressed. Someone had taken the time and care to tailor
the gear for me, and I wondered who. Either that or it adjusted to the body size of the wearer. Basically, the Hunters
wore a black bodymesh suit which covered everything but
hands, feet, throat, and head. The material was a flexible
synthetic patterned in octagons. I tried to knick the stuff
with the razor knife that was part of the equipment and
couldn't even peel a sliver from it.

A pair of shorts, a sleeveless overtunic, a wide equipment belt, and boots completed the uniform. Our wrist
gauntlets were disguised as ceremonial bracelets.

"You look like you've worn that all your life," commented Baldur.

I couldn't say much to that, and didn't.

Baldur gestured, and we slid to Sinopol "Now."

Sinopol of the present is nothing more than a handful
of hovels crouched around a shallow inlet of the Sea of
Tarth, a pile of brown heaps perched on a plateau above
the choppy black waters of the dead sea.

The Hunters of Faffnir had founded Sinopol a million
and a half years earlier. Then the high plateau was lower,
the air clearer, and the water dark green and filled with
fish.

For five thousand centuries the Hunters hunted and con-

quered the systems of the Anord Cluster. In the Five
Thousandth Century, the Hunters overran the Technocracy
of Llord, and there were no more conquests left in the
cluster. Anord Cluster is isolated by the Rift and impass-
able to large fleets.

Without conquest, the Hunters turned on themselves,
first on the fringes, then at the capital, and in the end, the
tallest towers of Sinopol were fused flat into a silicon block.

Sinopol the Fair in the Five Thousandth Century, the
Great Millennium, was ringed with the eight glass blue
towers of dawn guarding the corners of the city. For all
the brightness of the towers and walls, for all the armed
strength represented in the steelglass battlements, the city
laughed, breathed with the laughter of happy people who
sold the tools of war with a smile, their hair, that universal
blue-black, cropped short, and their eyes flashing as they
talked of the art of war and, sometimes, the war of arts.

Strangers were prey. The slightest offense under the
elaborate code duello led to a public challenge at any one
of the many corners arenas, where smiling Hunters chose
one of the two parties and laid bets on the outcome.

Strictly speaking, the Palace of Technology wasn't. It
was a city within a city, surrounded with a force screen
shimmering green in the dusk and gold in the sunrise.
Kilos of closed and cool arcades, scented year around with
the smells of a summer evening, were lined with store-
fronts.

Did a Hunter want battle armor? The nearest information corner contained computerized directories of the enter-
prises located in the Palace.

After this build-up, arrival in Sinopol came as a shock.
Baldur's rented room was a hole in the wall, a clean hole
in the wall, but a hole in the wall nonetheless.

Baldur wasn't in any shape to discuss the matter. I could
see why he wanted to get it over with. Under the body-
dyeing job, he was pale. I insisted he lie down on the single
couch. He did and was out in less than a unit.

The room could have been anywhere on a dozen planets.
Just a synthetic-veneered room with a couch, a table, a
chair, and a separate room with funny-looking facilities for
hygiene.

I sat down in the chair for a while, hoping Baldur would
wake up, but he just kept snoring away.

I stood up. Somehow the straight-backed chair didn't feel right. I studied it, but couldn't figure out why.

I checked the lock and bar on the doorway. The security equipment was dusty. Baldur rolled over, stopped snoring, and stayed asleep.

I'd had it. The mission's first step was to get some stellars, a pile of the local currency, in order to buy the generator.

Baldur hadn't said, but there was some reason why we couldn't or shouldn't steal the equipment outright. I accepted that, and checked my outfit over carefully.

I made my first break-out into a quiet corner of the Palace of Technology and popped out when no one was looking. As I began to stroll through those endless halls, I put a few pieces together.

Item: Only the biggest and toughest men walked alone.
Item: Women could and did walk unescorted.
Item: The smallest of the male Hunters were taller than me. Most were at least Baldur's size.
Item: Stellars were carried in sealed belt pouches like mine, attached with the same synthetic as the bodymesh.

Not much chance to liberate the coinage of the realm through cut-pursing.

A pair of young Hunters came out of a metal-mirrored emporium, their eyes swinging across the hall. The flowing script above the door they left proclaimed the store as "The Reflection of the Honorable Pursuit." A smoother translation would have been "War Reflects Honor."

The two Hunters didn't seem much older than me. They walked quickly. I moved aside, recalling Baldur's recommendations to avoid trouble.

They moved in the same line.

I started to avoid them again, then saw the pattern. If I kept clear of them, I'd be called for cowardice or its socially unacceptable equivalent. If I didn't, one or the other would brush me and claim I had insulted his honor by not recognizing his passage.

The corridor was wide, well-lighted, moderately traveled. The Faffnirians could smell a fight. People were turning in

anticipation before the two bully boys started their final
approach. Unless my neck was really at stake, sliding undertime with a crowd watching wasn't the best idea. All
we needed was an entire high-tech culture looking for a
stranger who disappeared in full view. Baldur, not to men-
tion Heimdall, would have my hide.

If I'd been Heimdall, or Freyda, or even Baldur, I might
have been able to plan a graceful way out. But I wasn't. I
just kept marching straight ahead until the thinner one,
and both were whipcord lean, like a Hunter of Faffnir
should be, brushed my shoulder.

"Honored young Hunter, I do believe you have conducted your passage with less than the requisite discretion,"
intoned the thin one. The elaborate phraseology somehow
underscored the deadliness of the game.

"Honored old Hunter, I do believe you have contrived
a lack of clearance in your own passage merely to reaffirm
your past glories." I responded. Better to be hung for an
eagle than a dove.

His eyes widened slightly. His companion smirked, I
thought.

"I regret," he retorted, "your passage from this veil will
provide such an opportunity, for the Hunters need young
hounds of spirit."

The "corner" arena was not far. Too close. After the first
flush, I'd been tempted to disappear and try to reason with
Baldur and company, but the thought of all the high-tech
goodies of Sinopol being brought to bear on Baldur and
me dissuaded me, as did the thought that Heimdall just
might have recommended a tour on Hell for calling attention to the Guard.

No. Better I fought out of it—if I could. I could always
dive at the last minute before the lean Hunter tried to cut
my throat—I hoped.

He folded his cloak and moved into the circle etched
on the stone glass pavement. All the pavements in the
Palace of Technology pulsed with a faint light, but the
"arenas" glowed reddish while the corridor floors glowed
faint yellow.

I folded my own cloak, studying him as I did.

The knife would be more of a hindrance than help. I
decided to throw it as soon as convenient.

"I favor the one with the spotted face."

I scanned the tanned smooth faces around the circle

before I understood the voice meant me. Damn! My
freckles hadn't been covered totally by the cosmetic job.
The two bullies had immediately gone for the difference,
just like Baldur had said they would.

"He's smaller."

"But to reach his age with such blotches . . ."

"At three-to-two."

The companion Hunter stepped into the middle of the
circle and began a spiel.

"Is there no other way for the two honorable individuals
to reconcile their differences?"

"I would accept only a profound apology, and that with
difficulty," replied the one I would have to kill or dive
from. That was right. No honorable blood-letting, scratch-
on-the-shoulder, old-chap stuff. One victor, and one body,
would result.

"An apology will not suffice, not for one who provokes
for empty reason," I snapped, not thinking.

That didn't sit well with the crowd. The mutter that went
around the circle turned opinion against me. These people
expected pointless duels.

I was experiencing cultural shock. I was not standing in
a blood-stained arena, on sand baked by a sun burning
overhead, with a blood-thirsty crowd jeering and cheering.

No, I was waiting in a wide, cool, and spacious corridor
with the scent of trilia flowers, or something similar, wafting
around me, with well-cloaked weapons shoppers stopping
for a casual look, as if it were the most common sight in
the world to see two young men getting ready to kill each
other.

Maybe it was in High Sinopol in the Five Thousandth
Century of Glory, but as a young, time-diving Temporal
Guard from Query, I had a few reservations about the
matter.

All too soon the formalities were over, and the Hunter
was circling in on me. At first, I counter-circled, trying to
ignore the running comments from the bystanders. I felt
slippery under the mesh armor.

"See . . . the mongrel backs off."

"Perhaps he is an imposter."

I couldn't help a shudder at the last. Imposters were
dispatched beyond the veil on the spot—if discovered.
Shuddering was a luxury, and almost my last one at that.
Seeing the distraction, the Hunter came in quickly, light on

his feet and perfectly balanced. His knife was like silver fire.

Somehow I avoided it and circled back.

"The young dog has speed. Most would have been gutted on the spot."

"If he is so quick, why does he let the other control the circle?"

Tactics were becoming clearer as we circled. Given the bodymesh armor, slashing was virtually impossible. Any successful use of the knife would have to involve a clean and incapacitating thrust.

Now, critical jeers came from the crowd, and not all were aimed at me.

"Can't you hunt down a dog, proud Hunter?"

Sooner or later, he'd get careless with my lack of offense, I hoped.

Sooner it was. Perhaps enraged by the crowd, perhaps thinking me an imposter, he came in with his knife too high. I threw my own blade at his face, and half-ducked, half-slid, blurring almost into the undertime, right around his arm. I snapped his knife wrist with the moves Sammis had drilled into me so many times and crushed his throat with an elbow thrust.

For a moment, I guessed I must have looked at the body stupidly.

"Have you ever seen a Hunter that fast?"

"So fast . . ."

"The knife was a decoy . . ."

The murmurs buzzed around the circle. The bets were paid, and the bully boy remaining, pale under his dark complexion, approached.

"Honored young Hunter, I apologize and regret any inconvenience you may have been caused."

I nodded curtly, choking down the nausea that was climbing up my throat.

Under the customs, I got the dead Hunter's weapons and his coin purse. The rest went to his clan or wife.

"I would be honored, Hunter of Honor," I managed, after receiving the dead man's knife, weapons belt, and purse, "if you would convey my understanding of the honor and bravery of such an esteemed Hunter to those who would be most concerned."

The ritual saved me. I wasn't sure I could have said anything original. The sanitary disposal flitter appeared before I had even crossed the red pavement back into the yellow corridor.

A few older Hunters were standing at a distance and speculating. I took the path toward the nearest narrow corridor, and the instant I was alone, slid undertime and straight for Baldur's room.

I made it to the funny-looking hygiene facilities and thoroughly lost the contents of my stomach.

Two blows, delivered as taught, and a young man was dead on glowing red stone glass. Everyone had smiled, especially the older merchant-type who had bet on me.

I recalled looking up from the crumpled body on the pavement to see him chuckling and collecting from a dour Hunter. What had triggered the nausea I didn't know.

Had it been the winning smile of the young lady after my glorious victory? Or the laughter? Or the realization that I had used techniques my opponent had no idea were possible? I'd cheated. Cheated him of his life, and no matter how I rationalized it, my own failure to avoid the confrontation played a big part in his death.

Baldur was standing at the door to the facilities as I washed up.

He understood, all right.

He nodded at the weapons belt and purse I'd dropped in the middle of the floor.

"Just like you, Loki. Had to snoop around and get in over your head."

"How could they? How could I?" I hadn't had all that much choice, but still . . . "I kept thinking that you or Heimdall could have avoided it. But me, no, I had to get into a situation where either everyone in Sinopol would be looking for me or where I had to kill someone."

I sat down because I realized I was shaking.

Baldur seated himself on the other end of the couch and leaned back against the wall.

"You know, Loki, you're probably the first Guard in centuries, besides Sammis maybe, who's killed someone bare-handed. I assume you used hand-to-hand."

I mumbled an affirmative, and he went on.

"Most of the Hunters of Faffnir retire after a single tour or die in some sort of combat. Don't put too much guilt on yourself. You seem to show some appreciation of life."

I was afraid Baldur might start preaching again. The feeling must have showed. He laughed.

"No, young killer, no sermons. One point. You killed one man, who possibly deserved it, and you feel the impact. Freyda, Eranas, Martel make decisions which kill, or leave unborn, millions. Odinthor, for all his heroics, never killed anyone face-to-face with bare hands. He just stood back and roasted them. Think about it."

I didn't want to think about it.

I opened the purse. Surprisingly, it was stuffed with stellar notes. Surprising, because I had not thought such a young Hunter would have carried so much. I handed them to Baldur.

"That's enough for us to go into phase two."

Phase two was gambling. Simple when I thought about it, and another reason why Baldur needed a good diver with him.

Casino-style parlors were scattered throughout Sinopol. We settled on one, Rafel's Bazaar of Chance, large enough so substantial winnings were possible and not overly conspicuous, plain enough that minor breaches of etiquette wouldn't be picked up.

My part started there. I jumped forward and recorded the payoff numbers on a chance gadget, logged them against the local objective time. Basically, the gadget was a gilded random-number generator, the kind that I could have gimmicked. It was honest.

"Of course, it's honest," pointed out Baldur when I returned back-time with the information. "Under a duel-based society, how long would a crooked operator last— unless he were the best fighter? Even then someone would eventually kill him."

Baldur had a point.

Since I couldn't occupy the same space-time twice, after I'd given Baldur the information, I jumped ahead over my time in Rafel's and waited for Baldur on the corner outside. Out of habit, I left myself wide-unit margins on both sides.

Seemed like forever before Baldur lumbered out of the casino, blue-black hair hanging over his eyebrows, but my enthusiasm for lone exploring was less than before.

He didn't say anything, just pushed on. We took a mobile slideway toward the Palace of Technology, drifting through the early evening like quiet ghosts among the laughing Faffnirians.

Two things struck me. Sinopol was clean. Even the term

immaculate could have been applied accurately. Second, establishments seemed to be open around the clock.

Like all imperial cities, Sinopol reeked of money, reeked of power—from the fountains that bent light around falling water which twisted in midair, to the men and ladies of leisure who paraded the streets flanked with bodyguards dressed in matched golden mesh armor and little else, to the clean air scented with trilia flowers, and overlaid with the impression of absolute bodily cleanliness.

In a moment when no one was close, I asked, "How can a society with such person-to-person dueling run an Empire that spans an entire cluster?"

"How would you keep a society lean and able to function over five thousand centuries?" he asked back.

High Sinopol contained more people than all of Query, it seemed, and probably had a hundred times the creative spark. For all the wealth and technology applied to the streets and corridors of the city, for all the fantastic decorations, I saw nothing of the overelegant, nothing of the decadent, of the Sertian. Not exactly austere was Sinopol, but not ostentatious either.

In the middle of a narrow corridor in the Palace of Technology, Baldur stopped abruptly. The script over the slit door stated "The Power Place."

Baldur faced me.

"Remember, nothing is perfectly safe. Once I verify that the generator is complete, be ready to grab it and dive, if you have to. Remember the generator. The generator is what counts, not me."

He sounded so damned gloomy.

"You're what counts," I responded. "Query can always get another generator."

"No we can't. This is a special order, and for some reason, none of these battle generators appear at any time later than this, and this is as far back as I can dive."

He made it sound like the last chance, like the Tribunes were serious about it. Just for one suitcase-sized fusion generator.

What a Hell of a mess. Only one man in the Guard able to identify and find the need, and only one place in reachable time where it could be found, and only a trainee with enough diving strength to cart it back.

The slit door to the generator shop remained sealed until

Baldur placed a black disc in the slot. He shoved me inside before the knife edges of the portal snapped shut behind us.

We stood in a bare room with a number of weapons nozzles pointed at us. The walls shimmered metallic blue, devoid of features beside the weaponry and five closed portals.

"Baldra, Hunter of the Outer Reaches, returns for what he has ordered, Honored Craftsman." Baldur practically groveled before the blank wall screen. I groveled too.

Energy fields crackled around the room, so much power concentrated that it probably bent the undertime. I could have made it out through the undertime before being fried —maybe—but there was no way Baldur could have.

The flow of energy waned, and another portal opened into a small showroom. Again no one was present in the room, but a blocky object, half-man-sized and covered with shimmering black cloth, rested on a table. Next to it was an open case with an attached shoulder harness.

"You may enter, Baldra of the Outer Reaches. With your friend."

Baldur stepped forward. I kept a pace or two behind him.

As the situation developed, I began to see why we couldn't have stolen the generator. I could have lifted it clear, but I wouldn't have had the faintest idea of what to look for. Baldur couldn't time-carry it, for all his superior physical strength.

What a tenuous web the power of the Guard rested on —a generator from Sinopol, a copier from Weindre, a food-synthesizer stolen from who knew where, and the Guard always reaching, always searching out the gadgets necessary to keep Query functioning.

Baldur made a quizzical gesture as he lifted the cloth that glittered with a light of its own.

I caught a glimpse of what was under the black cloth. It wasn't any fusion generator. The unseen observer reacted. The energy fields around us began to build.

I grabbed Baldur by the arm and slid undertime, diving forward.

I brought us out into real time near dawn in Baldur's room.

"That wasn't the generator, was it?"

"No. I don't understand what went wrong."

I did. Since it might have been my fault, I avoided the question.

"Baldur," I began hesitantly, "I may be able to salvage this. I may not, but I have an idea. I'll be back in a few units."

I slid out of there undertime before he could protest.

If I were right, the actual generator had been on the table under the cloth until a few units before we arrived.

My recovery was going to be tricky because I had a limited window to work with—basically the time I'd skipped over while Baldur had been gaming. I'd left the gaps there more out of habit than anything.

Hopefully, the operator/craftsman at The Power Place had set up the real generator before we'd won the stake at Rafel's. If not, I'd have to try another approach.

I lucked out. From the undertime, I could tell that something had been set out. But I didn't break-out—not then.

I needed a replacement. Searching fore-time a couple of days, after about thirty units subjective, I found a chunk of a light synthetic sculpture roughly the same size as the generator. It was piled in the back of what I judged to be a warehouse. No one was likely to miss it immediately.

Toting the synthetic contraption back-time to The Power Place, I located my time window and stored the sculpture nearby in a closet even further back-time.

Next, I wandered around the area undertime until I located the command or control center of The Power Place. Back fore-time I dived until the room was vacant, perhaps several days. When I broke-out, the whole place was a shambles. I fiddled around until I found the light-control levers on a side panel.

With another dive back to the sculpture and forward to my window, I located the control room, and with a quick flash-through, flicked off the lights for the entire Power Place.

I slid into the showroom where the generator—I hoped the real generator—was displayed, and lifted the shiny black cloth. It looked real enough. I made the switch and hoisted the real power equipment undertime just as the lights came on.

The damned fusion generator may have been trunk-sized, but I could barely hang onto it with my arms and hands for the instants of subjective time it took me to struggle back undertime to Baldur's room right after dawn.

I was staggering as I broke-out, but Baldur picked the generator out of my arms as if it were a toy.

I collapsed with a question. "Is that it?"

"That's it."

I explained how I'd made the switch.

"You made the switch *before* we got to The Power Place, but in subjective terms, it was afterward?"

I nodded.

Baldur was no dummy.

"That means that because you made the switch before in real time, you had to rescue me, which meant that you had to make the switch."

I wanted to get away from the circular logic. Because I'd made the switch, I had to make the switch. Fine.

"Baldur, I've got to go back and grab that carrying case. I can't possibly hand-carry the generator back to Query without it."

"Hold it, Loki. You say The Power Place was a shambles after you went fore-time?"

"Yes. Why?" What difference did it make?

"We'd better make sure that happens, too." Baldur handed me a silver cube the size of my foot. "Energy reflector. Drop it on the floor as close to our back-time departure point as you can. Diverts energy back to the source. That's an oversimplification, but after it works, you would be able to pick up the carrying case at your leisure."

I sighed, squared my shoulders, took a deep breath, and dived. Managed to get within a few units of the time we'd left the night before, made a flash-through break-out, and dumped the cube.

I waited for the energy flows to settle and broke-out maybe thirty units before dawn.

Baldur had understated the impact of his little cube. I doubted a single circuit in the entire Power Place would work.

Back in the room, Baldur loaded me up with the damned generator.

"See you later," he remarked as he dived.

For a moment, I wondered what he meant. But I recalled a bit of theory that Freyda had mentioned, and it made sense. Baldur had spent less subjective time away from Query than I had. All my doubling back and forth counted, which meant that Baldur would arrive back at the Travel Hall sooner than I would.

As I vaulted from time-path to time-path back toward Query, I couldn't help wondering about the implications of the time-twists I'd created in Sinopol.

The reason there weren't any suitcase generators later in Sinopol's time-line was simple. We'd tried to get one when we did because they didn't appear later. Because we'd tried to get one, we'd destroyed the possibility of later generators by destroying The Power Place. Baldur's energy reflecting cube had probably destroyed the inventor/craftsman, and with the secrecy of The Power Place, none of the other Hunter techs tried such a small generator.

So we had to do what we did because we did what we did.

I tried to figure out what came first. Had I caused the switch by imagining the energy build-up? Or had I reacted to an actual energy build-up/possible double cross and thus set in motion the entire set of events?

I gave up attempting a solution. In real terms, it didn't matter.

By the time I broke-out in the Travel Hall, Baldur had a small cart waiting for the generator. It went straight to the mech section.

I went back to my rooms and straight to bed.

VI

Dealing with Time, diving season after season, and knowing you could be time-diving objective centuries later has a certain effect.

No Immortal had ever died from old age or from any disease, bodily malfunction, or infection. The rate of spontaneous abortions was high.

All the same, outside of Odinthor, I'd never met a Queryan older than a half-million-plus, not that I knew, anyway, but training kept all of us from exploring past history or anything else to any degree.

My personal theory was that with the weight of memory, Immortals became more and more preoccupied with their personal pasts until they neglected the present. And accidents killed Immortals as easily as any other race, more easily than some.

If it hadn't been for the Temporal Guard, the last Queryan could have died millennia ago. The Guard babied Query, and at the same time it toughened and challenged the most able, intoxicated them with power, and cast them down when they used it against the Guard. That was the way I saw it, the way it was.

The rules were few, strict, and generally unwritten.

Theft was an automatic sentence to Hell. Had to be. Any Queryan could slide into any place big enough to hold him. A few of the Guard could do better than that. So there was no real way to physically safeguard belongings.

Some compensating mechanisms did exist. My diving equipment, for example, was stored in a chest which was

keyed only to my aura. The chest was locked, too heavy
for most to carry on a planet-slide, and too small to get
inside.

Our personal possessions were small and few. Living
quarters were similar. As a matter of custom, we respected
each other's private places, although some of the early
histories cited a period of lawlessness after the initial appearance of the time-diving ability.

All that didn't mean theft didn't exist; it merely limited
it because the stakes were high and the rewards few.

Who wanted to be an Immortal and chained to a rock
on Hell with eagles swooping and ripping at your guts,
grounded by a temporal restraining field and fed by a
bodily sustenance field that would not let you die? That,
or worse, was the lot of the convicted thief.

With the Temporal Guard doubling as the police force,
for most Queryans escape was impossible. When or where
could a criminal flee? The successful crimes were those
that went undetected.

Only the craziest, or the most desperate, stole. In practice that translated into idealists or ambitious Guards with
abilities good enough to avoid detection.

In a nutshell, Query could have been described as a form
of socialism or maternalistic family, but a relatively af-
fluent family. That affluence was reflected in both Guard
training and Guard functions.

With little violence and few property crimes, other
Guard functions in the domestic area became more important on Query than in other cultures. As part of field
training, we were assigned to functions such as weather
observation, local Guard duplicator offices, and to Domestic Affairs, with a longer stint in the Locator section.
Locator was the people-tracing aspect of the Guard.

Locator and Domestic Affairs are two functions of the
Guard not located within the Tower, not even in the
wings. When I thought about it, it made sense. The Tower
is out-of-time-phase, and few Queryans can slide or dive
into or out of the Tower from points on Query.

If a child is missing, or another domestic crisis crops up,
time can be important. The Tribunes felt that a direct
slide into either the Locator or Domestic Affairs sections
would speed up the resolution of the problem.

Basically, in Locator, four or five Guards sit on their
stools behind plain black consoles around an open stage,

waiting for upset Queryans to appear and pour out their Locator problems—usually a missing child, a childish prank, occasionally a missing parent.

Two or three of the Guards who sit and wait are trainees. That was how I found myself staring at a blank Locator screen one afternoon.

What a come-down it was—to spend the morning in advanced field dive-training, diving into a nowhere between stars and trying to orient yourself enough to dive back to Query without using the homing equipment and then to find yourself propped in front of a blank console, waiting, sometimes for nothing.

"Guard Loki!" the woman called urgently, breaking into my reveries. She knew my name because it was on the desk nameplate. "My daughter's disappeared. I can't trace her anywhere."

"Her name?" I asked politely.

"Kyra Dierdre."

"Birth date?"

"16 Jove 2,115,371 Orange."

I keyed it all into the console. Then I punched in the seeker controls.

"Back-time, One Red, South 34-337-45. EPB . . . Astarte."

I fed the coordinates into the microcircuits of my wrist gauntlets and time-dived right from my stool. For a ten-year-old to have gotten that far meant talent, and talent meant trouble.

The Guard didn't lose many, but it could happen. If the kid broke-out on an airless planet, I'd have to be there for the pickup within unit fractions to prevent physical damage.

Other things came into play. I'd heard lots of talk about looping time to undo death, but you can't do it. Dead is dead. The metaphysics of it consume pages of theory, but dead is dead.

Rescuing Kyra was standard. Under the Time Laws I couldn't make physical contact until after break-out, but I swept in behind her on a narrow black time-branch that led to the airless moon called Astarte. I came out right behind her, grabbed, and dived straight undertime. She didn't even have time for a breath of vacuum or a chance to see the black ash and the stars spilled like sugar across the sky.

Kyra's mother may have been surprised as we popped

into being before her, but she didn't show it. True Queryan stoicism—perhaps a touch of mist in the mother's eyes, but no tears, no visible emotion.

She did reach for the girl.

I forestalled her. "I'm sorry, madam, but she'll have to be debriefed before she can come home."

Once more, the stoicism. "When should I come back for her?"

"Two hundred units."

All that time, the girl hadn't said a word. They seldom do immediately after an experience like that.

I slid Kyra and myself to the training center stage. We had to walk through the narrow stone archway. It wasn't in the Tower either, but across the main Square of Quest from it. The room we entered was out-of-time-phase. I let go of Kyra's arm once we were inside.

She tried to slide. She faded slightly, but that was all she could manage.

"Sit down." I pointed to a comfortable stool facing the blank wall screen. She sat.

I triggered the series. Basically, it was similar to the briefing Gilmesh had given me the very first day of my own training, but worded more simply. Most children don't show any time abilities until puberty. They pick up planet-sliding by the time they can walk and talk coherently, which is why some Queryan homes with small children have inhibitors. The static patterns are enough to stop smaller children—most of them.

Kyra was caught by the screen. No great surprise, since a hypnotic field was focused on her to intensify the material. Standard hazard list was the basis—the dangers of suns, airless planets, black holes, blizzards, radiation, etc.

Simplified, but the Guard's indoctrination series for wayward children laid it on thick. Designed for the extraordinarily headstrong children whose will had outpaced the development of their rational faculties.

Two hundred and one units later, Kyra and her mother left the Locator section, presumably for home.

I smiled and sat down on my stool in front of the console. I keyed her name into the records as a likely prospect for the Guard. While she might not pan out, anyone that strong at ten was likely to be one Hell of a diver in another five or ten years.

My watch tour for that day was about up when Frey marched in and presented himself before my console.

He wasn't swinging the black light saber, and he was decked out in formal blacks, with his Senior Guard's four-pointed silver star positively glittering. My insignia was the gold and green of a senior trainee. At the end of the year, when I finished with Locator and Domestic Affairs probation, I was eligible for promotion to full Guard status, and I could wear the solid gold star.

The ranks were really quite few. After you became a Guard, centuries could pass before the next promotion. The Senior Guards wore the four-pointed silver star. Counselors wore black stars edged with gold, and the three Tribunes had black stars edged with silver.

When I looked at the Guards I came in contact with, I wondered who was selected, by whom, and why. Freyda was a Counselor, and likely to be a Tribune whenever Martel stepped down, or so the gossip ran. Baldur was a Counselor, but Gilmesh, who had more service than either and was in charge of Personnel, was only a Senior Guard.

Frey had been promoted to Senior Guard a few years back and had been assigned to run Locator/Domestic Affairs when Wolflen hadn't come back from a scout run to Atlantea.

Frey was in a hurry. "Report to Domestic Affairs as soon as you're relieved. Need a second stand-by Guard with hand-to-hand skills."

He was gone. No explanation. No questions about my availability. Just report to Domestic Affairs.

I wondered if I were getting a reputation as a stand-by muscler as a result of Baldur's report on the Sinopol dive.

I was curious. I'd only had lectures on Domestic Affairs and wasn't scheduled to do my probationary work there until much later in the year. Why had Frey ordered me as a back-up Guard? For what?

By the time Ferrin arrived to relieve me at 1050, I was itching to go.

Ferrin picked it up. He catches everything. Might not have been much of a diver, but if anything were in the wind, his long thin nose and keen ears were the first to find out.

"Know what's going on in Domestic Affairs?" I asked with a straight face.

Ferrin smiled, and his smile and too-big teeth lighted his face like a glowbulb.

"Heard Frey needs muscle. Didn't want to turn to Heimdall for it. You were selected, shining star."

I grinned back at him. Even though he was snoopy, and his lank black hair hanging over his forehead and his long nose gave him a vulture-like look, I had to like Ferrin.

"So why does Frey need me?" I had another question, stupid, but Ferrin could answer it, and I didn't need one of Gilmesh's sarcastic answers. "And why does he run both Locator and Domestic Affairs?"

"Do honey and soda bread go together?"

I thought for a minute, then shook my head.

Ferrin, ready to explain anything, plunged in. "Look, Loki, at what Locator does. Locator tracks people. Now what does Domestic Affairs do? Handles the police functions. And how could it handle the police functions without being able to track people?"

It made sense. I hadn't had to track someone wanted by Domestic Affairs, but Loragerd had told me the story of her second watch at Locator, when the Guard's special Domestic Force had gone out with stunners after a man who had tried to storm Martel's house with an ax.

Using an ax against anyone or his home is bad enough, and it doesn't happen very often, but to lift it against the High Tribune . . . the wretch deserved a term in Hell for something like that.

Only problem was he didn't get it.

The Domestic Force finally cornered him on a cliff edge under the Bardwalls, right below the Garthorn, but before they could stun him, he'd jumped off, and there was no way to match fall velocities, especially on Query. Besides, who'd want to for a nut like that?

I'd asked Loragerd if she knew more about the incident, but she didn't, only that the man had yelled something about the "tyranny of time" and screamed he was tired of being a "poor, dumb sheep."

No trial. The matter was closed.

"What's so hot that Frey needs me?"

Ferrin stopped smiling.

"I have not the glimmer of an idea, nor even the inkling of a conceptual hypothesis. Unfounded rumor would indicate that he requires someone with outstanding sliding skills and of a physical nature, someone who is not beholden totally to Assignments."

Whenever Ferrin used the double-talk, he meant he couldn't verify what he said, that he was guessing. His guesses were better than most Guards' knowledge. And translated—Frey needed a junior goon who might be expendable, and he wanted to round the goon up without asking Heimdall's help.

I reported to Domestic Affairs at 1103 and was promptly greeted by Frey, Gilmesh, and a Guard I'd never met.

"Loki, this is Hightel," noted Frey.

Hightel was stocky, broader than me, with rock-sandy hair, brown eyes. He seemed ready to burst out of his black jumpsuit. He smiled pleasantly. I decided he was the kind of Guard to be polite to.

"Greetings," I acknowledged, and bowed slightly. I couldn't resist pushing Frey a bit. "Could you explain what I'm here for?"

"Fairly simple," began Gilmesh as Frey stood there without uttering a sound. "We have to move a miscreant from detention to the Hall for Trial. Hightel would normally handle the situation, but there is the faint possibility that those sympathetic to the miscreant may attempt to interfere. You are present to insure that no one interferes with Hightel."

At that, he handed me a stunner, deliberately setting it on "full."

I didn't understand, but buttoned my lip. None of it made sense. If the miscreant was so dangerous, why drag a trainee, even a senior trainee, in as a second Guard? Frey was all too nervous, and Gilmesh too plausible. I took the stunner.

Miscreant was the official term for those non-Guard Queryans who violated the Code. This particular miscreant must be something.

While some detention cells were in the Domestic Affairs building across the Square from the Tower, most cells were in the lower Tower levels. Made sense, because the construction of the Tower inhibited sliding and diving. The power was there for the restrainer fields.

The field's a rather elaborate gadget, and how it worked I'm not certain. They'd been around as long as the Guard had. What they did was to scramble thought enough to prevent time-diving or sliding. Without something like that, it would have been impossible to confine any Queryan.

The four of us marched across the Square to the Tower, out of step, but who cared?

Hightel hadn't said one word. We marched down the ramps to the detention levels and still he said nothing. Frey pointed out the cell. Except for the restrainer fields, the thick walls, the windowless and barred room might have passed for a comfortable, if austere, apartment.

"The executioners arrive, with a young one to be blooded as well. Lead on, servants of tyranny," declared the prisoner. Even without the flowery speech, he didn't look like a miscreant.

Although we all had youthful builds and did not age physically, the man in the cell gave me the impression of middle age—tiny lines in the corner of his eyes, a spade beard, faded green tunic and matching trousers, and hand-crafted leather boots like my father made. He had light brown hair and a reddish beard, and his eyes sparkled as he spoke.

Neither Gilmesh nor Frey said a word. I did not either. Hightel did.

"Let's go."

He took the man by his arm. The prisoner couldn't slide or dive because he couldn't carry Hightel with him. If he did, Hightel would subdue him after break-out.

If anything happened to Hightel . . . but that was why I was there.

I noticed my palms were sweaty. I didn't know why. The trip had to be routine—just up the ramps and across the center of the Tower to the Hall of Justice. We didn't go outside.

In the Hall of Justice, the Tribunes were waiting—all three of them—which indicated it was important. Only took one to decide most cases.

I breathed a sigh of relief when the prisoner was settled into the red "Accused" box and the restrainer field was adjusted and trained on him. He didn't look dangerous, wasn't as big as me, but what do appearances indicate?

I eased myself into a corner of the section reserved for the Temporal Guard. The Hall of Justice is a magnificent place, lit with slow-glass panels brought from every type of colored sun in the galaxy, with seats enough for thousands, the whole Temporal Guard and more, and with the crystal dais for the Tribunes, the black podium for the Advocate of Justice, and the red stone box and podium for the accused.

Martel was the High Tribune, flanked by Eranas and Kranos. They sat quietly, waiting. The Advocate, silver mantle draped over her formal black jumpsuit, stepped to the podium.

I drew in my breath as I recognized Freyda, the Counselor and my advanced time-jump instructor.

"Honored Tribunes, honored Guards, honored citizens," she began.

I looked around the Hall. A handful of Guards and a hundred other spectators were scattered about.

The name of the accused was Ayren, and he was charged with civil disorder, personal violence, and treason. To me, that seemed like an odd combination.

Freyda offered the evidence—the testimony of a dozen witnesses, what holo records there were—with a low-key approach. All the testimony of the witnesses was taped, but they were on call should the accused contest the factual content of the testimony.

Ayren chose not to challenge anything.

According to the evidence, the frail man in the red stone enclosure of the accused had employed crude explosives to destroy the Domestic Affairs regional office at Trifalls, used a stunner stolen from the wreckage of the office to stun the first Guards who arrived to investigate, and had stood on the ruins preaching the overthrow of the Temporal Guard and asking every citizen to murder the next Guard he saw.

Fortunately, no one had taken his admonition seriously.

Finally, Ayren tired of stunning Guards and when the follow-up Domestic Force arrived attacked them with a crossbow taken from the Historical Museum.

One Guard, Dorik, had taken a bolt through the arm, but as Ayren was attempting to rewind the weapon, he had been stunned by the two remaining Guards, who carted him off to the Tower for detention.

As the Trial progressed, I became more and more confused. Ayren scarcely seemed crazy, but with each damning charge, each report of an assault, each violent action, Ayren either nodded agreement or failed to contest it.

At the same time, Freyda imputed no motives, just cited

each action, the corroborating evidence, and the applicable section of the Code.

Her summary was brief and concluded with the harsh statement that "Ayren Bly, Green-30, did destroy the property of the people of Query, did advocate the overthrow of the government by force, and did attack with intent to murder. The evidence is clear and undisputed."

Not terribly eloquent, but sufficient, considering the wealth of evidence she had displayed on the screens.

Ayren declined to offer counter-evidence and rose to offer a closing statement, as was his right.

Ayren stood behind the red podium. In the light from the slow-glass panels that lit the Hall, his eyes held the glitter of a madman's, and his voice was filled with the bitter fire of hate—or something, I guessed.

"Thank you, Advocate, Tribunes. My time here is worthless, a coin of gold buried in a charade of counterfeits.

"My speaking will not save me from Hell, nor will my words alter one iota the orbit of this doomed planet. But I must make the gesture, feeble as it might be, against the winds of time. For the winds of time do not die, but sleep, drowsing in the afternoon, waiting for the God of Time to wake them and change the face of this hapless orb. There will be a God of Time, and you will know Him, though you know Him not. And He will know you, and not all your power will stand against Him in His anger. He will sweep the mighty and the proud, and they will break into less than the dust of time. . . .

"Do not condemn me to Hell because I violated the Code. Do not condemn me because I assaulted your agents of repression. If you must condemn me, condemn me for speaking the truth. You have yourselves condemned the people of a once-mighty planet to be your sheep, herded by a few blacksuits, beguiled by an easy life and meaningless toys, while you tear down the galaxy to protect your poor pastures and preserve your waning power. For it wanes. . . .

"Send me to Hell for trying to save the sheep from the shepherds who are no more than black wolves. Send me to Hell, if you must, but do not call it justice. . . ."

There was more, but pretty much in the same vein— ranting and raving about the God of Time who would put down the tyrannical Tribunes and the awful evil Guard.

Poor bastard—didn't seem able to see the mountains for the boulders.

No one listened to him. Who would have, him spouting such nonsense?

After Ayren finished, he bowed politely to Freyda, to the Tribunes, and sat down.

The fire was fled from his eyes, and once more he was just a frail and tired man. For a single moment, I felt sorry for him.

The black curtain rose around the Tribunes from beneath the dais, but not for long. I didn't time it.

When it dropped, everyone stood for the verdict. Less than twenty spectators remained.

The slow-glass panels were damped, except for those focused on the Tribunes. Martel picked up the black wand from the holder and pointed it at Ayren.

"Ayren Bly, Green-30, the Tribunes and people of Query find you guilty as charged and sentence you to thirty years on Hell, and on your return to a full chronolobotomy, to enable you to serve Query as you are best able."

One of the spectators, a woman, maybe his daughter, contract-mate, collapsed. No one paid any attention to her as two Guards I didn't know joined Hightel. All three grabbed Ayren and marched him out.

Still no one noticed the fallen woman.

I walked over. She was clothed in a bright green jumpsuit which flattered her tan and golden hair.

I picked her up and laid her out straight on the bench, wondering if I should cart her over to the Infirmary. She seemed to be breathing normally, but was pale underneath the tan.

She recovered before I'd decided what to do, stared at me, and sat up, shaking slightly.

"Are you going to send me to Hell, too?"

"What on Query for?" I stammered.

"You're one of *them*. Isn't that what you do to everyone who doesn't agree with you?"

"Only those who blow up buildings and try to kill innocent people."

"No Guard is innocent."

I was getting fed up with the conversation. I'd been worried about her, and she, whoever she was, was treating me like I was the criminal.

"So it's all right to blow up people you don't like if you can just pin a label on them? That justifies it?"

It didn't even register. She glared at me, practically hissed, "Did you ever wonder what the past was really like? Did you ever ask yourself why we don't have heroes any more? Did you ever ask yourself why you do what you do? Not you! Not your type!"

She marched off and left me standing there.

What could I have said? That I intended to be a hero? I didn't. So really, what was there I could have said?

VII

The first independent mission the Guard dispatched me on
was a search on Heaven IV.

Although I'd finally gotten my four-pointed gold star
and the status of a full Guard, as a rule search missions
weren't assigned to such junior Guards. I'd thought Freyda
might know and had hunted her up to ask the question.

She was leaving Personnel when I caught up with her.

"Why a search on Heaven IV for me?"

"It's not for your charm, dear Loki. You're the only
young Guard left who can handle a split-entry. Anyway,
it's a simple mission."

She gave me a wry smile as she left me standing there.
Freyda could always leave me speechless in those early
years.

I headed for Assignments. Heimdall, the Counselor who
ran Assignments, had carefully placed his console on a low
platform with two lines of smaller consoles radiating out
from his.

Ostensibly the arrangement allowed Guards consoles to
study the briefing materials while being close enough to
Heimdall to draw on his experience.

Interestingly enough, the access keys to the briefing files
could only be actuated in the Assignments Hall, or by the
private codes of the Counselors or the Tribunes.

Heimdall pointed to one of the consoles at the far end
of the row.

"Heaven IV."

I pulled the stool up to the console screen and attempted

to absorb the information on Heaven IV. The briefing was simple enough.

A periodic sampling of the "religious" literature from Heaven IV mentioned miraculous appearances and disappearances from the skies.

To the suspicious Tribunes, any strange disappearance indicated the possibility of time-diving or planet-sliding which needed further investigation. Because of the lag in reporting, the reputed events had taken place some three hundred years earlier. My job was to confirm or deny.

Heaven IV is at the edge of the area regularly searched by the Guard, closer in to galactic center, and an odd planet to boot. The angels had a loosely held social structure, basically non-tech, and for good reason, since they were peak dwellers.

They shared Heaven IV with the goblins, who were surface dwellers in the hot, and it was hot, lower levels. Heaven IV is a metal-poor, rugged planet with a thick, graduated atmosphere.

The rest of the briefing was technical.

After struggling through it, I headed down to Special Stores, where the techs fitted me with a full-seal warmsuit and supplied me with a miniature time-discontinuity detector. Supposedly, the gismo was designed to point toward sudden changes in time fields, which would enable me to track down the case of the mysterious disappearances.

How did a population of ten million people support such high-tech gadgets? We didn't. We bought or took them from various times and places, like Sertis, Sinopol.

Stealing takes effort, information, hard work. For example, scattered throughout the Guard were linguists who knew virtually every form of every language in use in each high-tech humanoid world in our sector.

Whenever a new one turned up, the Guard dispatched someone with skills to learn the lingo. On the linguist's return, he or she was hooked into the input side of a language tank, and the information became available to the entire Guard.

The business of getting specific technology can be cutthroat at times, like when Odinthor wanted a series of miniature weapons and manipulated the warriors of Ydris from mid-tech to high-tech with back-time tampering. After he obtained the supplies and the production equipment he needed, Odinthor went back and blasted the culture into savagery, partly with the assistance of his brand-new pocket thunderbolts.

The thunderbolts were handy, but I wondered about the purchase price.

When I had all the gadgetry in hand, I pulled on the warm-suit, taking the standard diving equipment out of my chest with care. In the midafternoon, the equipment room we junior Guards shared was empty. So was the Travel Hall. I liked it that way.

The time-dive back to the Heaven IV of three hundred years earlier was uneventful, smooth as silver, and break-out was on the dot. I expected that of myself, tried to avoid sloppiness. I always have.

The sky of Heaven is blue, bluer than the bluest sky of Terra, bluer than the bluest sea of Atlantea. And the pink clouds tower like foamed castles into the never-ending sky.

Angels on wide spread wings soar from cloud to cloud, half-resting on the semi-solid cloud edges on their flights to and from the scattered mountain citadels that rear tall into the domain of the angels.

I looked down, and I could see a hell under the dark clouds below—the sullen heat, the red shadows of the surface, and the squat black cities of the goblins.

I had the split-entry technique down pat, and I hung there with my toes tucked into the undertime, poised in midair.

After long units just soaking in the feel of the unlimited skies, I studied the time-discontinuity detector dial which I was wearing above my wrist gauntlets. The needle was supposed to point toward any discontinuity.

Every once in a while it would quiver, and I'd duck understream to narrow the distance. Whoever or whatever was causing the disturbances was doing it in short bursts, like a planet-slide. After having wasted more than a hundred units, I still hadn't succeeded in narrowing the area.

So I marked the real-time coordinates and set them into my gauntlets. Then I dived back fore-time to Query.

The Travel Hall was deserted. I packed up my gear and started out of the Tower to get a hot meal and a good night's sleep. Hanging in chill midair, warm-suit or not, was tiring, even for me.

Freyda intercepted me as I was heading for the West Portal. I answered the unspoken question.

"No. Took me all this time to get within a revolution or two and half a planet. The detector's pretty rough."

She nodded, inclined her head questioningly.

I knew what she meant. We walked out of the Tower of Immortals together. It was against custom to slide out. Only a few Guards could, anyway, and for some reason, I didn't want to let on that I was one of the few who could.

So we walked out onto the ramps leading through the fireflowers that sparkled in the late twilight.

Freyda stretched out her hand, and I took it, and we slid to her city quarters, high in the Citadel.

She insisted on cooking, and for being a Counselor, Freyda's a good cook. Very little from the synthesizer. She used simple food, simple recipes.

A contract wasn't in the offing, not between a junior Guard and a Counselor. Not age differences, but power-of-position differences.

Sometimes we talked together. Sometimes we slept together, but most times we went our own ways. We never talked policy, and it was probably a good thing for me we didn't.

For all her apparent gentleness, Freyda believed in the Tribunes and their powers, the Guard, and the system as it stood with heart, soul, and body.

"Heaven IV, Loki?" she asked as we lay across from each other on the two low couches. The view of the Tower from her rooms in the Citadel was picture perfect. The spire of the Tower glittered like an arrow of light poised in front of the hills.

The Citadel was one of the few multiple-dwellings left in Quest and dated as far back as the Tower itself. Many Guards kept rooms there, as well as retreats elsewhere on Query.

I had two rooms on a much lower level with no view. Too cramped for me, and I knew I'd have to get a more private place. But I had all the time in the world and was spending my days exploring the tangles of time. I put things off.

Spent a lot of time on mountaintops, in the quiet high forests under the Bardwalls. I've needed alone-places as far back as I could remember, and before that. My mother told me I was sliding into strange corners around our isolated mountain home even before I could complete a full sentence.

I was retrieved five times by the Locator section before I could talk, or so I've been told. Some of that might have been parental exaggeration, but I doubt that. They didn't exaggerate much. Maybe I was a late talker.

"Loki?" Freyda asked again. I realized I'd forgotten where I was, with my thoughts out on the empty needle peaks of the west continent.

I picked up a fistful of nuts before answering her question.

"Blue. Never seen such blue," I mumbled while chomping.

"I remember it," she said softly. "Years ago, Ragnorak took me. You're so like him, Loki. I couldn't hold a split-jump, and he held me there in the air so I could see it— the cloud towers, the angels. If we were only angels, instead of the temporal administrators of the galaxy . . ."

"Just part of it," I reminded her.

She shook her head, and her eyes seemed less deep.

"How do you like being a god, Loki?"

"No god, just a simple Guard."

She laughed, with a tinge to her voice like a harsh silver bell and a sweet one at the same time. "No guard, just a simple god is more like you."

"Then you're a complicated goddess."

Times, she was all flame, like me, and times she was colder than the ice computer on Frost. Never knew which would come, fire or ice, but that night was fire, perhaps foreshadowing the future.

Freyda was gone when I got up the next morning, and that was strange—for her to leave her rooms to me. On those few times when I had stayed the night before, she'd at least awakened me before she left.

As I thought about it, I realized that she'd never been to my quarters, nor had I ever been to her retreat, not even when she'd had me for dinner back when I had been in basic training.

I knew she had a place in the hills overlooking Quest. I'd heard Heimdall saying it had a fabulous view, but I'd never been there at all. You can know so little about your lovers, I guessed, even your very first.

I had to get back to the Travel Hall, back to Heaven IV, before Heimdall rattled me for goofing off. After gulping down a few swigs of firejuice, some cheese, and a piece of fruit, I cleaned up and pulled on a new black jumpsuit Freyda had brought back from Textra for me.

Heimdall was checking the logs in the Travel Hall and smiled that brilliant and meaningless grin of his when I walked in.

"Back to Heaven, or from it?"

I shrugged. We all had to put up with his crass mannerisms. He was good at trend projections and organizing assignments, but was a lousy diver. The older Guards called him "all-seeing," not quite mockingly.

I thought he talked too much and too sharply, but that could have been because I disliked him.

"Heaven IV," was all I said.

He didn't respond, and I went into the equipment room and suited up.

If anything, the blue sky was bluer, and the cloud towers pinker. All in the mind. I'd dived back to a point just a few units after I'd left the day before.

I was in the right real-time. The needle on the detector kept twitching and jumping.

After fifty units sliding around the blue skies, feeling colder and colder, warm-suit or not, watching angels soaring, occasionally fighting with those black ice lances, ducking under the darker shadows of the pink clouds, I decided I was making little or no progress.

I back-timed and broke-out far enough earlier to see if I could discover when the time-discontinuities started. So wrapped up in my own thoughts was I that I slipped out under a cloud shadow right next to a pair of youngsters of opposite sexes, engaged as such youngsters are often wont to be.

After the shock passed—me seeing them, and them seeing this wingless being looking much like them standing in midair—I shrugged it off and decided to confuse the issue. I threw a thunderbolt from my wrist gauntlets at a passing bird. Perhaps it was an eagle, but I vaporized him with one bolt.

Then I smiled at the pair and slid elsewhere—more carefully. No one would believe them if they reported, I hoped.

I dived back up to Query and popped out in the Travel Hall. After storing my gear, I located Heimdall. Not difficult, because he was reigning over the Assignments Hall from his central console.

I explained.

Heimdall called in Freyda, Frey, Gilmesh, and Kranos.

I explained again.

"Sterilize the whole atmosphere," recommended Heimdall.

Freyda frowned at that.

Frey—Freyda's son by her fourth or fifth contract—was walking around the consoles twirling the light saber. He'd picked that up from some obscure group of galactic-wide do-gooders from near the end of back-time limits. Watching his nervous gestures, I wondered who his father might have been. For that matter, I wondered how Freyda had entered four contracts. I couldn't see her in one.

Frey stopped pacing.

"How about a gene-trace?"

"What?"

"Go fore-time. If the trait expands, you could locate a lot of angels with the trait. You aren't trying to find a diamond in a swamp. Stun one. Take a tissue sample and bring it back. The gene laboratories on Weldin ought to be able to synthesize a virus that's fatal to that one gene."

"Ingenious," muttered Heimdall, "but how do you propose to isolate that one gene from all the others? You all may be going to elaborate lengths just to exterminate the race."

"If the biological engineers on Weldin can't discover the right gene, no one can," Frey pronounced dogmatically.

I thought there were holes big enough in Frey's plan to march the whole Guard through, but no one was asking my opinion. I decided not to volunteer it.

"See what you can do, Loki," announced Heimdall.

I hadn't had much to eat before I'd left that morning; so before I headed back to the Travel Hall, I slid out to Hera's Inn for a bite or three.

I picked out a scampig filet from the synthesizer and wolfed it down with a beaker of firejuice.

Patrice was the only one in the Guard equipment room when I got back to the Travel Hall. She was finishing her suit-up.

"Destination?" I asked casually.

"Sertis. Where else? Do they ever send junior Guards anywhere but to pick up machinery and delicacies?" Her blue eyes were cold.

"It'll get better," I said inanely.

"It better." She left without another word.

I couldn't figure some people out. As I strapped on my warm-suit and other gear, I wondered, Didn't everyone have to start at the beginning? But did I? Within a year of getting full Guard status, I was on an independent search. Patrice was still being a porter. Sometimes I was, too, though.

On Heaven IV, the sky was still blue, a thousand years fore-time, the clouds pink, and angels flew.

Fewer angels than centuries before, it seemed, but plenty.

I checked the time-discontinuity detector. Not once did it quiver.

I quartered the planet, spent another fifty units, but not even a twitch on the detector.

There was a different feeling about this time, a feeling of aftermath, but I couldn't pin it down. Something had happened, I was convinced.

I dived further back-time, the real-time equivalent of Query "Now."

On break-out, I found plenty of angels, plenty of pink clouds.

Some of the pink cloud towers struck me as angular, regular, as if they'd been shaped.

I slid into one, found it hollow and filled with angels bearing pink ice lances. I dropped undertime before my presence registered, I thought.

Something was brewing. The discontent, if I could call it that, permeated the endless skies.

Half the angels had the pink ice lances, and half were carrying black ones. The black lancers and pink lancers avoided each other.

I ducked undertime and emerged about a year later, more from curiosity than anything. Everything was over, but the moans. Damned few angels anywhere.

I back-timed about a half year and broke-out in the middle of a pitched battle of the pink lances against the black lances.

I didn't believe it. All the information on Heaven IV stated that the angels were pacifists, and that only the goblins below had warlike traits.

But believe it or not, I was hanging in the middle of a war raging across the skies of Heaven.

I studied the time detector and found nothing.

I had a good idea I wasn't going to find a thing, but I coppered my bets by trying a good double-dozen time/ locales for spot checks. Nothing.

That's what I told Heimdall and Freyda.

"So now what should I do?" I asked.

"Drop it," ordered Heimdall.

I had a funny feeling that the whole mess was self-fulfilling, but wasn't sure I could explain why. I didn't try, either.

"Loki, Athene needs another Guard." Heimdall dismissed me.

As a very junior Guard, with no permanent assignment, I was shuffled from pillar to post. Often it was Maintenance, sometimes Assignments, where Heimdall had me help prepare briefing tapes, but most often it was Special Stores.

Not just for me, but for all the unassigned Guards. Special Stores was in charge of procurement, responsible for getting the items we couldn't make by sending Guards off to buy, beg, borrow, or steal whatever was necessary.

Not that it was a bad section to work for, although the planets and times we saw were all stable and settled, and the junior Guards like me all dealt in cash transactions, but after a while I wondered.

The more senior Guards came up with the cash and did the "steal" operations. Most non-time-diving peoples store valuables in locked enclosures. It's very simple for a trained Guard to dive directly inside and remove a portion of what passes for currency.

Usually we don't take much. What with our simplified culture, low population, and the use of the duplicating technology, we don't need too many items.

After my fifth or sixth trip to Sertis to buy power cells, however, I had some questions. Some items don't duplicate. Power cells are one, and the Guard who tried it was likely to end up with a few holes blown in him.

Perhaps because it was so late in the afternoon, perhaps because I was unhappy with the outcome of the Heaven IV mission, I wondered a bit too loudly for Counselor Athene.

"Can't we ever make anything?" I'd asked Halcyon.

We'd just finished checking the posting sheets to discover we'd been assigned a trip to Sertis for power cells.

"What do you mean?" asked Athene.

I must have jumped. I hadn't realized anyone else was around.

"Well—uh—seems like we have to gather a lot from everywhere, and that we make nothing."

"There is that," Athene said.

Halcyon stepped back and said nothing. The twinkle in her eye told me I was on my own. Not nastily, Halcyon's not like that, but sort of a now-you've-stepped-into-it look with mischief in it.

I decided I should have followed Halcyon's example and kept my mouth shut, but it was too late.

"Who do you think ought to make all the materials we import, and how?" Athene asked in her gentle voice.

Athene was one of those deceptive-looking Guards. Taller than me, slender as a willow, with softly curled hair like spun gold, a small nose, together with a soft voice, a stubbornness harder than the Bardwall granite, and slate-gray eyes that could burn hotter than a nova—that was Athene. I didn't think she ever forgot.

"Do you have any suggestions, Loki?"

"Maintenance," I suggested lamely, forgetting my resolve to keep my mouth shut.

"Not a bad idea. I wonder what Baldur would think about it."

I didn't care for the tone of speculation in her voice.

"After you make your pickup this afternoon, Loki, I'd like to talk to you again."

I noted the rest of the details from the posting sheet, signed for the Sertian currency, and trudged down the ramp toward the Travel Hall.

From nowhere, Halcyon joined me.

"You had to open your head, didn't you?"

"Wasn't too sharp," I admitted. "I wonder what she's got in store for me when we get back."

We didn't say much as we got ready to dive. What was there to say?

Sertis is high mid-tech or low high-tech, that is, the time locale we were posted for.

Once during training I asked why we made so many trips there, but Gilmesh answered my question with a question: How much can you carry on a dive? And that's the problem. So far the Guard hadn't run across any mechanical time-diving equipment. Just people, and that meant that anything that got carried across time was carried by some poor Guard, usually some poor junior Guard or trainee.

Needless to say, that limitation had a profound influence on the culture I grew up in.

The dive was uneventful, boring, in fact.

Halcyon and I made the pickup, turned the two cases of power cells over to the Special Stores supply desk, where a Senior Guard named Quetzal logged them in and shooed us away.

Halcyon decided to have dinner. I wanted to face the music with Athene before leaving for the day.

I presented myself at the archway into her corner of the Special Stores Hall.

"Loki, our talk will have to wait. Martel has announced his decision to step down."

I didn't understand, and my face must have mirrored my lack of comprehension. I just wanted to get it over with.

She straightened and explained.

"If Martel steps down, we need to select a new Tribune."

Everything clicked. The ten Counselors and the Counselor-elect proposed by the Senior Guards would determine the new Tribune. The three Tribunes would then select among themselves the new High Tribune. That was an oversimplification, but a rough explanation without going into the various ballots and classes of ballots or the single right of refusal by the two remaining Tribunes.

The Senior Guards balloted for a Senior Guard to become a Counselor. Then the eleven Counselors and the two Tribunes decided the new Tribune.

Athene was getting prepared for her part in the selection so she didn't have the time to put a junior Guard through her logical wringer, for which I should have been grateful. I wasn't. I wanted to get it over with.

More to delay her than for any other reason, I asked, "Have the Senior Guards selected the new Counselor?"

"No. I suspect Heimdall will be the one they pick."

She didn't elaborate. I couldn't see Heimdall as Counselor, but since I wasn't a Senior Guard, it wasn't any of my business.

The Counselor selection process was over in a couple of days. How couldn't it be? Of the two hundred Senior Guards, all but a handful were on Query. The others were recalled quickly, and with everyone able to meet in the Hall of Justice, they picked Heimdall, just as Athene had predicted, within a few hundred units.

In the meantime, the Guard functioned. While it didn't happen too often, picking a Tribune wasn't such a big deal to the average Guard. At least, it wasn't to me. The office, rather than the holder, generated the respect.

With all my rationalization, I wasn't particularly happy to see Heimdall picked as the new Counselor.

I did not know all of the Counselors, and some I knew as Guards, without knowing they were Counselors. I was familiar with Freyda, Athene, Baldur, who'd taught us Maintenance as trainees, Odinthor, and, of course, Heimdall.

Baldur had never said a word to indicate his position, and I couldn't recall him wearing the gold-edged black star of a Counselor. Maybe he did, and I hadn't noticed it.

The second day of the selection, while the eleven Counselors and the two Tribunes were holed up picking a successor to Martel, I had lunch with Loragerd at Hera's Inn. It's always been a favorite with the younger Guards.

"What do you hear about the selection? How do they narrow it down from thirteen?"

"Loki, sometimes you're so naive." She smiled and reached across the table to ruffle my hair. I liked it when she did that.

"What do you mean?"

"Not a real choice at all. Probably already narrowed down to one or two. I'd say Baldur or Justina."

"Justina?" The name was familiar, but I couldn't place her.

"You know, the stern, let-us-do-what-is-right-for-the-people type who runs Observation? She gave us the indoctrination on the Weather Service, but left all the training up to Pertwees."

I had a hazy mental picture of a dark-haired woman, stiff, cold, and full of herself, a female version of Heimdall, in a way.

"Didn't know she was a Counselor."

"Can you imagine any Guard running such a tedious operation without some reward?"

"Some of the satellites are pretty run-down," I mentioned, recalling the one Sammis had stuck into my Attitude Adjustment test. "Where did they ever get them anyway?"

"Loki, sometimes I think you do your best to forget history, especially if it doesn't square with legend. They predate the Guard, relics of our own mid-tech past. Can you imagine us building one now?"

I couldn't, but I was more interested in the selection. I changed the subject back.

"Which one do you think they'll pick?"

Loragerd took a sip of the dark ale she liked so much before answering. She was still wearing her hair as short as the first day we met as new trainees.

"Baldur. He's fair and doesn't pick fights."

Made sense to me.

We were both wrong. When we reported back to Assignments, after lingering at lunch, Heimdall was back in his high stool on the platform, with his brand-new gold-edged black star.

"Who?" we asked in unison.

"Freyda," he answered, understanding the question. He seemed pleased, but who wouldn't after having been elected Counselor.

Glammis was sitting next to him, smiling broadly. That was one of the few times I'd seen her smile, not that I ran across her very often. She was the assistant supervisor of Maintenance, usually quite reserved. She and Heimdall spent a lot of time together, but Loragerd had told me that they'd never been contract-mates or even shared quarters.

Heimdall must have been in a good mood. He beamed at Glammis, even smiled at us.

"Loragerd, you can take off the afternoon. Loki, as far as I'm concerned, you're free also, but I understand Athene wants a word with you first."

I didn't think the Senior Guards or Counselors ever forgot anything.

Athene was expecting me, and she didn't waste any time.

"Loki, I've been thinking. I've had a chance to talk it over with Heimdall and some of the other Counselors, the Tribunes, and we all agree you need a permanent assignment."

I waited for the other boot to fall. Except for Ferrin, no one else out of my trainee class had been made permanent. Maybe it wouldn't be too bad. I felt I could take Special Stores, Assignments, even the Weather Service, or Archives.

"**Ma**intenance."

I must have cringed.

"It's not that bad. Baldur says you're one of the few newer Guards with any mechanical aptitude at all."

Why was Heimdall so interested in keeping me out of trouble?

"When do I report?"

"I'd say today, but it's the nearest thing to a full holiday. Make it first thing in the morning."

I bowed and said thank you. I was a bit dazed. Like Patrice had said years ago, divers didn't work in Maintenance, especially not crackerjack divers. And I was becoming a damned good diver, if not the best. Everyone said so. So why had they all decided to stuff me away in Maintenance?

I ran down Loragerd at Hera's Inn and asked her the same question. She wasn't terribly sympathetic, but that might have been because she and Halcyon had been comparing notes, and I'd burst in.

"You're favored with one of the first permanent assignments, while Halcyon and I cart perfume and power cells around, and immediately you run here to tell us what's wrong with it. What did you want? Special assistant to Freyda in view of your past services?"

Loragerd was high on the dark ale, I figured, but the crack hurt.

"That's not it at all."

"Not completely, anyway," chipped in Halcyon.

Loragerd brushed Halcyon's comment away with a wave and turned full face to me.

"Sometimes you're so dense. Don't you see? All support jobs are dull. Do you want to lug supplies across time and keep records for Athene? How about keeping reports for Gilmesh in Personnel? Or would you rather listen to citizen complaints at Domestic Affairs in between hearing Frey's boasts?"

I had to chuckle at the last. Loragerd always made so much sense. Why couldn't I see it that way?

She reached over and touched my arm briefly.

"Other things will have to change, too, Loki. Remember that."

What did she mean?

Loragerd switched the subject to the selection process. I didn't have a chance to comment. Halcyon looked peeved for a moment, but relaxed as Tyron and Ferrin wandered over.

"You know," began Tyron, dumping gossip on the table like a chunk of rockwood, "there's a rumor that the first person selected to be Tribune refused the election."

"Who was it?" I snapped.

"Was it Justina?" asked Loragerd.

"Corbell? Athene? Baldur?"

Tyron shrugged. "I don't know. No one's saying, but it's never happened before."

"But that sort of thing wouldn't be in the Archives," protested Ferrin.

I sipped my firejuice and let them discuss it. Despite the furor over the rumor, I was thinking about reporting to Maintenance. No one really understood. What diver really wanted to stand ankle-deep in oil and grease?

I left early, while the others were still singing and talking.

First, I slid up to a little ledge under Seneschal, high in the Bardwalls, and stared at the silver rivers in the canyons below. That ledge was the sort of place where I intended to have my own private retreat someday. A place where the only sound was the occasional hiss and flap of a night eagle or the whistling of the wind. In my thin jumpsuit, I soon grew cold and slid back to my own quarters in the Citadel.

After a solid night's sleep, I reported to Baldur the next morning with my heart in my hands, so to speak.

He didn't let me voice my misgivings, and, sitting back in his plain stool, he started right in.

"A lot of Guards have the feeling that Maintenance is grubby, that we work ankle-deep in grease, oil, grit. Now take a good look around . . ."

Baldur stood a good head and a half taller than me, and with his light blue eyes and silver-blond hair, looked like a gentle sort of giant. His voice was mid-toned, a light baritone that cut through noise and distractions without being raised and without annoying. Baldur was instantly likable, yet conveyed solidity. But somehow no description really did him justice.

That morning, as he outlined Maintenance, I wished they'd selected him Tribune, forgetting that if they had, he wouldn't have been running Maintenance.

Baldur led the way to a corner area, well lighted, with

a clear worktable and a comfortably padded, high-backed stool.

"Here's your space. The work you'll start with is replacing or repairing microcircuitry in wrist gauntlets and stunners. They get banged up so often it's simpler for us to repair than replace. Within the year, you will be able to rebuild any microcircuitry you can see from scratch. Then we'll go into more elaborate work."

That sounded elaborate enough.

The technical side was straightforward. Baldur demonstrated the console reference guides for the information on gauntlets and stunners, the micro-magnifier and step-down microcircuit waldoes, and pointed out the bin where what I had to handle would be placed.

Next came a guided and detailed tour of the Hall, and we ended up back in his spaces.

"Sit down." He pointed at a vacant stool. I sat.

"Why is an understanding of machinery and electronics important to a Guard?"

"Because a Guard can't use to its fullest capabilities equipment he doesn't understand." That's what he told us in training.

Baldur laughed.

"Well, you do remember those lectures. But there's more. I may say some things which will surprise you or shock you, but try to keep them in context.

"First, the Guard is composed generally of a group of polite barbarians. Second, barbarians have a tendency to destroy what they don't understand. Third, most past Tribunes have historically understood that, from Sammis Olon on. Fourth, most Guards don't. Now, do you know what I mean by a polite barbarian?"

I didn't have the faintest idea, but decided to guess.

"Someone who is polite, but doesn't understand."

"What's polite? Understand what?"

I shrugged.

"Look at it this way, Loki. Most Guards know that if you push the stud on a stunner and point it at someone, it knocks them out. Why?"

I shrugged again.

"Then how did someone discover how to build one— by trying every possible piece of electronic gadgetry in the universe?"

I must have looked as blank as I felt.

Baldur grinned. "Pardon me if I get on my podium, but I can get intense on this subject."

I nodded, wondering where he was headed.

"I'll cut it short for now. It takes an understanding of physiology and electronics to build a stunner. On Query we don't have that knowledge. Do you understand the simple chemistry behind a projectile gun? A linguistics tank? That's what I mean by barbarians. Every culture has its barbarians, but in the average culture when there get to be too many barbarians and too few individuals who understand the technology, the culture collapses.

"On Query, no one understands the mechanics of every-day life. Nor that the Guard structure is all that really maintains our way of life. In the Guard, basically three functions are critical—Maintenance, the data banks of the Archives, and Special Stores.

"One of the reasons I give trainee-lectures is to empha-size that point, but it's gotten harder and harder to get across, even in my lifetime. A related problem is power. Stored power can't be run through a duplicator. So we import generators, as you may recall from our episode on Sinopol, and power cells. Maintenance has to repair that equipment."

Baldur paused, studied me, and sighed.

"I can see I've just about overloaded your rational faculties. We talk more later."

That was my first day in Maintenance.

VIII

Wrapped in furs and close against a young lady with smooth, cool skin, I was dreaming, flying lightnings across a twilight sky. Though Loragerd lay by me, she was not within the dream, as I strode across massive black mountains to pull down night.

Fires streamed from my fingers and the stars paled to nothing against the light I wielded. . . .

A faint hum came from the clothes strewn behind the couches, leading me from the dream. I wondered if someone were calling, but let myself slip back into the clutches of sleep, drawing Loragerd closer.

Her black, pixie-cut hair was fluffed slightly, and the warm fragrances of trilia and cinnamon drifted from her body and enfolded us in the early morning.

Suddenly, two Guards I didn't know were shaking me out of my sleep.

Instantly awake, I threw the smaller Guard off my shoulders and into the wall. I'd seen him before, a brown-haired ferret who usually followed Heimdall around the Tower.

The other Guard had plucked Loragerd out of the furs and had his paws all over her. She was white-faced and wearing nothing at all.

The first Guard was still crumpled in the corner, trying to regain his feet. The pawing one saw me coming and dropped Loragerd like a lava-stone.

"Heimdall—needs you now—in Assignments," he stammered.

"So—was this necessary?"

78

I wanted to take both bastards and drop them over Sequin Falls.

"Heimdall sent us," apologized Ferret-face, as if that excused anything and everything.

"And how did he know where we were?" I asked without thinking.

Nobody answered me, and I realized what a stupid question I'd posed. Heimdall had sent them over to Locator to get the coordinates and in they'd slid.

Looking at the pair, I noticed they were both bigger than I was—much bigger, but I hadn't even noticed it before.

"So scram," I growled. "We'll get there when we're dressed, and that will be sooner if you get out of here."

The two exchanged glances, looked back at me, and winked out as they slid, presumably back to Heimdall.

I put my arms around Loragerd, who was shaking. Though the room was warm, I could feel her shivers and the goose bumps on her normally satin-smooth skin.

We didn't say anything. What was there to say? We'd overslept when we should have been on duty. Junior Guards have very few rights.

As we dressed, I thought Loragerd gave me an appraising look, a strange sort of glance, but I could have been imagining it.

She went to Linguistics, which was her permanent assignment, and I made for Assignments.

As I marched up the ramp from the West Portal of the Tower, I could sense a tenseness that tightened as I approached the Assignments Hall.

I could have cut the silence with a light saber, Frey's or anyone else's. Heimdall was slumped in his high stool, and the blackness poured from him like a river.

As he caught sight of me, he straightened, opened his mouth as if to shout, then clamped it shut. He waited an instant, then began curtly.

"Glammis was on Atlantea. Fifty centuries back. Locator tag wavered, just went blank."

That meant the Locator console was receiving a signal, but not linked to Glammis's thought pattern, which meant she was dead, deep-stunned, or near death.

I stared at Heimdall. The whole morning made sense. If there'd ever been anyone Heimdall was close to, it had to have been Glammis, the slight woman with the stern

face and dark curly hair. Why had Glammis been on
Atlantea? She usually presided over the machine shop's
daily operations with an iron hand. Baldur supplied the
philosophy, Glammis the work.

She seldom went into the field, but Baldur had mentioned that she'd once been considered a crack diver, centuries ago.

"You want me to bring her back?"

He nodded. I understood. Heimdall wanted ability, not
just any diver. So Heimdall had sent his troopers after me.

"Information?" I snapped. I had a couple of units, if
that.

"End console."

If I hadn't known Heimdall better, I would have sworn
the iron Guard's voice was ready to crack.

In a funny way, I had to admire him. If it had happened to Loragerd, I'd have gone off half-cocked no matter
what. Heimdall knew his limits, understood he couldn't
rescue Glammis, and had to stand by helplessly as he tried
to round up help.

Glammis's mission had been simple, according to the
console. The mid-island people of fifty centuries earlier
had developed a broadcast power transmitter. The results
were strange, to say the least, since the output at the re-
ceiver was greater than the input. But for reasons unclear
in the surveillance reports, the project had failed when the
generator quit producing power and later exploded.

Glammis had been so intrigued with the possibilities,
considering that power is one of our main problems, that
she had decided to make the dive herself. Wasn't too surprising, when I thought about it. Divers who understood
mechanical theory were few and far between.

I got the directional output from the console and headed
for the Travel Hall.

No waiting for languages, cosmetics, or special equipment—I threw on a stunner, equipment belt, and wrist
bands and dived.

A fast recovery, if at all. I wasn't happy about it. Mes-
sengers who confirm bad news are likely to become the
recipients of gratuitous violence.

Atlantea was a strange planet, although every planet has
some peculiarities. Atlantea has shallow seas and metallic
deposits, with no moons and no tidal forces to speak of.

The combination's not supposed to occur, but that's the way it was.

And Glammis was down.

I red-flashed the back trip, homing in on Glammis's signal from her Locator tag and power packs.

Sometimes the line between death and unconsciousness is terribly fine. If Glammis died, subjective time, before I had dived clear of Quest, she was dead, but if there was any spark, she had an outside chance.

I was aiming for a break-out point right at the instant her Locator signal had shifted from active to passive. A risk, but probably worth it.

Undertime doesn't really have a color, but it feels gray, and your vision is limited. You can see "outside," the real objective time, but it's muddled, like looking up from beneath the water, silvered over and wavering, with flashes of light darting across your field of vision like minnows.

Time tension, like water tension, exists at the moment of break-out when you are showered with a spray of moments that slide off you with the emotional shock of icy rain.

Except this time I bounced back undertime as soon as I broke-out, my head reeling with the impression of time mirrored in time. I slid sideways fractionally and came out in a corridor.

The stench was ozone. The building atmosphere spelled out "powerplant."

The directionals on the wrist gauntlets pointed toward a door closed and barred. The bar had melted, in effect welding itself to the frame.

No one was around.

The feeling of time being warped grew as I walked up to the door. I grabbed the crossbar and dived. The bar came with me; the doorframe didn't. That's how the Law of Discrete Particles works. If the bar had been the same material as the frame, nothing would have happened.

I still couldn't slide or dive into the room, for whatever reason. I broke-out, dropped the bar, forced open the door—it was a sliding type that had a tendency to jam—and walked into the generator room.

The place was a mess. Two control stations were a fused mass, and I didn't need more than a quick glance to see that the two controllers were dead.

With the currents of time swirling around me, it took

every bit of concentration to walk across the ceramic floor to the dark-haired woman sprawled on her back. She was alive and breathing. But her mouth hung open, and her wide green eyes were empty.

I picked her up, hoping she didn't have any physical injuries, and caught the time-tide swirling out of the generating equipment to throw us undertime and fore-time toward Quest.

I suspected that Glammis had literally lost her mind, but I'd leave that determination to the medical techs.

Rather than trying to make a dive and a separate slide, I broke-out with Glammis right in the Infirmary. I staggered into the critical care section as Hycretis came running.

Hycretis devoted his attention to Glammis, as if I weren't even there.

I stood there dumbly for a long moment, wondering why the room was vibrating, before I understood my legs were shaking. I plopped down on the edge of a vacant bed at the end of the ward and closed my eyes.

"Damn you, Loki! Damn you!"

I felt myself being shaken like a rag doll. Was it a nightmare? I tried to roll over in the bed, but the buffeting wouldn't go away.

"What did you do? God you would be, Loki, and deprive me of my only joy! Torment me, would you, young god, with an empty shell?"

Like a slowing top, the universe began to settle, and I woke up fully to find Heimdall grabbing my harness, shaking me, and screaming, tears streaming from his eyes, and saliva drooling from the corners of his mouth.

"Answer me! Answer me, would-be god!"

Heimdall slapped my face, and this time it hurt.

He had me just by the harness. I slid behind him with a quick dive barely under the tension of the "now." He was still holding an empty harness and staring at the vacant space where I had been when I cracked him a solid one from behind. He went down like a breaker, foaming at the mouth, but out. Out cold.

"Wouldn't you say that Heimdall was suffering from strain?" I asked Hycretis.

Both Hycretis and the two storm troopers holding him appeared stunned, for some reason.

"Let him go." I gestured at the two Guards.

They released their hold on the medical tech, but he didn't say anything.

"I think Heimdall was under too much stress," I announced, "and that all he really needs is a good rest."

I turned to the two thugs. "You two watch Heimdall and make sure his rest isn't troubled by anyone—except maybe the Tribunes."

That would occupy them for a while.

"Hycretis, give Heimdall a muscle relaxant or whatever you deem suitable, and maybe a mild sedative."

This time my words registered, and he nodded.

I checked the objective time. Seemed like I'd been gone forever, but the wall clock said one hundred units elapsed from the moment I'd left the Travel Hall. I'd have bet ninety units had been my sleep recovery time.

"Glammis?" I asked Hycretis.

"Physically, fine. Her mind's wiped clean. How I don't know. Thought patterns of practically an unborn child."

The Glammis we knew was gone. Heimdall had been right.

"Did you tell Heimdall?"

"How could I not tell him?"

I thought about the two thugs guarding Heimdall's bed. Right. How could he not?

Another question was why I hadn't noticed how Heimdall was employing his private army. That could wait.

I knew the answer to the power problem Glammis had been investigating, I thought. Baldur would know if I was right.

I went down the ramps to Maintenance not quite at a run.

Baldur glared at me as I stood respectfully outside his area, taking deep breaths, waiting, and refusing to go away.

"All right." He touched a stud on his console. "What is it?"

I recounted my travels to Atlantea, from the funny generating room where I'd rescued Glammis to the time currents and my diving difficulties.

". . . and I don't have a thing to go on, but if I had to guess, I'd say they're tapping the time-tides and wrenching time out of its flow."

When I began, Baldur had a half-bemused, let's-humor-Loki look on his face. By the time I finished, he was run-

ning his stubby fingers through his white-blond hair. He
did that when he was excited. "Fascinating concept, fascinating, but dangerous. Let me think about it, Loki. Let me
think about it."

As far as he was concerned, I had ceased to exist. Baldur
was back in his world of numbers and concepts.

While I was deciding what I ought to do, I walked back
over to my own work space and began to finish cleaning
and running maintenance checks on a faulty copier that
Frey had brought down from the Domestic Affairs weapons
storeroom.

The duplicator wasn't faulty. Frey was. He'd tried to
copy some sort of hand weapon with power cells in place.
Luckily, the power pack had been almost drained, or
Hycretis would have been scraping Frey and his light
saber off the nearest wall.

Boring—that's what it was. In spite of the light pouring
in from the long windows and the airiness provided by the
high ceilings, milling out the melted junk and replacing
the circuits one by one was a tedious task.

All in all, I enjoyed being able to fix things, seeing a pile
of metal turned back into a functional machine. As Baldur
had pointed out, repairs were usually more efficient than
sending trainees and junior Guards all over time to pick up
more and more hardware.

As I finished the copier and rolled it back to the front
where Frey's flunkies would pick it up, I realized someone
was standing in the shadows.

Loragerd. After the Glammis pickup, the incident with
Heimdall, Baldur's comments, she'd slipped my mind.

"Are you all right?" she asked as I came up.

I could feel my throat tighten. Here she was, waiting
for me, after having been pawed, assaulted, and forgotten—asking how *I* was.

What could I say? I just shook my head and held her,
tightly.

"Loki." She leaned back and wiped my cheeks. "I'm fine,
just fine. Heimdall was after you, worried about Glammis.
You handled everything except you. Freyda came and told
me to take off early and find you. I did."

I couldn't say anything. What could I say?

After my first fling with Freyda, our relationship had
cooled, but she still worried. Imagine, sending Loragerd to
look after me.

Imagine, Loragerd caring how I was. Me?

Ridiculous. Except I stood there in the afternoon shadows of the ancient and time-protected machines holding Loragerd and shaking.

We had a short dinner at Hera's before going back to my rooms.

All night long, I kept waking up, wondering if someone would appear out of nowhere and grab me. Loragerd slept better, I think.

On that long night, with my arms around Loragerd, wondering about the chain of tomorrows that loomed ahead, I kept recalling the shock of the morning. Seemed longer before than the same morning.

I was going to get a place, even if I had to build it stone by stone, that no one could slide into. Thinking that, knowing it would be so, in the early morning silence, I drifted into sleep and did not wake again until the wake-up chimed.

Loragerd and I had some juice, some fruit, and dressed.

She left for the Linguistics Center before I was quite together, but within units I was headed for Maintenance. I made the Tower in a quick slide and hustled down the ramps from the West Portal to see what Baldur had come up with.

From the look of his area, he'd been there all night. The circles under his eyes were blacker than ever, but he gave me a smile. "Most intriguing problem, most intriguing, Loki, but I suspect a self-resolving one."

"What do you mean?"

"I've checked the files. Glammis located this device fifty centuries back, and the records show the station was abandoned. Obviously, it was unsuccessful. The Atlanteans succeeded in transferring some energy across time. I've postulated a theoretical basis for the mechanism."

"I'm lost," I admitted.

He beamed faintly because I'd pursued the question. "If your conjecture is correct, and I suspect it is, the total of mass and energy, energy really, since mass is a stabilized form of energy, and that's simplifying it grossly, does not need to be constant.

"The Atlantean powerplant was diverting energy from the nearer time levels. That was why you couldn't dive into the area immediately around the generator."

Baldur stopped and gestured an end to his response, lifting his bushy blond eyebrows as if the conclusion were evident.

I didn't feel like guessing.

"And?"

"There is a definite limit to the energy easily available to the generator. Within a few years, seasons, perhaps days, the generator will stop delivering power. It's really an energy concentrator more than a generator."

"The damned thing will quit by itself?"

"Right. And . . ." Baldur launched into a detailed explanation of how and why which I listened to with my thoughts elsewhere. I'd have to go back and check the Atlantean generator over a period of years before making a final report.

I've always disliked loose ends.

After that I was going to discover the location I'd visualized for my private retreat—where Heimdall and his thugs couldn't track me down.

Baldur wound up his technical dissertation.

"Then I'll dive back and check out your theory."

"You doubt everyone, don't you."

I grinned. He'd caught me out.

Baldur dismissed me, and I marched up the ramps to the Travel Hall. I should have checked in with Assignments, but I could claim I was acting under Baldur's orders if anyone complained.

Ten years fore-time from my pickup of the disminded Glammis, I came across not a malfunctioning power plant, nor an empty structure, but a fused and leveled pile of rubble, glazed over as if by a tremendously hot energy source.

I tried to locate the exact point of destruction, but couldn't. In one instant, five years objectively after Glammis's near demise, the complex stood, vacant and nonfunctional. In the next unit remained only the glazed pile of junk.

No matter how I concentrated in the undertime, I couldn't identify that fraction of a unit when the destruction occurred. Between two instants in the undertime, I could only sense what I'd call a vortex, a whirlpool of time, an instantaneous unleashing of power striking from between the threads of time, yet a power totally separated from the Time surrounding those instants.

I recorded the results on the portable holo unit I'd carted along for the purpose and dived back to the Travel Hall.

A few trainees were popping in and out of the Hall, but no one I had to account to.

I took the holo unit and cornered Baldur, not that it was hard because he seldom left Maintenance during the day.

"Not surprised," he commented tersely, for once trying to get rid of me. He'd solved the problem. I was the doubter. "Time recoil, showing the limits to which energy can be transferred."

I wandered back to my own area, thinking it over. I didn't understand the why of it, but that's the way time is. You can only bend it so far before it strikes back.

Ferret-face was waiting for me.

I glared at him. He cowered. Damned if I knew why. He was an experienced Temporal Guard with the power of Heimdall behind him.

"Heimdall would appreciate seeing you in the Assignments Hall."

I wondered about Ferret-face's politeness, but that's not the sort of question you can ask.

Heimdall was back behind his desk, as if nothing at all had happened the day before. His eyes were a bit bloodshot. That was all. Intent as I was on Heimdall, I overlooked Freyda at first. She was standing a few steps to the left of Heimdall.

"Honored Tribune, Counselor." I gave them both a half-bow.

Heimdall pointed to the chair on the platform next to his console. I plunked myself into it. Freyda sat down next to Heimdall.

Heimdall nodded at Freyda, deferring. She accepted whatever invitation it was and began. "Commendation for your recovery of Glammis. While she will need a total re-education, there was no lasting physical or genetic damage.

"Second, the Counselors have recommended that you be assigned to take over as assistant supervisor of Maintenance. Glammis will not be able to resume her duties for some time."

Brother, was that an understatement. Glammis would take years to recover her skills, and there was no guarantee the stimuli of her second childhood would lead her down the same mech-oriented path as her first.

Although Baldur would continue as the overall supervisor of Maintenance, I'd have much wider latitude—and more to do. The whole thing also demonstrated the thinness of the pool of Guards with mechanical talents.

I thanked both Heimdall and Freyda for their confidence, vowed to follow the high standards of tradition, bowed, and was dismissed.

Back down the ramps to Maintenance I ambled, musing over the latest turn of events.

The first thing to do was to move into Glammis's old spaces. Several days passed before I was satisfied with the results. By that time the repairs had piled up, and that meant working late for a good ten-day. I didn't feel that should be a permanent state of affairs.

Baldur agreed. "What do you suggest?"

"That you request the trainee with the best mechanical aptitude from the current third-year class for a hundred units a day."

"Fifty," replied Baldur.

"I'd also suggest more routine maintenance help from the second-year trainees, like you used to require."

"If you want to run the operation, fine."

Surprisingly, Heimdall agreed.

Narcissus was the third-year trainee, and I ended up by giving him the same spiel Baldur had fed me—except I wasn't quite so successful.

"You seem awfully sure, Loki, and I guess I believe you," was Narcissus's reaction.

I must have had some reaction to his doubts. He gave me the strangest look.

"I believe you. I believe you."

I admitted to myself that I wanted to tweak him with a thunderbolt to get my point across, but I didn't believe I'd considered such a drastic alternative seriously.

That spring plodded along into summer before I got things running the way I wanted, before I had much free time for my second and more personal project—locating a site for my own personal retreat.

I must have looked at every cliff ledge in the Bardwalls before I settled on a location. I'd figured out what I'd needed before doing my surveying. The location had to be physically inaccessible except through an undertime slide right inside the structure. I intended to build the exterior stone by stone in order to put it out-of-time-phase—like the Tower of Immortals itself. That way only someone

with innate directional senses and the ability to dive into
an out-of-phase building could get there.

I settled on a site under the peak called Seneschal, a
small ledge jutting from a sheer cliff. Although Seneschal
is a quarter of the way around the planet from Quest, I
figured I could cope with the sun and time differential.

Construction wasn't what I'd expected. My father had
built his own home, and if he had, I knew I could. But I
might not have been so eager, not if I'd known the years
it would literally take.

Each heavy chunk had to be quarried, cut, and trans-
ported by hand with a time-slide to the site of my Aerie.
Aerie, that was what I decided to call it, perched as it was
over a sheer drop from the needle peaks to the canyons
deep below, nestled over the lightning storms that blasted
the lower levels of the deep valleys.

During the days, I worked at trying to increase the
ability of Maintenance to do more repairs. While it was
too early to draft him, I had my eye on a second-year
trainee named Brendan, who had a sense for mechanics.
In the interim, I struggled with the overflowing repair bin,
and with Narcissus, who had the unnerving habit of
polishing metal to look at his reflection, rather than to
clean it for repairs.

Both Maintenance and the Aerie struggled along.

I wasn't building a castle on the heights. The Aerie was
scarcely that—just two levels, three rooms, plus a kitchen
and a hygienarium. The structure was what took the effort, especially warping each stone, each beam, out of
time. It was worth it. On the evening when I moved in the
last of the furnishings, stood on the glowstone flooring,
and watched the sunset below, I swallowed hard to try to
push down the lump in my throat.

I had built something lasting, something of beauty, and
with my own hands. My own hands—that was important.

IX

In the midday sun, a dwelling crouches in an overgrown meadow, its back to a dry creek bed. On the far side of the dry gulch, a forest begins.

The blotchiness of the unfinished wood and the dusty permaglass testify that the dwelling is vacant. Tattered lynia flowers droop their violet fronds across the barely visible stones of the walk, those that the moss has not already crept over.

A breeze whispers its course across the open ground with the restrained promise that it will whistle when the clouds now hugging the horizon arrive later in the afternoon.

From thin air, a young man wearing a one-piece black jumpsuit appears in front of the structure.

He gawks at the building, at the dust-streaked panes, the overgrown stone walk which leads nowhere, as if he had not expected the desertion.

After a moment of hesitation, he walks briskly up the low steps to the porch and the door.

"Greetings!" he bellows. A gust of wind heralding the clouds in the distance ruffles his bright red hair as he waits for a response.

The arched door opens at his touch.

He steps inside, and the hall echoes as his black boots strike the floor.

The house, for it could be termed that despite the years of desertion, is small, with hygiene facilities and a pair of bedrooms on the upper level and three rooms on the main level.

Dust blankets the simple furniture, the once-polished stone and wood floors that shine beneath the covering bestowed on them by time.

So well-built and preserved is the structure that the dust seems out of place.

The man in black, his face smooth and unlined enough to be scarcely more than a youth, tours the rooms in silence.

He returns to the front hall, face blank, shaking his head.

"Locator was right," he comments to no one because there is no one to hear him. "Totally vanished. Left everything, and didn't tell me. Not even a note."

He shakes his head again.

Then, after stepping onto the narrow stone front porch and carefully closing the heavy door behind him, he vanishes into thin air.

The clouds and rain have not yet arrived, but they will.

X

Maintenance could be a challenge, as well as a pain in the neck.

The Guard attitude toward machinery made it difficult. Frey and his people were the worst. They used and abused equipment until it broke, pounded on it to see if it were truly broken, threw it in a storeroom or unused corner to gather dust until it was needed again, and then and only then carted it down to Maintenance with a request that it be repaired immediately.

The first few times that happened I made the repairs without comment. The next dozen times, I grumbled, suggesting that Frey send equipment when it broke, rather than waiting.

One fine winter morning, after a frost, when the air was clear and I had a breathing spell, I surveyed the Hall and watched Narcissus overpolish the sides of an auxiliary generator.

Hopefully, I'd get less spit and polish and more repairs out of Brendan in the months ahead when he completed training. Once Brendan arrived as a permanent assignment, I'd see what could be done to track another trainee into Maintenance.

In the meantime, I was struggling along under the repair burden and not diving nearly as much as I would have liked.

As I was speculating about the future, Ferrin arrived with a set of battered Locator portapacks. Ferrin never carried gear down from Domestic Affairs.

I smiled.

"Oh, skilled god of forge and iron, of the fire and the energies that flow," began Ferrin lightly.

Ferrin got fancy when he'd rather not be doing whatever he was engaged in.

"Skip the rhetoric. What's the dirty work?"

"Frey wants these immediately. No more than one hundred units. Need to track down a malefactor, and he's headed fore-time outline—beyond the finer capabilities of the base units. Remember that Bly character? Some woman bushwhacked Hightel and Doradosi as they were bringing him back from Hell for a chronolobotomy."

Bly? It took a moment before the name registered. And the woman who attacked Hightel and Doradosi had to be the one who had collapsed at Bly's hearing.

"Ferrin . . . how long have these been lying around in your storeroom not functioning?"

I picked one up and blew a cloud of dust from it.

"Couple years, probably."

I slid off the stool, leaving the Locator packs on the bench, and marched across the Maintenance Hall. Baldur was in. I'd seen him earlier.

"I've had it! Had it! This is the twenty-first time in the past three years Frey has done this. I've recommended, suggested, begged, pleaded—everything. Let him do his own repairs."

"He doesn't know how," Baldur said calmly, as if he were used to Guards banging his workbench every day. "Glammis had the same problem, you know."

I didn't understand. Baldur, of all Guards, should understand. He was the one who had taught me the value of maintenance, of care.

"Are you unwilling to make the repairs?" cut in a new voice, and I knew it was Heimdall's from the tone of menace in the question.

"No, honored Counselor," I replied, turning to face him and bringing my voice under control, "but I do feel that a disciplinary action should be brought against Supervisor Frey for the continued misuse of Guard resources."

Ferrin's mouth dropped open. Heimdall was silent. Baldur smiled a smile so faint it wasn't.

"We could take this up informally with one of the Tribunes," suggested Baldur. It wasn't a suggestion.

Heimdall, who had appeared ready to speak, closed his mouth.

The four of us marched up the two ramps from Maintenance to the Tribunes' private Halls.

Eranas invited us into a sitting chamber and summoned Frey.

Frey arrived with murder in his eyes.

"I should be supervising the hunt for an escaped malefactor, but I am waiting for equipment which should be repaired and apparently is not, and now I find myself summoned here."

"Perhaps Loki should summarize the charge," commented Baldur.

I went through the whole thing, how year after year Frey never took care of anything, how I'd recommended, sent notes, pleaded, and how the situation never changed.

"So you refused to repair the Locator equipment?" cut in Eranas.

"No, honored Tribune. I refused to repair it until note was taken by the Tribunes that this type of procedure is not only detrimental to Maintenance, but inhibits the timely performance by Domestic Affairs. Even if I had started immediately on the damaged equipment, it would not be ready now. And the Guard Ferrin informed me that the defective Locator packs have been known to have been damaged for years, yet were never turned in to Maintenance for repairs."

"I see your point," said Eranas drily, "but we really don't have time to play around with this. Guard Loki, you will, of course, attend to repairs immediately."

He turned to Frey.

"Senior Guard Frey, you will consider yourself reprimanded, and after the conclusion of your search, will inventory all your equipment within the coming season to assure its function. You will eliminate unnecessary equipment and turn all necessary but non-functional gear over to Maintenance for repairs."

Frey was white, sheer white, whether from rage or fear, I wasn't certain. I knew he'd hear about it from Freyda as well.

Heimdall hadn't said anything.

I could read between the lines as well as anyone. If I'd had repairs to do before, they were going to be as nothing compared to what would be landing in my in-coming bin.

Repairing the Locator packs wasn't all that difficult; it

took maybe fifty units after I got back to my spaces. I sent Narcissus across the Square to Domestic Affairs with them.

I wished that had been the end of it, but what made Frey's attitude toward me even worse was that Ayren Bly escaped, didn't register on the locator screens anywhere, as if he'd vanished from the galaxy.

Frey was called on the glowstones for that, and Eranas made the point that it might not have happened if Frey had taken better care of his equipment.

Needless to say, Frey wasn't speaking to me, and for some reason neither was Heimdall, I guessed because in a strange way he and Frey were friends. Frey was a disciple of Heimdall's, and, like Heimdall, felt that Guard discipline should be stronger, that a more authoritative leadership was required, and that the routine dirty work ought to be done by non-Guard Queryans.

After the turn of the year, Baldur spoke to the Tribunes and Brendan was assigned to Maintenance. That was before Frey had gotten his equipment housecleaning fully underway, and for a time, I thought I might be able to keep ahead of the busted junk flowing down from Domestic Affairs.

But the word spread, and I started seeing long-broken equipment coming in from odd places like the Archives, and Observation. Nobody else wanted to end up shamed like Frey.

The hours I spent got longer and longer, and the sleep became less and less.

I shouldn't have tried to undo a century's neglect in less than a year, but where would I have put all the junk? Besides, Eranas kept dropping in to check on me.

Usually, I staggered into the Tower bright and early, right after dawn, but the morning came when I slept late. Not that I had slept well, but the shadows of the canyons below were already shrinking into black traceries when the midmorning sun hit me full in the face.

Even with the continuing lack of sleep, I had been a sound sleeper and early riser, but that night or morning my dreams had been filled with visions of crimson skies and screaming night eagles tearing at my guts.

Most mornings I could have overslept my own time limit by fifty units and still arrived before I needed to, but I'd overslept more than a hundred.

I was halfway down the ramp when I met Heimdall coming up.

"Loki's here at last! Good day, night owl, or is it night eagle, perched up in your hidden Aerie?"

"Good morning, honored Counselor."

Heimdall wasn't through, and blocked my path on the ramp.

"Being in charge of repairs in Maintenance, taking advanced instruction, living up to your responsibilities aren't too important, is that it?"

I kept my mouth shut. Heimdall was out to get me.

"Rather go out and fly with the angels of Heaven IV than stay in and do the dirty work? Rather blame others when your own lateness could be the cause? Is that it?"

The glint in his eye told me he knew it was unfair and was daring me to refute it. Damned if I would.

I could sense someone heading down the ramp from behind me, but Heimdall was so intent he didn't look up.

"Lateness shows no respect for the Guard and its traditions, and you show little enough, Loki."

"Enough," cut in Freyda's voice from behind me.

"Don't take the youngster's case, Freyda," boomed Odinthor. "He may have all the talent in the universe, but he needs discipline."

By this time Baldur had shown up as well.

"Loki," spoke up Heimdall, and his tone was all business, no malice, which set me further on edge.

I nodded.

He handed me a wrist gauntlet.

"Frey says the tracking functions are off. He's replaced what he can, and it still doesn't function. Nicodemus can't figure it out either. Obviously, replacement isn't the answer. Needs to be fixed."

I took it.

"Frey needs it today, before you leave."

Set up, I thought, and no way out. Heimdall had provided the scene, with all the props, even the rationale why Frey couldn't fix it himself.

"Now I certainly hope you'll find time to do it right," was his parting shot, "since you've made such an issue about the importance of directional and locator equipment."

Dumb statement by Heimdall. He couldn't find his way out of the nearest system without an electronic arsenal

and five different directional fixes. Neither could Frey.
But because I was late, I'd have to shove everything else
aside to fix what was obviously a problem gauntlet, which
meant more time. And I'd end up working even later for
days or falling further behind with Eranas always looking
over my shoulder.

I could have protested again, but I didn't think either
Baldur or Eranas would have stood for it—especially not
when I'd been late.

I carted the gauntlet to Maintenance and dumped it on
my workbench, although the continually cleaned and ster-
ilized surface no more resembled a conventional bench
than I did Odinthor.

Suppressing a groan as I took in the overflowing "in"
bin, I called up the gauntlet specs on my console. On the
off chance the malfunction might be simple, I placed the
wrist band in the diagnostic center, punched the stud, and
waited.

"No circuit malfunction," the console informed me in
its precise flowing script.

That figured. The gauntlet didn't work and didn't seem
to have anything wrong with it.

I scanned the area around me. No one around. Ducking
behind one of the old behemoths that bordered my space,
I slipped on the gauntlet and dived backtime, watching the
dials and the directionals.

Sure enough, at about a quarter million back, they began to fluctuate. Since it might be a function of diving
speed, I forced myself fore-time until I felt shrouded in
the bright blue of high-speed fore-diving. I braked just
short of break-out and checked the dials. The face of the
indicators was black.

I broke-out of the undertime right where I'd gone under.
I didn't see anyone nosing around so presumably my un-
toward dive had been unnoticed.

Back at my bench, I tossed the gauntlet back into the
diagnostic center, black indicators and all.

I punched the stud and was greeted with a fizzling sound
and a totally dead diagnostic center, followed by heat and
the smell of burnt and fused electronics.

> Item: The gauntlet hadn't done anything to the
> center before my dive.

Item: The dive had created enough power to
     overload the center, but hadn't burned me.

As it dawned on me, I looked down. Down at the insulation laid over the out-of-time-phase flooring. Of course, I
wouldn't get burned, not in Maintenance. I shivered. The
innocent-looking gauntlet didn't seem nearly so innocent
any more.

With all that in mind, I began to break down the gauntlet step by step. It was close to midafternoon before I
found what I knew had to be there.

Someone had removed the power source insulators on
one side and wired a microfilament antenna across the
underside of the gauntlet. If I'd broken-out anywhere outside the grounded confines of the Maintenance Hall, I'd
have been lucky to escape with as little as severe burns
around the arms and wrists—if not worse.

Since Heimdall didn't know the extent of my diving
ability, the gauntlet had to have been a damned setup.
Without a time-dive the problem couldn't be detected, and
since no one had been burned, it wasn't a real problem,
but a phony one foisted off on me.

The more I thought about it, the madder I got. Heimdall
wasn't just out to bury me under a pile of work. He was
out for blood, and if that was what he wanted that was
what he was going to get.

First, I fixed the gauntlet, after carefully recording how
it had been altered. Then I refixed it, with his microfilament antenna keyed to a false boss. If anyone besides me
wore the gauntlet and didn't set the boss correctly, they
were going to get the treatment that had been scheduled
for me.

Late afternoon arrived before I completed my micro-
engineering, but I knew Heimdall would still be waiting in
Assignments.

Heimdall was at his desk, leaning back in his high
padded stool.

"Heimdall," I said respectfully, knowing that the failure
to use his title would infuriate him, "I think I've got it
fixed."

"Just think?" he snapped. "You should know!"

"I've rechecked the calibration, which was defective.
I've replaced the power cell which was sending an uneven

flow to the instrumentation, and replaced the missing insulation."

"Are you sure it's fixed?"

"As sure as I can be without a test of some sort."

"Well," drawled the master of the sarcastic, "you don't think I'd let Frey try it just on your say-so, do you?"

"No. But would he trust it even if I said I'd tested it?"

Heimdall frowned. "I see your point. Tell you what. Let's go over to the Travel Hall. You test it, and if it seems all right, I'll test it, and then Frey should be satisfied."

Heimdall could be so smooth sometimes.

I trooped after him, down the ramp, and out to the Tower wing.

I slipped on the gauntlet, adjusting it, and making sure the false boss was in the correct position.

The dive was uneventful. I broke-out on back-time Almaraden to pick a bouquet for the all-seeing schemer, but Heimdall laid them aside when I presented him the flowers.

"You didn't notice anything unusual about the gauntlet when you fixed it?" he asked worriedly as I handed it to him. I'd already twisted the boss to its "loaded" position.

Strangely enough, Frey arrived at the Travel Hall about that time.

I decided Heimdall needed a push. Besides, I didn't want Frey to get zapped. Frey couldn't have put the gauntlet on without help from his mommy or from Heimdall, let alone rewired the microcircuitry.

"Heimdall," I began, knowing he'd be irked again by the lack of formality, "it was a simple job. Some fool had left some stray filaments running along the inside of the gauntlet. I cleaned up the loose ends, checked the insulation, and made the recalibrations. I did what you asked for, the way you asked for it, in the time you asked for it, and it works fine.

"I know you have better things to do than stand and check the quality of my workmanship, and your talents are better suited for those. So if you're done, why don't I just give it to Frey and let him check it out?"

If Heimdall handed it back to me, I could twist the false boss before Frey made a dive.

That strategy went sour with the arrival of Sammis and Wryan. Wryan had caught the end of my remarks and chuckled. Heimdall turned and glared at her, but the way she returned his look—no way I could describe it—Heimdall was shamed on the spot.

I had this sinking feeling in the pit of my stomach, but it was too late. The results couldn't be that bad, I figured.

Heimdall yanked on the gauntlet, without looking at anyone, and disappeared.

As he broke-out at the far end of the Travel Hall, the gauntlet exploded off his wrist, and blood and fire spewed all over everything.

"Loki!" he screamed before he collapsed.

I slid to the end of the room, catching his still form before he even hit the floor, and made a second undertime slide straight to the Infirmary. Had to have been less than two units between Heimdall's return to the Travel Hall and the instant Hycretis started transfusions with his shattered wrist and broiled arm under the tissue regenerator.

About that moment, the floor rose up and struck me down.

When I woke, I was in the cell-block under the Tower. Lovely place it was, with a single bright and recessed light in the ceiling, solid glowstone bunk without furs, barred doors, and a handy-dandy automatic restrainer field to scramble my thoughts and keep me in.

When I'd seen Ayren Bly years back, I hadn't anticipated being on his side of the bars. What was done was done.

Having nothing better to do, I tried concentrating hard enough to negate the scrambling effect of the restraining field. Didn't seem to take too long before I could shut out the automatic nature of the scramblers and slide into the corridor outside the cell. I heard footsteps and slipped back into my cell.

I got back where I was supposed to be just in time. Freyda, Odinthor, Eranas, and two hefty Guards I didn't know arrived to march me up to the Hall of Justice.

Since it was a Guard affair, the proceedings weren't public.

Freyda, Kranos, and Eranas, as Tribunes, sat up on the dais facing the Hall. I was placed at one side in the red-railed box reserved for the nasty malefactors. Frey was seated across from me behind the silver podium reserved for the prosecutor. Although the Hall could accommodate thousands, only a few Guards sat in the front rows.

"An informal Guard procedure," announced Eranas in his raspy voice.

Frey bowed and scraped, and the two Guards yanked me to my feet so I could bow and scrape. And I bowed and scraped.

"Counsel for the Guard requests disciplinary procedures for Guard Loki."

I was on my own. Under disciplinary procedures, I didn't rate counsel, not that it would have mattered.

"Senior Guard Loki," I began, automatically promoting myself for no good reason except that I was angry, "declares his innocence by reason of extreme provocation and fear of grave physical and bodily harm threatened by Counselor Heimdall."

Odinthor, sitting in the front row, snorted loudly and looked at Eranas. Eranas nodded at Frey.

Frey climbed to his feet, for once without the light saber, and made it very simple, and he was good at being simple.

Loki was a Guard. Loki was responsible for important repairs. Instead one Loki had booby-trapped a gauntlet which had harmed a Counselor seriously.

Frey used the big wall screen sparingly and basically to display shots of Heimdall collapsing in a shower of fire and living blood, followed with a shot of the poor assaulted Counselor lying in the Infirmary surrounded with all types of medical support equipment.

As Frey continued, I realized the dope had been used. He honestly didn't know that the gauntlet had been double-trapped for me.

Finally, it was my turn.

"Tribunes, my defense is simple. First, Heimdall intended that what happened to him should happen to me. Second, he waited for perhaps seasons for an excuse to administer such an assault disguised as routine Maintenance work. Third, when my repairs were completed, he knew there was a chance I would still be hurt and he forced me to test the gauntlet."

"Can you prove any of this?" rasped Eranas.

"Yes, Tribune. First, I carefully recorded the internal structures I found in the gauntlet I received from Heimdall, and the records from my diagnostic center will show that the gauntlet was altered to focus time energy on the wearer. I suggest you examine the records before they become unavailable."

Eranas might be thinking of stepping down, but he was nobody's fool. He disappeared straight from the dais, presumably time-sliding straight to the mech shop.

"We wait," noted Freyda. She looked at her son.

Eranas was back in place at the center of the Tribunes in a handful of units. "Loki, you are a damned fool. Heimdall may have deserved what he got. But without order, the Guard has nothing, and if your example were followed, there would be no order—"

"But—" I protested.

"But nothing!" rasped Eranas. "Heimdall will be in the Infirmary for another ten days. You will spend half that time on Hell, and the other half recovering from Hell."

He flipped the black wand out of its holder and jabbed it at me to emphasize his point. Neither Kranos nor Freyda had said a word.

I started to my feet to protest, but didn't get very far. It felt like the entire Hall of Justice hit me in the face.

I came to in Hell, or rather, on it.

The sky is a scarlet black so bloody deep it curdles your soul. The ground is all sand and rock, and little scavenger rats scurry out from under the rocks to bite with needle teeth anything that is there to bite—insects, grubs, legs, toes, arms, what have you.

I couldn't see much of that, chained as I was to a large black chunk of mountainside. Could barely think, because the Guard hadn't taken many chances. This time, unlike the period in the cell-block, someone had set an entire bank of restrainer fields up and focused them all on me. I wasn't thinking the same thoughts twice, but four or five times, and in fragments.

Somewhere I was being supported by a concealed cellular regenerator, but the water tube in the mask that covered most of my face didn't function.

The restraining fields prevented enough coherent thought to keep me from time-diving off the planet of the damned, and the regenerator gadgetry was supposed to keep me in one piece.

With all that, I still could have dived clear, but clamped as I was to the black stone, I couldn't carry the whole mountain with me.

Every so often—I couldn't keep track—a large night eagle

would come screaming out of the scarlet night that was day and rip a hunk out of me. I didn't see much, not with the face mask protector, the partial helmet, throat guard, and extended breastplate.

Not mercy, but practicality. The regeneration gear can't keep a body together if the eagles get the eyes, head, throat, or some large mess of guts.

Strapped there to suffer as these lovely beasts and birds rip away, most victims have a tendency to scream. I did too, until I was too hoarse to continue. Some things I'm not proud about.

Gravel-throated, whisper-voiced, unable to move, unable to scream, unable to dive, a cold fire built within me, focused on the absolute injustice of Guard justice, and between the lapses of consciousness, between the stabs of pain as a scavenger rat nipped off a toe, snipped through an Achilles tendon, I concentrated on my future, my destiny. . . .

If I had to strike, strike I would not until I wrenched bloody suns from their orbits. . . . by god, by Hell, by the eagles of night screamed and ripped, ripped and screamed. And screams from my dry throat merged with theirs and the blackness.

XI

I woke up in the Infirmary, alone, cellular-regeneration equipment attached to both arms and legs and with heavy wrapping around my all too tender mid-section.

Glowstones and slow-glass, white panels and sunlight, all came out gray in my sight.

I slipped back into sleep, and dreamed.

A man in black, the black singlesuit of the Guards, and a man in red stood on mountaintops facing each other across a cloud-filled chasm. Gray clouds framed the scene; no sunlight intruded.

The black man threw thunderbolt after thunderbolt at the red man, who never responded, never ducked, accepted each blast without moving, without effect.

With each cast, the man in black laughed. Each laugh infused the clouds beneath his feet with a darkness, a growing ugliness. The clouds of darkness began to climb from the depths below, to tug at the feet of the man in red, who stood as if asleep, untouched, unmoving. But his eyes were open, unseeing.

With a laugh that echoed through the gray skies, that shook the clouds until they trembled, the black figure leaned forward and released a last thunderbolt, terrible in its power, a yellow sword that shone with blackness, mightier than all that had come before.

The sound of the laugh reached the man in red and his eyes filled with knowledge, and, as they filled with understanding, that last thunderbolt struck his shoulder, and he staggered, dropping to his knee, swaying on the mountaintop.

Someone touched my shoulder, and I woke.

Loragerd was sitting in the stool next to the high bed.

I tried to croak something.

"Not yet," she said softly, laying her hand on my forehead.

There was plenty I wanted to know. No Guard should lose consciousness so quickly on Hell. I couldn't say much, but Loragerd filled me in. The Guards who dragged me off to Hell had been Heimdall's friends and hadn't been especially careful about the breastplates or throat guards.

Eranas, crafty old schemer, had figured as much. He, Kranos, and Freyda had waited until the damage to me became apparent, recorded the scenario on holo, and rescued me.

Evidence in hand, they'd held another Guard hearing, discharged the Guards involved, one of whom was my ferret-faced acquaintance, confiscated their equipment, and subjected them to that surgical procedure which insured they would never dive again.

Underneath my cocoon of bandages, I shivered.

The Tribunes had let me go to the point of death, destroyed the lives of Guards who disobeyed, and never made it public.

I drifted back into sleep, half-exhausted, half-sweating, with Loragerd stroking my forehead.

Four days dragged by before Hycretis let me out of the Infirmary. Baldur insisted I take another four before showing up in Maintenance.

Surprisingly, the backlog wasn't bad.

"That's because Baldur came over every night and whipped off a bunch of repairs," Brendan explained.

In my absence, Brendan and Narcissus had been in a dive or die situation. Narcissus had done neither, just plodded along, polishing away.

Brendan had dived, right into the business end of Maintenance, and learned plenty on his own, though he was still strangely lacking confidence in his own abilities.

Somehow, the backlog didn't seem quite so impressive, quite so overwhelming, not that I took it for granted or didn't keep whittling it down. A new perspective, I guessed.

Some scars heal quickly; some do not. Heimdall had set me up. Foolproof. If I'd done as I'd been told and goofed, I would have been dead. If I'd fixed it properly, played it straight, then Heimdall would have delivered the message that he could dispatch me at any time.

Heimdall got out of it with a slightly bruised arm, but two Guards who followed him were permanently disabled, and the only one who'd stood up to him was sent to Hell.

The more I reflected, the angrier I got, but it wasn't the unthinking anger that had gotten me into the mess.

I set myself the goal of mastering every piece of equipment in the entire Maintenance Hall—dating back to the Twilight/Frost Giant Wars. That would be one step, I decided.

The second step would be more difficult, but I put some stock in the dream Loragerd had interrupted. I identified with the man in red. I needed to wake up, but that meant becoming vulnerable, and if I did, I needed to learn my own full capabilities.

I petitioned Sammis to tutor me in everything he knew about hand-to-hand and weaponry.

Sammis had been around awhile, just how long no one seemed to know. He had done the "attitude adjustment" course for trainees as well as the combat training. The basic hand-to-hand instruction had been where I'd discovered that I could half time-slide and speed my movements while staying in the "now."

Sammis could detect that skill, I had discovered, much to my chagrin, while he could not do it himself.

I hadn't believed him, and it had showed on my face.

Sammis challenged me. "Go ahead. I'll stay put. Go on."

I had been upset at being put down in front of Ferrin and Patrice, perhaps because they had done so well in the classroom stuff. I hadn't thought, just charged Sammis, sliding at the last instant and figuring to come out behind him.

Instead of surprising him, my chin had arrived on his open palm. From that point, I had concentrated on the basics with Sammis.

Now, with Heimdall waiting in the shadows to do me in if I gave him half a chance, I needed more than basics. I wanted everything he could give me.

For once, I decided to do it formally. I went to Baldur and asked his permission to spend part of each day training with Sammis to improve my skills.

"No problem, and I'll enter it on your training record in the proper doublescript," Baldur said, almost kindly.

I was confused.

He smiled. "Loki, you're feeling that you've neglected something, and that you need more skills. Your work here is superb, and I think the Guard would benefit from your efforts to broaden your capabilities. Let's leave it at that."

Sometimes Baldur left me with the feeling that he saw much more than he let on, but I didn't want to push it.

He must have gotten to Sammis before I did, because Sammis said, "Of course"—with a catch.

The catch was that he and Wryan worked as a team, and that as a team they would teach me. "Besides, it would take two or more to really force you to upgrade your skills," Sammis noted.

Always the veiled hints, the messages within messages. I had never thought how many times this sort of information was passed in the Guard.

Working with Sammis and Wryan, even for just a hundred units a day, was more pleasure than toil.

Each of them sensed what the other was about to do and reacted.

One night at Hera's, Verdis told me that they predated Odinthor in the Guard. I hadn't thought that much about it, didn't have a chance to draw Verdis out because of the noise, and didn't get back to it.

With my usual tactfulness, the next afternoon I broached the subject in what I thought was a suitably oblique manner.

"Odinthor has been hanging around the Tower for centuries. When did he last take a diving mission?"

Wryan screwed her elfin features into a wry grimace. Sammis stroked his chin and looked at the equipment room floor. Finally, he answered. "I couldn't rightly say, but I think the follow-up work to the Twilight/Frost Giant Wars."

My jaw dropped open. Two million years back. "How . . . his mind . . . I mean . . ." I stammered.

"Not that bad," commented Wryan. "Even when he started, he never had much of one."

Sammis glared over at his partner.

"You're older than Odinthor," I snapped at Sammis.

"No." He grinned. "But she is."

I looked at Wryan. Never would I have guessed it. With Freyda, and I knew Freyda was only a couple thousand

years old, I could see the darkness of age behind the clear
eyes.

"You two are still taking missions."

They glanced at each other, back at me.

Wryan spoke next. "Who wants to sit around and let
their mind rot in front of a useless fireplace or an unused
console? Keep young by doing."

"But—you could be Counselors, Tribunes . . ."

Dead silence. Sammis pointedly stared at the floor once
more. Seemed embarrassed. Why did he seem so upset,
shy, flustered?

"Loki, you rush in, don't you?" Wryan asked gently,
humorously, but her smile held a trace of sadness.

"You two confuse me. My span is measured in tens of
years, not hundreds of thousands, like yours."

There was something I was missing, but damned if I
could figure out what.

"Perhaps we were," concluded Wryan briskly. "And
now," she changed the subject, "you've got more to learn
about knife-work."

She and Sammis started buckling on protective armor. I
stood there holding mine.

Tribunes . . . Sammis and Wryan . . . when . . . and then
it hit: the Triumvirate! Odinthor and the two others, the
first three Tribunes, with the other two the only Guards to
strike down Odinthor.

I started to strap on the armor, but my motions were
slow because my thoughts were stirred up.

Only Odinthor remained from that glorious time of great
deeds, I'd thought, but there were three left, maybe more.
If so, Sammis and Wryan had operated as a team for over
twenty thousand centuries, incredible as it sounded.

The legend was all I had to go on, because the Archives
records of that period had been sealed by the Tribunes who
had followed the Triumvirate. Why was unclear.

According to the tales, the Triumvirate had created the
structure of the Guard, with the Counselors and the three
Tribunes, to fight the menace of the Frost Giants. More
than half that early Guard had perished in the centuries-
long battle, and in the end, entire systems had been reduced
to molten slag.

As I recalled the legends, I realized there was no real
"afterwards." Nothing mentioned what had happened. The

War was won, and life went on. We had won a glorious victory, right?

I put down the armor. "I can't practice."

Wryan looked at Sammis. He nodded. She smiled.

"How about Loratini's?" she asked rhetorically.

We stowed the armor and slid.

I'd never been to Loratini's Inn, the oldest Inn on Query. You had to be invited to be welcome. Rumor was that no Counselors, Tribunes, or trainees were ever invited.

An odd place, it seemed to me, with separate balconies for each table, with each balcony, maybe twenty in all, set in stone and overlooking the Falls. Officially the Falls were called Loratini Falls and had been well visited once upon a time.

The three of us sat around the circular table. I had opted for firejuice. They had beers. Wryan's was dark, and Sammis's light.

"What do you know about the Twilight Wars?" asked Wryan.

"Only the legend. But when you said you'd been Tribunes, something clicked. And there was another question, too. I mean, there was no conclusion, no real ending to the legend."

Sammis snorted.

A pair, a real pair, they were, like a set of gauntlets perfectly matched. Even looked alike. Both with the light brown hair, the faint, tiny lines close to the corners of their eyes, with pointed chins and elfin faces, though Sammis's features were a shade heavier. Wryan was physically bigger.

Both had piercing green eyes, set off by even tans. All of us tanned easily and fairly darkly with a bronze cast.

The more I thought about it, the more confusing it became. There I was, sitting with two people who I figured were former Tribunes, who'd controlled the entire Guard and who had given it up to work for millions of years at standard Guard assignments. Why? And why didn't anyone say anything?

"Because," Wryan answered my unspoken question, "Odinthor is the only one left who knows the full story. Let's just speculate, say it might have happened this way."

I shifted my weight in the stool and listened.

"Odinthor is the strongest diver—except for you—the Guard has ever had. Unfortunately, his morality is non-existent, and his directional senses were worse. Too much of the early Guard was tailored for him, from the elaborate directional aides in the wrist gauntlets to special homing beacons, because he was the only diver strong enough at first to break the para-time barriers of the Frost Giants. But let's guess a little more about the Twilight War and add a bit to the story, remembering that it's only a story."

Wryan paused, and Sammis continued where she had left off even though a word had not passed between them.

"Believe it or not, the War created the Guard."

The War started when parts of Query started freezing solid, instantaneously, according to the legend.

". . . but none of the divers could get close to the Giants. As the Giants traveled through space and time, they warped the time around themselves and sustained themselves with that energy. The backlash was the freezings. The first problem was to find the home or base of the Giants . . ."

Sammis kept talking, and I found myself being drawn into the story.

I wasn't sure I should believe any of it.

The Frost Giants stood only a head or so taller than the tallest Queryans and were not giants in any real sense, though they had four arms and considerably more mass.

The Frost Giants demonstrated another adaptation of the time-diving talent, noted Wryan as she took up the tale. While they had definite range limits, a Giant could time-dive to any point in the galaxy which existed during his or her or its own objective life. Giants seemed to have lived several millennia.

I hadn't asked for a dissertation on the Frost Giants, but remembering my training thrashings from Sammis I decided to let them make their point in whatever obscure fashion pleased them.

Giants went through two phases. In childhood they were planet-bound until they physically matured, had children, and then became fully adult. Adults gained the ability to time-dive and place-slide. If the maturing "child" did not inherit the talent, he, she, or it died of old age within the century.

In maturity, the Frost Giants needed no gross physical food, but absorbed the heat energy around them with each dive. How they "drank" it without burning themselves up, none of the Queryan scientists could figure out.

"Yes, we had scientists," explained Wryan.

The more the explanations went on, the more confused I got.

"The Frost Giants were big, and when they matured, if they matured, they could time-dive, and when they dived they fed and took all the heat energy from where they dived, which left some planet or locale with a frozen chunk. Is that the idea?" I asked.

Sammis nodded and kept talking.

At that time, time-diving was a talent still new to Query, not more than a thousand years since it had first popped up.

Queryan spaceships had investigated and placed bases on the two other closest system planets, and the scientific community was hoping for a break-through on a faster than light drive.

The first awareness of the Frost Giants came when half the base on Thoses was frozen solid.

Wryan took over the story and summarized the summary.

The Queryan planetary government, really a titular monarchy—whatever that was, I thought—had sent an expedition out to Thoses to investigate—and found nothing.

In the meantime, the base on Mithrada, the innermost system planet and the one next toward the sun from Query, had begun reporting abnormal temperature drops all over Mithrada.

Some bright scientist suggested programming all the locations into a computer, which was promptly done, to see if the results could be used to predict new occurrences. Some military type, having too much gusto, decided that it wouldn't hurt to lob a thermonuclear weapon into one of the predicted probability areas, provided it was unsuitable for anything else. The "experiment" was a great success, and from the results, potted a Frost Giant.

At which point, the military headquarters on Query was frozen solid with the High Command still inside.

The longer the story got, the more questions I had.

At the same time, interjected Sammis, the Government Time Research Laboratory, under the direction of Dr. Wryan Relorn, had been employing the few hundred really good time-divers to scout out possible interstellar colonies —since it was obvious the majority of the Queryan people could not travel in time or use the ability to move in space.

Dr. Relorn theorized that the ability to time-dive was inherent in most Queryans, but because of the special limitations of the relatively inflexible Laws of Time, they didn't realize their potential, or thought they were hallucinating.

"None of this is in the Archives," I tried to point out reasonably.

"Let's just keep calling it a story," said Wryan, "just a made-up story."

"All right. But we've got Frost Giants freezing chunks of Query because somebody bombed one of them and a few scattered time-divers under a nutty doctor . . ."

"She's not that nutty," said Sammis quietly.

I'd almost had enough. Now Sammis was insinuating that his partner Wryan was Dr. Wryan Relorn and that she had sailed to the rescue of Query by forming the Temporal Guard, right? Sammis and Wryan were good Guards, and maybe they'd been around since forever, but nothing matched. I must have muttered my objections half-aloud without realizing that I had.

"No. That came later," said Wryan. "Try to understand, Loki. Millions of people lived within kilos of where we sit. All they knew was that the more the government tried, the worse it got. Each new attempt to fight the Frost Giants, even to discover what they were, resulted in more of Query being frozen."

"So what happened?"

"Everything collapsed. The King was torn apart in the Square, right where the Tower now stands. People can stand anything but uncertainty, and everything was uncertain." Her voice grew even more intense. "Can you imagine living in a city with millions of people, none of them able to dive or slide, not knowing if there would be food for your next meal, or whether you would be frozen solid in the next instant? Knowing that whatever the government did, it didn't matter? Believing that the time-divers could save you, but that they wouldn't, and that it was all the government's fault?"

"People just don't do that!" I protested.

They both just stared at me, and I began to feel how old they really were. For that instant, the masks of youth that covered the depths of their eyes slipped, and I saw another kind of Hell.

"Just say they did," I temporized. "What happened next?"

The people left in the city of Inequital stormed the Time

Labs and the family housing of the divers. Most of the divers escaped, but their families did not.

Mass diving disrupts the web of time and can be detected, and the Frost Giants slid in where the remaining divers had fled. Most of Inequital was frozen and pulverized.

After the riots, the famines, the diseases, and the Giants, perhaps two hundred time-divers and 100 million Queryans were left. It was too big to visualize. Within a space of a few years, the population dropped from a billion to 100 million. Nine-tenths gone.

A diver named Augurt Odin Thor came to Dr. Relorn and suggested building a community of divers, supplied with the remnants of the high mid-tech wreckage, and using the divers to raid the rest of the Galaxy to put Query back on its feet again.

With chaos reigning, the alternatives seemed worse.

The diver who located the most promising planets to steal from was called Sammis Olon. After the first divers' camp had been built below Mount Persnol, the youth had appeared from nowhere while Dr. Relorn and Odin Thor were talking.

The three had worked as a team. Odin Thor had recruited divers. Dr. Relorn had supervised the project and organized the technology. Sammis Olon kept scouting. The disappearance of the Frost Giants, though no one knew then that was what they were, had allowed the situation to stabilize—

"Disappearance?" I interrupted.

"For a while," said Sammis. "Now do you want to hear it or not? It's only what might have happened."

I shut up and listened some more. The shadows crossing the mists from the Falls were getting longer, but my fire-juice was still nearly untouched.

With the disappearance of the Giants and the influx of new talent, more organization of the divers was not only possible, but necessary. Since Odin Thor had been a Naval Marine, he suggested a military organization called the Temporal Guard.

Dr. Relorn vetoed the idea, but not the name, and suggested a looser organization, roughly communal. Odin Thor saw he was in the minority and capitulated.

During the short transition period of around fifteen years, the old central city of Inequital was razed, and the Tower of the Guard, later called the Tower of Immortals, was started with the new knowledge of time-warping and the construction techniques that remained from the last of the Queryán high technology.

I still wanted to know how the legend of the Twilight/Frost Giant Wars got started.

As the rebuilding of Query along the line of self-sufficient individual communities progressed, it was becoming apparent that many Queryans were not aging and either they or their children or both had the time-diving ability.

"Remember, Loki, there was a time when we were not Immortal. Remember that when you become a god," Wryan said.

Sammis glared at her before going on.

Far-roving divers under the direction of Sammis Olon kept running across traces of the Frost Giants. Finally, an isolated Frost Giant popped up on the edge of the new city of Quest and froze one family.

Odin Thor seized the opportunity to rally the divers into a crusade against the Frost Giants, with him in charge, naturally, and with the divers behind him, offered a nominal split in the leadership to Sammis Olon and Dr. Wryan Relorn.

With a fait accompli staring them in the face, with the anger of divers who had lost one family to the Giants, the doctor and the young scout capitulated.

Finding the Giants was the easy part. In the undertime, they left a trail vibrating with energy. The difficulty lay in figuring out what to do once Odin Thor's Guards found the individual Giants. Past experience indicated that no known energy weapon short of a thermonuclear warhead or a dreadnought class laser was effective.

Sammis and his scouts combed the high-tech cultures of the Galaxy as far back and forward as they could reach, bringing back weapons and weapon-making machinery.

In the end, with all the grubby persistence that the Guard personified, Sammis Olon himself found the device —nothing more than a glorified sun-tunnel with special circuitry.

I looked at the two. It was almost evening, and the shadows were so long they were beginning to merge into twilight.

"It doesn't end there, does it?"

"No, unhappily," said Wryan.

Wryan condensed the story of what followed into units. "By tossing a sun-tunnel linked to a sun into the proximity of a Frost Giant, with an alternation between the sun and the near absolute zero of deep space, an energy resonance was created which effectively fragmented the Frost Giant. Odin Thor was overjoyed, equipped his best Guards with the units, and they all went hunting.

"How many Giants they got before the Frost Giants realized a hunt was on, I don't know. But the remaining Giants knew where the hunters originated, and all descended on Query.

"The western continent was the heavily populated one, even after the riots and the rest. The Giants froze it solid from sea to sea. The Guard baked and blistered it into a cinder with the counterattack. Another eighty million perished.

"I suppose they thought we were ants, and they'd stirred the anthill. I don't know. Odin Thor and his crew drove them off, and when the Giants dove clear, those that were left, the Guard turned the Giants' home planets into slag with stolen planet-busters and chased the adults. Chased them to the end of the galaxy and back for a hundred years, picking them off one by one, even while the reforesting and the rebuilding of the planet Query was begun by the Guards who stayed behind.

"And when Odin Thor returned from his mindless genocide, Dr. Relorn and Sammis Olon were ready for him."

"Ready? Mindless genocide?" I didn't understand.

"Genocide," returned Wryan. "Odin Thor never tried to communicate, not even with the children, who were no threat. He destroyed them all, four planets' worth."

"So what did the doctor and the diver do?" I asked in spite of myself.

"Why," answered Sammis, "they made Odin Thor the great hero of the Temporal Guard, and the three of them resigned to pave the way for three elected Tribunes to carry on the work of planetary reconstruction." He stopped to clear his throat. "Remember, this is only one way it could have happened. Maybe it did. Maybe it didn't."

Something clicked.

They both got up abruptly. "Stay as long as you like, Loki. Don't be late tomorrow. You need more work with the knife."

I scarcely felt them leave as thoughts swirled through my mind.

No glorious Twilight/Frost Giant Wars? The cataclysm

that struck Query brought on by our own stupidity? Why would they tell me such a fantastic tale? Why on Query would they?

I watched the stars above the mist for a while, listened to the roar of the falling water, and tried to digest it all.

What kept coming back was the question of motive. If it weren't true, why had they told me? And how could two people tell a story like that, as if they'd lived it, if they hadn't?

I toyed with the long-dry and empty beaker that had held too much firejuice for my own good, attempting to puzzle it out. The story was true or it wasn't.

At some point, I gave up and slid back to the Aerie.

Even there, I couldn't sleep, tired as I was. Gazing down into the deep valleys, knowing what caused the fused and splintered canyon walls, I asked myself about the revenge taken on the Frost Giants by Odinthor. What had it cost him? Did revenge always turn on the revenger?

I was different. That was how I answered myself. No thoughtless pursuer like Odinthor, at least, not after my taste of Hell. No, I was different, and I would have my revenge on Heimdall.

Would that be enough?

Was revenge on Heimdall really what I wanted?

With the questions piling up in the early morning hours, I drifted into an uneasy sleep.

XII

A long morning, one that stretched out under the high ceilings of the Tower as if it would never end—that was what the day promised.

Most technical peoples think that time passes at a uniform rate. It doesn't. Any good time-diver knew that. A chronometer will measure intervals precisely, but not the passage of time.

Scientists explain the variance, if they try at all, by citing biological eccentricities, anything but the real answer, which is that time just doesn't pass at a uniform rate. In most places, it doesn't vary much, it's true, but time is not an interval.

What is it? It's time. Simple answer, but the most accurate.

On that morning when the time dragged out, I left my work space to find Baldur.

Baldur wasn't in his space. One look, and I knew he wouldn't be back.

Baldur never left loose ends, and his old-fashioned writing platform was bare. Only a few standard manuals remained in the shelves by his stool.

I tiptoed over to the writing platform and opened the single drawer. Empty. The whole space was empty.

I debated trying to track him down before letting the Tribunes know, but decided against it. Better to keep playing it safe and not give Heimdall and company any free shots.

I rushed up the ramps to the Tribunes' chambers and asked for Freyda or Eranas.

I was tapping my feet by the time Eranas appeared.

"Baldur's left. Permanently."

"How do you know?"

I told him about the tidy way in which all the loose ends were tied up, about how that would square with Baldur.

"I can't say I'm surprised, Loki," Eranas mused. "Thank you."

He turned to go.

"Aren't you going to do anything? Locate him?"

"For what? As a Counselor, he can leave any time he wants to. And how could I compel Baldur to do anything? Should I?" He smiled at me. "If you found Baldur, what would you say?"

Eranas walked back into his chambers, leaving me there open-mouthed.

After thinking a unit, I crossed the Tower and walked into Personnel to tell Gilmesh.

"Figures," he growled. "On your way back to Maintenance, take this."

He thrust a dented wrist-gauntlet at me. "It's Lorren's. Damned fool left it on during hand-to-hand with Sammis."

Lorren was Gilmesh's latest addition, a young blond trainee with an insipid smile. I couldn't help but smile at the thought of what Sammis could do to a trainee's arrogance.

The corridors of the Tower were quiet in the morning. I waved at Loragerd as I passed the Linguistics Center, but she didn't look up.

Back in my own work space in Maintenance, I dumped the wrist-gauntlet on the bench, sat down on the high stool I liked.

Baldur was gone. That was it, and whether Eranas or Freyda or Heimdall cared, I had to find out why.

To locate Baldur, or see if I could, I needed his assignments file and a locator check. The question was how to get either. Gilmesh ran Personnel and didn't seem interested. He'd agree with Eranas. On the other hand, Eranas wasn't going around announcing Baldur's disappearance. So maybe I could play it dumb. Once again, I might be risking a bit, but safer to play dumb aboveboard than sneaky and get caught.

I needed an entree, so to speak. I got to work on Lorren's gauntlet. Took a few units to put it back in shape, principally because I replaced the microcircuitry lock, stock, and barrel. Wasteful, but quick. Later I'd have to break down the damaged modules which I'd set aside and fix them. I didn't care much for total black-boxing as a standard repair technique, but it did come in handy when I was in a hurry.

Gilmesh was a creature of habit, and one of his habits was sipping cuerl at midmorning with Frey and Heimdall.

With the gauntlet in hand, I trotted up the ramps to Personnel and loitered around the bend in the corridor until I heard the quick clump of boots heading toward the small lounge where the Senior Guards often took a break.

Time to present Lorren with his gauntlet.

He was sitting at the small console in the back corner, with his blond hair hanging over his heavy brows and that insipid smile planted firmly and unwaveringly on his face.

"Here's your gauntlet," I announced.

Lorren nodded, without even opening his mouth.

"I need to run down Baldur's whereabouts. Can you run out an update on his past assignments?"

"Need Gilmesh's approval."

"Look. Baldur is my supervisor. If he's upset at my running him down, he'll take care of me. You don't have to worry about it."

Lorren shook his head.

I picked the gauntlet up from his console.

The smile disappeared, to be replaced with a half-pout. "What are you doing?"

"If you don't want to cooperate, fine. As a full Guard, I can require any trainee to fix his own equipment."

"But it's fixed," protested Lorren sulkily.

"I black-boxed it, as a favor."

We stood there. Lorren thought about it. Gilmesh certainly wouldn't let him off from his duties to fix the result of his own carelessness. He'd have to come down to Maintenance in his free time.

"All right, if you're going to be that way about it."

He punched a series of commands on the console. I held on to the gauntlet. When he handed me both the print-out and the tape, more than a few units later, I let go of the gauntlet.

I left, hoping I didn't run into Gilmesh on the way out.

In a corner farther down and around the corner, I took a look at the print-out. The earliest dive entry date was over

two hundred centuries back—real time. I hadn't thought
Baldur had been with the Guard twenty thousand years,
but I supposed it wasn't all that surprising.

Frey wasn't around when I marched through the archway into Locator. I hadn't planned it that way, just happened. Ferrin was doing most of the work anyway.

Without any doubt, Ferrin was the worst diver in memory to have passed the Test, but he more than redeemed
himself in the running of the locator system.

Ferrin was the one who rearranged the rotation system
for all trainees, Guards, and Senior Guards by figuring the
actual diving abilities into the schedule. That way, there
was always a strong time-diver on locator duty.

"Ferrin, can you run a locator cross-check for me?
Baldur went off without explaining some heavy Maintenance scheduling and, frankly, I need some of his technical expertise."

Ferrin's eyebrows lifted.

"Loki, since I am a literal-minded administrator, and
since you undoubtedly have a worthwhile purpose, far beyond my meager powers of comprehension, I will indeed
facilitate your search."

I restrained a smile. A diver Ferrin might not be, but
he knew I was skirting legality. Ferrin, perhaps more than
anyone I knew, could smell a fish. But he knew, and I
mean *knew*, what would hurt the Guard and what wouldn't.

He slipped off the stool, took the tape data-bloc and
eased it into his tracer console.

"This is totally unnecessary, and that's one of the reasons I'm happy to do it."

I couldn't believe that. Baldur disappearing and a tracer
unnecessary?

"I'm a snoop, Loki. Surely you remember that. That's
why I can keep this place going—because I know more
than I'm supposed to. News does have a way of spreading,
you know."

He turned back to the tracer screen. "You take a look."
I looked.

The console had printed in its stylized script, "No present trace. Individual does not register outside previous
locales."

Baldur couldn't disappear. Not like that. But the console said his back- and fore-time traces existed only in the

places his assignment tape said he'd already been. Ergo he'd disappeared. Right?

"Loki," said Ferrin, "whatever Baldur's done, he deserves to be left alone. If he went to all the trouble of disguising his trace enough that we can't locate him, you can certainly see he doesn't want to be disturbed. And if he were dead, the change in the signal would show."

"Maybe," I noted, still suspicious.

"You suspect everyone and everything. You should. But nobody disliked Baldur. Nobody, not even Heimdall."

What Ferrin said made sense. I didn't want to believe that Baldur, who was so concerned about the future of Quest and Query, would off and take a dusting.

I left the data-bloc with Ferrin, pocketed the print-out, and headed back to the Maintenance Hall.

I didn't get much time by myself before the Tribunes arrived—all three of them—Freyda, Eranas, and Kranos.

After scrambling off the stool, I bowed slightly in welcome.

"We have a problem," began Eranas.

"With Baldur's disappearance, the Guard is left without a Maintenance supervisor with the appropriate knowledge and seniority. While no one doubts your unquestioned ability, to say nothing of your skill as a diver, your impetuousness and lack of seniority are equally demonstrable. At the same time, no Senior Guard having mechanical talents is available, and it will be a number of years before you will be eligible for Senior Guard status."

Eranas obviously wanted some acknowledgment from me.

"I understand the problem."

"We explored a number of alternatives, including making you the nominal head of Maintenance with supervision by the Tribunes personally. But the unwise precedent that could be set by making a junior Guard a department head and the fact that such supervision could be somewhat time-consuming . . ."

In short, young fellow, I translated, you've already given us too many headaches.

". . . leads us to another temporary expedient, which we will review on a periodic basis. Assignments and Maintenance will be consolidated under Heimdall, but you will in fact take charge of the daily operations of Maintenance."

All three waited for me to react.

I couldn't say I was surprised. No other Senior Guard would have touched the job for anything if what Loragerd had told me about the gossip was half-true.

"Not much I can say, honored Tribunes. While Heimdall and I certainly have not seen eye-to-eye in the past, I am confident we will develop a working relationship of mutual understanding."

Translate that any way you want, I thought.

"So long as that remains a working relationship," commented Kranos in his deep bass voice, "all of us will be pleased, I'm sure."

I bowed slightly once more.

"I appreciate the trust you have put in me."

With as little ceremony as when they arrived, the three left.

One of two things would happen, I decided. Either I would be swamped with trainees to avoid a recurrence of the present situation or they'd leave me alone as long as I kept out of trouble.

After the entourage of higher-ups departed for their sanctified quarters elsewhere in the Tower, I studied the print-out of Baldur's past assignments.

On the average, he had taken a diving assignment once a year, and that worked out to over twenty thousand. The physical print-out was notational, with all the assignments and the duration, objective and subjective, on a line or less. Twenty thousand assignments meant twenty thousand lines, or a few hundred thin pages.

I was searching for a specific kind of listing, however, and decided to assume for my first tries that no foul play was involved, that Baldur had left voluntarily.

How was I going to find him when the locator tag system couldn't?

The locator got a fix on every fore- and back-time point where a diver is or has been. The "now" position was determined by eliminating past assignments with a cross-index, which was why the records of all dives were so rigorously maintained by Personnel.

Further, the rules of Time are inflexible. No diver could occupy the same time slot in more than one place in the same solar system. I never understood why a diver could occupy the same time point in different systems, but that was the way it worked. Baldur couldn't have time-dived back to a time/place where he'd been once—*unless* he broke-out at the end of that earlier dive. I hadn't asked for differentials, and Ferrin hadn't suggested it, which struck me as suspicious, after the fact.

Baldur was hung up on doing constructive work, which meant a mid-tech culture and some place he wanted to stay for a while. My first step in trying to track down Baldur, after polishing off the routine maintenance waiting in my bin, would be to program my idea of Baldur's ideal home into the Archives Data Banks and request a list, hard copy.

Great insights aside, I still had a day-to-day job to get done. The Maintenance "in" bin was strangely full. A lot of it was real junk, dusty, unused for decades. Coincidences like that weren't.

I rated a midday break, despite the workload, and took the time to trot up to the Guard section of the Archives instead of sliding out to an Inn or the Aerie for a bite to eat.

I'd already decided to ask the Data Banks for the narrowest search possible, figuring I could widen it step by step if the parameters didn't touch on one of Baldur's earlier assignments.

Sitting there in the golden glow of the black-walled cube, waiting for the screen display and ready to punch the print stud, I wondered why I was so determined to track down the gentle engineer.

Another thought struck me, and I asked the Archives data system if anyone else were indexing the same data.

"Affirmative," scripted the screen.

"What command?" I pursued.

"Duplicate all requests, LKI-30, Red."

I struck the side of the cubicle, hammered my fist against the unyielding plastic, but the sharp lance of pain up my arm dissuaded me from further banging. That plastic was hard.

If they wanted to know what I was up to, I'd give them more than enough information. Scramble their schemes that way.

In the meantime, the information began writing out on the console screen. All in all, about two hundred time locales matched.

I ordered a print-out, then went ahead with my decision to muddle the waters by widening the search. I lowered the tech level by one magnitude, which boosted the numbers considerably.

The second list was lengthier, as well it should have been, with over two thousand time locales.

I cancelled the hold on the first grouping, ordered a print-out on the second, and left the second list on recall hold for my personal code. I hoped that would give the impression that I'd found what I wanted in the second grouping, rather than the first.

I ambled back down the ramp to Maintenance. The repairs piled in the bin were still waiting; they seemed to have grown in the short time I had been absent. Some variation of the theme that idle hands make easy work for careless time, I guessed.

Another thought occurred to me as I pitched in on a portable atmosphere generator which had definitely seen better days—uptime Terran manufacture, lots of plastic, excess back-up circuits to cover the sloppy construction— Baldur had been a Counselor, even though he had avoided most of the meetings.

Maybe, just maybe, he'd gotten tired of the plottings, the maneuverings, and what have you. But I couldn't be certain.

I plowed through the work on the regenerator, finished it off, improving the workmanship in the process, and started in on a set of camp barriers, followed by a child's deep space suit that hadn't been used in centuries.

I gritted my teeth and did the best I could, making a pretty good dent in the pile. Some of the easier garbage I farmed out to Narcissus and Brendan. Sooner or later I was going to get ahead of it because even Frey couldn't break it as fast as we three could fix it.

When I left the Tower at twilight, I smiled at everyone I passed, even Heimdall. I time-slid to the Aerie, the two sets of print-outs stuffed into my thigh pockets.

At the Aerie, it was still afternoon, but I'd grown used to the sun-position differences over the years.

I set the print-outs on the table next to the permaglass window and grabbed some fruit and nuts from the keeper, along with a beaker of firejuice.

I pulled up the stool and started in on a quick comparison of the Archives' short list against Baldur's assignments. At least ten matched—requiring dives and explorations and searches of ten planets. By the time I made ten time-dives, someone in Locator, and by then I felt everyone was monitoring my every move, would figure out what I was doing.

Dive smart, not often, Sammis had said. I might have to do some thinking about this, I figured as I munched my way through the print-outs.

I laid out a couple of assumptions. Number one: If Baldur really liked one area culture, he would have made several dives there on some pretext or another.

I went through the ten assignments that matched the data-bank short list and came up with two systems that Baldur had visited often.

The Atlantean Empire on Terra, twelve centuries back real objective time, was the first. The second was the third early mech period of Midgard, five centuries back. Both were well within Baldur's limited time-diving range.

My guess was Midgard. The Atlantean Empire of close back-time Terra, as I recalled, had been a casualty of a unique natural catastrophe which wiped out all chance of such a pass-on.

Midgard was a relatively small and dense planet, and the back-time era where I suspected Baldur had gone to earth was relatively underpopulated, but it would take forever to search each "industrial" center for hints.

So I curbed my impatience and leaned back to watch the flashing threads of the silver rivers below, resisting the urge to chew through my fingernails. Didn't have much practice at analytical thinking, but maybe it was time to start.

> Item: Baldur liked to think and to work with his hands.
> Item: Baldur disliked the continual time-tampering of the Guard.
> Item: Baldur could make an impact in any early mech culture.
> Item: No winds of time-change had accompanied his departure.

Possible conclusion: Baldur was playing a longer-range game, and the closer to real objective "now" his destination was, the less likely his objective would be discovered.

Thinking done, I stood up and unloaded an insulated

warm-suit from its sealed pack. I had it half on before I stopped.

I kept forgetting. I had all the time in the world. No one else was searching for Baldur, and I didn't have to find him that night.

Was I deluding myself? Would it be easy to pace myself, take some time? Or was it that I already knew the answer? Or did I want time to come up with my own answers? I stared into the morning hours, asking questions I could not answer, walking, watching the flickering silver of the far-below rivers as they glittered against the darkness of the canyon's night, pacing in front of the permaglass—wondering.

The dawn snaked its way over Seneschal all too soon after I had crawled into my furs, and later than I should have risen, but I managed to grumble myself together and onto my feet. From there it was only a few units until I slid to the Tower and walked into Maintenance.

During the day, the backlog shrank a bit more, perhaps because Heimdall and company were running out of things to have repaired. Never had so many odd pieces of equipment been in such good condition.

During the midday break, I wheedled a language refresher out of Loragerd, but had to promise to be careful on Midgard. I hoped she wouldn't say anything, but I couldn't do much searching for Baldur if I couldn't speak the lingo, something I'd forgotten the night before, for all my serious deliberations.

Right after a quick evening meal, I pulled on the insulated suit and dived from the Aerie, straight back to Midgard and the time of Baldur's last objective time assignment, in the city of Fenris. The wolf-city was more like a town, with narrow streets and open sewers. A half-day local, five taverns, and six smithies later I knew nothing more than when I started.

I time-dived back to the Aerie and fell into the waiting furs for a few hours sleep.

I made it to the Tower and into Maintenance at my regular time, a feat in itself after my night explorations on Midgard. As I studied the new additions to the repair bin and congratulated myself on making all the ends meet, Loragerd cornered me.

"I've been thinking."

"Dangerous occupation, thinking."

She avoided the hint. "I know Baldur's disappearance has upset you, but are you going to chase his ghost all over the galaxy?"

I turned on her, grabbing her shoulders before I realized I'd even moved.

"Ghost! So he is dead! How do you know?"

"Loki! Loki! Stop shaking me. I'm here. I'm not your enemy. I don't know what happened to Baldur."

"You said ghost, and people who are alive don't have ghosts."

I let go of her shoulders and found she was inside my arms, holding me. Holding me, for Guards' sake.

"Loki, for such a strong man, you're such an idiot."

I stood there for long units before I remembered to put my arms around her. At that, she stepped back out of my arms and brushed something out of her eyes. She cleared her throat, and the sound was swallowed in the morning emptiness of the Maintenance Hall. "Why is it so important for you to find Baldur?"

"Because it's not like him to disappear."

"From what you've told me, it is just like him. No fuss, no outcry. You're the one who likes the theatrics."

That hurt, even from Loragerd, and she must have realized it. She looked at the glowstone floor.

We avoided looking each other in the eyes. I gestured toward the two stools in front of my bench. "There's something more on your mind," I observed.

"You'll never love anyone, and you know it. You may be fond of me, or want Verdis, even Freyda. But you won't let yourself love."

"What does that have to do with Baldur?"

"Everything. Baldur loved. He loved everyone. And he couldn't stand it anymore. He left. He didn't tell Freyda, or Eranas, or Heimdall, or Odinthor, or you."

"How do you know?"

"Because they've been following you, tracking you, wondering if you can find Baldur, half-hoping you can, half-hoping you can't."

"They don't have any ideas?" I snapped.

Loragerd brushed whatever it was out of her eyes again, cleared her throat, and went on. She seemed hoarse. "Freyda said . . . she said you ought to let the poor bastard alone."

"What?" Manipulating Freyda wanted someone left alone?

"I'd better go, Loki."

"You just got here."

"You have work to do, and so do I."

She slipped off the stool into the quiet side lights and was lost in the shadows within instants.

Why had she come down to see me? Had she been trying to tell me something? Sometimes, none of it made sense.

I dropped off the stool, walked over to the bin, and studied the backlog piled there. With the exception of the shield unit, Brendan and Narcissus could handle it all.

Despite my intentions to farm all of the repairs out to Brendan and Narcissus, I ended up working straight through. Not much left to do by the late afternoon.

After picking up a quick meal at Hera's Inn, I tried to puzzle it all out as I watched the sunset from the Aerie.

Baldur gone, and no one able to track him, no one wanting to. Loragerd's puzzling appearance in the Maintenance Hall and that business about my not being able to love anyone. That had hurt.

Sammis had said to dive smart and not often, but as the sun dropped lower and cast a red light on the snowfields of Seneschal I found myself suited and ready to time-dive back to Midgard. Another night, another city—this time, Isolde.

My luck, skill, whatever, wasn't any better in Isolde.

Somehow the days and nights passed. Fifteen cities, towns, villages, and no sign of Baldur. Fifteen days consisting of two days and a couple hours sleep—a day at the Tower, a day on Midgard, and what sleep I could get, the pattern repeating day after day. Fall was coming, but I didn't notice much of the mild change in season.

The morning after my last dive to Midgard, and I knew it was my last because there wasn't anywhere else to look, I was staring blankly at a warm-suit powerpack connection block.

"Loki."

I knew the voice, and swiveled on the stool to greet Freyda.

"My lady."

She seldom beat around the bush. She didn't then.

"Haven't you tried enough?"

"Enough on what?"

"Baldur. What else?"

"What did you do to him?" I tried a glare, but was too tired for it to make much of a dent in Freyda's composure.

She shook her head slowly. "In such a hurry, trying to solve the universe as if you had no tomorrow. I'd hoped . . ."

"Hoped what?"

She smiled faintly. "That is neither here nor now. I thought I might be able to help you. Why do you want to find Baldur so badly?"

"Because he shouldn't have disappeared."

"Did you know Ferrin has tried every possible Locator cross-check? That includes comparing the time-length of past assignments, trying variations on Baldur's Locator tag signal, and sending Sammis back- and fore-time with portable Locator packs."

I swallowed that without commenting. No wonder the Tribunes had been content to let me poke around Midgard. They knew he wasn't there. "And you let me waste time . . ."

"Would you have believed me without trying it out yourself?"

I wasn't sure I believed Freyda then. "So what do you want now?"

"For you to stop wasting your energy chasing a ghost."

"What did you do to him, or with him?"

She looked at me for a long time, eye to eye, and her gaze never wavered. "I was the second choice to replace Martel—a very distant second. Baldur was selected on the first ballot. He refused, without explaining. If you want, I'll even open that section of the Tribunes' private records to you."

Put in that light, I had no reason to disbelieve. I didn't understand, but Freyda was telling me the truth, at least, the truth as she knew it.

"Why?" I caught myself about ready to pound on my workbench. "Why would he just walk out on everything?"

"I have an answer, but I think you'll have to find your own, Loki. Guards are human, all too human, for all our experience, all our age, and all our abilities. You can't be a god and be a human, not both, and stay sane. Somewhere you make a choice. Baldur chose one way, and I may have to choose another. You will, too, if you haven't already."

The words whirled around in my head, just words, disconnected from any reality.

Looking into the darkness of the shadowed and shielded machinery, asking why, and not having any answer, I let the time ebb and flow past me before I understood that Freyda had left.

I wondered if she had even been there.

Was her appearance a creation of my own mind?

Baldur had dropped from the sight of the Guard, had turned his back on us, and I had to accept that. But the question that kept digging at me was why he'd gone. If I really understood why, I might have been able to figure out where. The only places he'd shown any great interest in were like Terra, and personally I thought the Terrans were just like us, too damned ruthless for someone like Baldur.

I shrugged as I considered it. The change winds didn't blow far backwards, and there was no way to track Baldur, or anyone, through all the fore-time possibilities.

Baldur was gone. I had to accept that. The old names were fading from Query. Martel had stepped down. Odinthor was a shadow of himself. My grandfather Ragnorak had been missing for centuries.

How did an immortal die? Did immortals die, really die, or live out meaningless lives on dustballs in the void?

The ranks of the immortals were thinning, it seemed, replaced with the techs like Ferrin, Verdis, Loragerd.

XIII

I was perched above my workbench, pondering over the possibility of changing the layout in Maintenance when Nicodemus tiptoed in.

Never did understand why all the trainees walked into Maintenance as if they were treading on eggshells. I was always civil.

"What is it?"

"Counselor Heimdall would like to talk to you, sir."

"I'm not 'sir,' Nicodemus. I'm Loki, first, last, and always."

"Yes, sir."

As Nicodemus stood there waiting, stiff, as if I were going to snap his head off, I climbed down from my high stool, brushed my hair off my forehead, and straightened my black jumpsuit. I followed Nicodemus up the ramp to Assignments.

Heimdall was waiting, calm, assured, with his long black hair in perfect place. He was frowning though, and kept pulling at his chin.

"Problems?"

"Think so, but not certain. That makes it worse."

He flicked his long fingers over the console in front of him while I stepped up on the platform and settled myself in the lower stool across from him.

"You know Patrice?" he asked without looking away from the screen.

"Went through training together."

"Good diver, I gather."

"I don't know about her evaluations, but my impression was that she would be good."

"Sammis agrees. Makes this disturbing."

I wanted to ask what it was all about, but I bit my lip. Heimdall was usually so direct I wondered if he was playing on my impatience.

I waited.

"Locator has a fix on her. Twelve centuries back. Toltek. Supposed to have returned two days ago. Sent Derron after her, fully equipped. He hasn't returned either."

"Toltek? Derron?"

"Best diver from the Domestic Strike Force."

The assignment Heimdall was setting me up for was shaping itself as nasty, plain and simple. If Frey's most accomplished goon couldn't rescue one of the better divers in Scouting . . .

He hadn't answered my question about Toltek so I asked again. "Never heard of Toltek. Should it be familiar?"

"Toltek?" Heimdall seemed amused. "No. Out beyond Faffnir. Small cluster. Patrice did the preliminaries from deep space, then orbit, brought back some holo shots. Went in for a closer scan."

"And never came back, and you sent Derron. And he never came back. Now you want a double rescue?"

Heimdall's fingers flashed over the console again before he answered. He didn't look straight at me.

"May not be that simple. Archives evaluated the holos Patrice brought in. Signs of mid-tech culture, maybe even high-tech."

High-tech civilizations are rare, a handful in the time and area spans surveyed by the Guard. I shivered. I knew what was coming. "High-tech?" I asked.

He nodded.

"With two lost, if I don't succeed, you'll recommend cutting the Guard's losses?"

He nodded again.

Clear enough. If I didn't drag them out, at some back-time point a planet-buster would be funneled through the undertime to Toltek.

The process would automatically destroy the planet and the Toltekians, but not necessarily an alert Guard. We'd have a chance, but how much of a chance depended on circumstances. I didn't like that prospect.

Sounds cruel, but it wasn't. With really good divers scarce, the Guard couldn't afford to have them whittled down on rescue attempt after attempt. And we weren't organized for massive assaults. All in all, a second attempt was worth it, but not a third.

If necessary, the Tribunes would regretfully order a planet-busting. They had done so before. Be less messy if I recovered Patrice and Derron.

"Briefing?" I asked, mentally trying to catalogue what I might need to take along.

Heimdall tapped several studs on the console, got up, and pointed to the display.

"Restricted," he explained. I didn't question that, although I probably should have.

I sat down in his stool, on edge about his standing behind me, and watched the script and holo shots unfold in front of me. Patrice had blown it. Obvious even to a dunderhead like me. You take it easy with planetary cultures that build lots of structures which can be seen from space.

Toltek was too regular. The forests, rivers, coastlines fit into a definite pattern. Any culture which shaped a planet for aesthetic purposes had one Hell of a lot of power to spare.

"Stinks," I commented to Heimdall, more to get his reaction than to state the obvious.

"Forego your rescue and recommend immediate destruction?" he asked in a level tone.

Common sense said yes, but I wasn't about to be the one who decided to destroy an entire planet. "No. I'll see what I can do."

According to the data Patrice had recorded, the air was breathable, if high in water vapor and oxygen. The temperature was a touch high, and gravity heavy, but not enough to bother me. I needed a small Locator pack to trace Derron's and Patrice's shoulder tags, plus demolition cubes to cover our tracks if I succeeded.

"When are you leaving?" Heimdall interrupted my planning with his question.

"As soon as I gather what I need," I replied, slipping off his stool and heading out the archway toward the ramps.

I stopped by Maintenance to pick up a small laser cutter and some spare power cells in case Derron and Patrice needed them. I sent Brendan over to Locator to pick up the portable locator packs and told him to meet me at the Travel Hall with them.

I reached the Travel Hall before Brendan and began to assemble what I needed. Compromise was the order of the day. I started with the black bodymesh armor I'd worn to Sinopol and put it on under a standard jumpsuit. I added the laser to the equipment belt, plus a stunner, some additional ration-packs, and a knife.

By the time I finished, Brendan arrived with the locator packs.

"Ferrin says good luck."

I had to grin. "If you see him—don't make a special trip—tell him that luck is a luxury too chancy for me."

Brendan just nodded. Seldom could anything I said surprise him.

I ambled out into the Travel Hall from the equipment room, taking my time. Finally, I dived, smashing through the time-chill and arrowing out and back-time toward Toltek.

I took a flash-look at the planet from altitude.

Patrice's holo hadn't conveyed the greenness of the place, from the green atmosphere, to the long green grassy stuff that covered the regular fields, to the persistent green cliff walls that outlined the symmetrical green sand beaches.

After three, four, five flash-throughs around the edges of the daylight cities, I had not gotten a glimpse of a native, although the evidence of continuing planetary maintenance was everywhere evident.

Nocturnal—that was my next thought. I flashed through the undertime, nightside, and was rewarded when I passed over a beach on the nightside. I came back for another look.

Several figures were standing on the glowing green sand under the stars. I stood on the sand, silently, for several units trying to make out the shapes—definitely not humanoid.

Abruptly, I was seized and shaken. That's what it felt like, but there was nothing around. Just as suddenly I was tossed head over heels onto the sand.

My whole body vibrated. The shaking and the high-pitched whine that accompanied it made concentrating hard as Hell, but I knew if I didn't slide quickly, I wasn't going to be sliding or diving anywhere. I managed to blot out the distractions and stagger undertime. As soon as I did, the shaking and the whine disappeared.

Too close—way too close.

As usual, dumb old Loki had slid right in and announced, "Here I am." I hung in the undertime for a subjective unit or two to try and get an impression of the Toltekians.

Not humanoid, that seemed certain. Through the time-tension barrier, I could make out a solid "trunk" with pseudopods, I thought, propelling it, and with a fringe of tentacles at the top. The "trunk" glistened like the cliff walls around the beach, which made me think it was solid.

I plunked myself over to an isolated spot on Faffnir, settling on a knoll above the lifeless black sea. I sat down on a raised and smoothed chunk of ironglass which probably dated back to the fall of High Sinopol.

In the atmosphere of quiet antiquity, in the afternoon light of Faffnir, I began to put together what little I'd picked up.

Item: Toltekians were nocturnal non-humanoid.
Item: I was assuming the beings I'd run into were Toltekians.
Item: They had picked up my appearance within unit-fractions and shaken Hell out of me.
Item: I had barely managed to think my way undertime with the scrambling my thoughts had taken.
Item: Most divers wouldn't have gotten clear.

My first guess was energy projection, but I hadn't felt the power, and with my sensitivity to high-energy concentrations, I should have.

Second guess was directed sonics. If the Toltekians were a sonic-based culture, that would explain a number of things. They could have picked up my arrival, my breathing, and reacted. I postponed further thought while I pulled a ration stick out of my belt and munched it to settle my shaking legs.

If my assumptions were correct, and I saw no reason why they shouldn't be, the Toltekians could maintain such a sound attack for only a limited time. Patrice and Der-ron should have escaped and reported. They hadn't.

I knew of only two ways to imprison a good diver—either scramble his thoughts or tie him to a chunk of something too big to carry into a dive. The second method was likely, particularly if Patrice and Derron had been rendered unconscious with the initial sonic blast.

I reached down and checked my own equipment-belt for the laser cutter. It was there.

Knowing the kind of Guard employed on the Strike Force, I'd have bet that Derron had homed in on Patrice's signal—tried a frontal assault of some sort. The Toltekians had apparently been ready for Derron and potted him as well.

Sitting there in the early afternoon light of Faffnir, I decided that waiting wouldn't solve my problems. I didn't know of any equipment back on Query that would provide a defense against sonics. So it seemed like speed was the best answer—speed and a willingness to zap a few Tol-tekians along the way.

I checked the Locator packs and activated them, diving undertime toward Toltek. The signals led me under one of the larger structures on the northern continent. Both sig-nals were from the same point, from what seemed to be a solid rock or stone chamber well underneath the city above.

The objective "now" for Patrice and Derron was close to local midnight. I could have waited until "day," but that far underground I doubted it would make a difference.

With both the darkness and the undertime barrier, I couldn't see more than shadows, but the picture I received was of two figures chained to opposite sides of a long wall with Toltekian sentries posted or planted at each end. A long pointed weapon was aimed at one of the captives—Derron probably.

Hit and run was my idea, to slide up from the under-time behind one sentry and stun her, him, or it, then to do the same to the other, disable the weapon gadget with a thunderbolt, cut the two Guards free, leave a set of demolition blocs, and depart. The charges would make a thorough mess of the chamber and cover our tracks as well.

I slid from the undertime behind the Toltekian sentry closest to the gadget gun and thumbed the stunner. It hummed. Nothing happened. The sentry stood. At that instant, both sentries "screamed" and the whole dungeon began shaking. I dropped the stunner and threw a thunderbolt at the far sentry.

All that energy bounced off him, skittered around the tentacles—purple tentacles. But the sentry shrank back, wincing. In the intervening instants, the sentry I'd failed to stun had turned toward me, "screaming," and grabbed at me with his tentacles.

For a fraction of an instant, the vibrations distracted me, but I mentally pushed them away and slid around the grabby Toltekian. I threw another thunderbolt, this time at the weapon. The pointed nozzle wilted, and the sentries froze at the flash. A deep gong chimed in the background, and kept chiming.

So far, I'd alerted the entire city and accomplished nothing. I was beginning to see red. Damned if a bunch of tree-snails were going to stand in front of Loki!

Light! That was the answer. They didn't like light. I began firing off thunderbolts in every direction, pulling the laser cutter off my belt as I dashed/slid toward Patrice. She was out cold, slumped against the chains which linked her to the wall. Her arms were tight against the stone, and the links of the chains were shaped stone which seemed to be the same material as the walls. That explained plenty. I cut through two sets of links and let her slump to the floor. Then I fired off another round of thunderbolts in the general direction of the two sentries and slid to the other side of the chamber.

Like Patrice, Derron was unconscious. It was harder to cut the chains from his arms because he was bigger than me, bigger even than Baldur, and had his whole weight resting against them.

I used the cutter to blaze through one while I threw a bunch of lightnings behind me. I had the feeling that more Toltekians were closing, ready to enter the chamber, but I finished the second set of links and let Derron collapse on the rock floor. I could hold him, but not carry him.

I glanced up in time to see a procession of Toltekians coming through the oval door with a high-speed glide.

I froze them in place with all the power I could throw and as the chamber flared with that light, I saw that they were unlimbering some ugly hardware.

I flash slid to the other side of the dungeon and tossed Patrice over my shoulder, glad she was small, and slid back across to Derron. Using my free arm, I blasted the Toltekians again, concentrating on light. The thunderbolts may not have caused them physical pain, but all the power I was tossing blinded them and made a mess of their equipment.

Before I picked up Derron, I had enough presence of mind to yank out a handful of demolition cubes, one at a time, ripping the set tab of the corner of each one as I scattered them across the chamber. With the last cube gone, I grabbed Derron around the waist and forced my way undertime.

Forced, because it's difficult to carry a cooperating and consenting adult undertime, let alone two unconscious ones. The unconscious mind resists *any* change; it has a tendency to lock itself into the here and now, wherever it is. But I managed, clearing the undertime of Toltek as fast as I could. I struggled fiercely to get as far as Faffnir, and Faffnir was only a fraction of the time and distance home. I broke-out on the knoll I'd found earlier, not that I'd been looking for it, but somehow we ended up there. Local time was late afternoon, with a breeze sweeping in from the sea, carrying an ancient tang of metal.

Legs quivering, I eased both Derron and Patrice down and laid them out so they'd be as comfortable as possible on the hard ground. Both were breathing and had no obvious physical injuries. I sat down on a low hump next to them. Didn't have any choice. My legs refused to support me any longer.

I dug out my ration sticks and gobbled two bone-dry before I even thought about being thirsty. After a few units, my body stopped trembling, and I began to take stock. Patrice and Derron, unmoving, slept like small children. I surveyed my own gear. Both my wrist-gauntlets were fused and inert plates.

One arm, my left, had a red line. I peeled back my sleeve slightly to trace it, but the scratch only ran up to a point below the elbow, like the fine scrape of a briar-thorn. I dismissed it and checked through the rest. Everything was accounted for except the stunner I'd dropped.

"Unnhh," someone groaned.

I glanced at the two Guards. Derron was breathing, but

not moving. Patrice was shaking her head and trying to get up.

She was wearing a canteen; she was more thoughtful than me. I unstoppered it and helped her take a small swallow. For several units, she sipped and pulled herself together.

I waited.

"Hell! Had to be you, blood and thunder. Break-out and assault the sentries and cart everyone off. I suppose you blew up the planet after you left."

"Patrice!"

"Did you?"

"No, just part of the city, or whatever it was. That's a guess. Took everything I had to drag you two here."

"Where's here?"

"Faffnir."

She cocked her head. "How come they didn't get you with their shaker-upper?"

"Almost did." I told her about my experience on the green sand beach at night.

"No reinforcements? And after *that,* you decided you could handle it?"

In retrospect and put that way, it did sound stupid. "Why not?" I replied, not wanting to admit it.

Patrice was about to tell me, but Derron started groaning, and I was spared another lecture about my impetuousness. After a few units, Derron started asking questions. From the tenor of his comments, I gathered he'd been in a lot of tight spots. "Never seen anything like it—those trees, snails, didn't react to stunners, warblers, thunderbolts, nothing," Derron lamented. "How did you manage it, Loki?"

I didn't have any answers. "Just lucky, I guess."

"You blinded them, is that it?" pursued Patrice.

"I tried."

Patrice climbed to her feet, studied the area around us for a long unit or so, then jumped, pointed at a near-by rock.

"Loki! Quick! Throw a thunderbolt! That rock! Don't think! Fire!"

I fired and blasted the rock into powder.

Patrice turned absolutely white, sat down in a heap like a pile of stone fragmenting into gravel.

Derron looked around as if he'd missed something. "I don't get it," he said.

I was afraid I did. But I didn't have to think about it right then.

"Must be seeing things—better get back, before Heimdall thinks we're trapped here," said Patrice. Her color was returning.

Hycretis insisted on putting all three of us through a barrage of diagnostics and retaining us for a night's sleep in the Infirmary before he'd let Heimdall debrief us.

After eating and cleaning up the next morning, the three of us walked over to Assignments.

Nicodemus intercepted us at the archway into the Assignments Hall. "Counselor Heimdall would like to see you individually, starting with Guard Patrice. He suggests that Guards Loki and Derron avail themselves of the lounge."

I shrugged. Derron looked off balance.

Patrice smiled faintly. "Don't worry," was all she said.

Why should I have worried?

Derron and I wandered down the corridor to the vacant Senior Guards' lounge and sat down. For a time, neither one of us said anything, just sat there, me looking up at him, him looking down at me. But he wasn't looking, not exactly.

As the silence grew, Derron cleared his throat. "Loki?"

"Yes."

"Remember one thing, no matter what happens. I'll never cross you."

Odd, that's how I saw it. There was a seasoned Guard who'd been tracking down malefactors for centuries, who outweighed and overtopped me, asking me to remember that he'd never cross me.

"I mean that," he insisted.

"I'll remember," I promised, when it became obvious that he was sincere. But why was he worried? Just because I'd somehow thrown a thunderbolt without gauntlets? A thunderbolt was a thunderbolt, and both kinds killed.

We sat for a few units longer in the low stools before Patrice tripped her way out the archway and down the corridor.

"Derron, Heimdall wants to see you next."

"See you around, Loki," he said as he got up.

I stood and bowed slightly. "Good diving, Derron."

He deserved that much.

Patrice waited for Derron to enter the Assignments Hall.

"You never told me what was on that rock, or why you screamed yesterday."

"Nothing. There wasn't a thing on the rock."

"Why did you scream? You're as cold as ice in the crunch."

"So you wouldn't think before you acted."

"I don't understand." But I did, and didn't want to admit it.

"I know. You don't understand anything, and it may be the death of all of us, but I'll be damned if I'm going to answer your stupid questions for you. You have to find the answers. I hope you have time to discover them, because part of you doesn't want to admit you can."

"You're playing games!" I was getting angry. Patrice was just like the rest of them, hinting at this and that, but never just coming out and saying it.

She half-turned away. "I'm reporting back to Scouting, but I'll give you a question. Didn't you check your gauntlets on Faffnir before I woke up? Check them again. Think about it."

Hints or not, she made sense, and I didn't like that either.

Brendan had carried all my equipment down to my bench for repairs because Hycretis wouldn't let us go. After Heimdall finished with me, I could go over the gauntlets again. Didn't take long, but Heimdall didn't come to find me. Nicodemus did.

Heimdall was leaning back in his stool right where I'd left him the day before—had it only been a day earlier?

"Derron and Patrice have filled me in on what happened to them, except for how you got them out of the dungeon. The Toltekians 'screamed' when you appeared and that knocked out Patrice and Derron, I gather."

I told Heimdall what I'd done, from the point where I'd broken-out on the green beach at night till the time when I'd staggered onto the knoll on Faffnir with Patrice and Derron in tow.

He nodded as I recited, muttering at one point something about "sheer brute force." A matter of opinion, I thought. At least I hadn't used any more force than necessary, nor had I destroyed the planet.

I stopped.

"You all agree on the sonic control," Heimdall noted. "What sort of follow-up would you recommend?"

"Do we need any? I'd have to revise my earlier judgment. I don't think the tech level is as high as I figured."

Heimdall punched out a code on his screen, then leaned back so I could see the picture that formed.

The holo shots zeroed in on one of the Toltekian cities. As I watched, a whole section collapsed in on itself, thundering silently down into a pile of rubble.

"Sammis went out last night to get a series of follow-up shots. I thought you might have left a trail." He laughed, a short bark that wasn't expressing humor.

"Sammis does agree with all three of you that further retaliation is totally unnecessary."

I repressed a sigh of relief.

"There's one question that hasn't been answered, Loki."

I stiffened.

"The Toltekians 'screaming' stunned two of the best divers in the Guard. You were hardly affected. Why not?"

I had been wondering about that myself. "I don't know. The first time, on the beach, it was hard, really hard, to get undertime. The second time I was mad, wasn't thinking about it, and it didn't seem to affect me as much. I don't know why. Hycretis gave me some hearing tests, but the tests showed my ears are as good as Derron's."

I shrugged. What else could I do? "I don't know, Counselor. I just don't know."

Heimdall accepted that, or seemed to.

"Is that all?" I asked.

"That's all."

I got up from the lower stool and went out through the main archway. Started down the ramps to Maintenance, but I wasn't watching where I was going and barely avoided crashing into Sammis.

He smiled, but I hadn't the faintest idea why. "Keep it up, Loki."

And he was on his way.

I was mulling over what Patrice had said about the gauntlets. Unfortunately, her hints made sense, too much sense. I'd checked my gauntlets on Faffnir before Patrice had awakened, and I was certain they were so much fused metal. I knew I could tell busted equipment from functional. And if they were fused, how could I have thrown a thunderbolt at that rock unless I didn't need gauntlets?

Broken gauntlets were so much useless metal. But so what? A thunderbolt thrown at me would have been just as fatal. Dead is dead, natural or mechanical.

I brushed past Narcissus and headed straight for my bench. The gauntlets were on my bench, fused.

A chance remained. One might be operational, for all the melted exterior. I removed the power cells, cutting one out with a laser. I placed the left gauntlet in the diagnostic center.

"Non-functioning," the console scripted out, following the diagnosis with an extensive list of malfunctions. The right wrist gauntlet was diagnosed the same way. It made sense, for all my unasked questions. I just didn't like it.

Derron was another question. Why would an experienced goon, two heads taller than me, one of the biggest, toughest-looking Guards, insist he'd never cross me? Any thunderbolt from a gauntlet was as deadly as mine, and maybe more certain. I didn't know how much, if any, control I had.

Heimdall hated my guts, I sensed, but had been nothing but polite and courteous.

That evening came quickly, but tiredness even sooner. No matter what I thought, diving, and especially rescue diving, took a toll. By the time I'd cleaned up the last of what I'd tackled from the repair bin, I was ready to head for the Aerie, a meal, and a long night's sleep.

It couldn't have been more than fifty units after I'd walked out the South Portal of the Tower that I was wrapping myself in sleeping furs and feeling my eyelids close.

Most nights I slept without dreaming, or if I did dream, I didn't remember. Once in a while I had a dream so vivid it was real, no dream at all. I could tell that kind was a dream only because the subjects were so unreal. The dream I had after the Toltek rescue was different, if it was a dream.

Some sense of energy, of power, a tingling in the air around me, pulled me from sleep, but I felt so light, so filled with energy, I knew it had to be a dream. It couldn't be happening, not when I'd fallen asleep so exhausted.

With the exception of the muted radiation from the glowstone floors, the Aerie was dark. I looked around, half-sitting, trying to puzzle out what had brought me out of deep sleep. Nothing, no one—but an uneasy feeling grew, centered on a point in the middle of the room.

I eased to my feet with a fluid motion so swift it had to be unreal. The walls, each glowstone, the permaglass overlooking the cliffs, all stood out in the darkness in relief, outlined with an energy reflected from—somewhere. I walked across the room, hovering above the glowstones, trying to pinpoint the sense of danger. I couldn't explain it, but the energy that outlined the room, the same energy that filled and refreshed me—that unseen force that coursed through my veins like fire—was the danger. As I waited, at the absolute center of the Aerie, a point of starlight burned, pulsing, pushing its way out from the undertime. The room filled with blinding light, heat, and power.

Without thinking, I gestured, pushed the light back where it came from, banished it into the undertime. I couldn't have explained how, but I did. I wanted it gone, and it was. Real time wavered for a few instants, rippled by the vanishing energy, before stabilizing, and the remaining energy lingered in the Aerie, the outlines which had put everything in relief fading slowly. The heat dissipated more slowly. I felt sleepy, filled with warmth, and I curled up on top of my sleeping furs.

When the sun struck me full in the face at dawn, I was curled on top of the furs. The Aerie was warm and the dream clear in my mind. As I uncurled, I felt better than I had in seasons, relaxed and refreshed. After wondering if the dream had anything to do with it, I washed up, dressed, and downed some biscuits and firejuice, ready for a quick slide to the Tower and the work that was waiting.

The Tower was quiet, the ramps vacant, when I arrived, earlier than normal, and bounded down the incline to Maintenance.

I had zipped through several routine jobs by the time Brendan rushed in.

"Loki, have you heard the latest?" He stopped and whistled. "Where did you get that tan?"

"Tan?" The time on Faffnir hadn't been long enough to darken my already tanned face that much more. Was I more tanned?

I decided to brush off the question. "What's the latest?"

"Sun-tunnel blew on some of Frey's Locator personnel.

Hycretis has them closeted in the old wards of the Infirmary. Hush-hush, that sort of thing, but Lynia had duty last night, and I wouldn't let her in until she told me."

Lynia must be his contract, but Brendan hadn't mentioned her before. He was too young, by custom at least, to enter a full contract.

"Told you what?" I was thinking about Lynia, barely out of training.

He laughed. "Loki, were you listening?"

I grinned back at him. "Sort of. Lynia had to work late . . ."

"No, she had duty, and Hycretis and Gerrond had to work most of the night patching people up. Some of the divers were badly burned. Must have been one hot tunnel."

"What were Frey's people doing with a sun-tunnel? How many were there?"

"Lynia said five had to stay in the Infirmary. One of them was screaming 'impossible' over and over. Nobody would say why."

"Strange," I commented. "Very strange, but it won't clear our backlog."

Strange wasn't the word. Sun-tunnels could be dangerous, but normally only took a diver or two, not a whole team. I felt a vague fear rising in the back of my mind, like a wave. It couldn't have had anything to do with my dream. Besides, who'd want to poke a sun-tunnel into the Aerie?

Coincidence, that was all. Then too, maybe I'd just had the dream because my subconscious had somehow tuned in on the disaster.

"About that tan?" Brendan asked again.

"Spent the day before yesterday on Faffnir."

"Oh."

And that was the end of the questions.

In any case, Brendan, Narcissus, and I had more than enough to do. It was time to get on with reorganizing Maintenance and reducing the backlog that had been dumped on us.

XIV

Seasons, years, can pass before a Guard knows it, even an impatient one with a purpose. Much had to be done, and there were few enough Guards to accomplish the mere monitoring of our corner of the galaxy as it was.

Through it all, I kept puzzling out the old equipment and machines in the Maintenance Hall, determined to uncover the principles behind each old design. Not so direct was the self-imposed goal of increasing my own personal abilities. At first, the harder job was working with Sammis and Wryan. As the seasons passed, however, the daily sessions became less than daily, and then less than that.

Finally, Sammis called a halt. "You know more than either of us, or both together, probably more than any Guard ever has, and far too much for your own good. Too much ability, too much knowledge, and not enough wisdom. Take a break. Let a little time flow around you."

By then, I'd decided that the answer didn't just lie in physical abilities. Some of the stunts I attempted after that were doubtless stupid, like catching thunderbolts and trying to tap solar flares through the undertime. Not that I spent a whole lot of time on experimental stuff.

I picked up a new trainee along the way, a woman named Elene, who rated somewhere between Narcissus and Brendan in ability. Another redhead, but with a calmer disposition.

Took some pride in the fact that we had everything in the Tower working. Heimdall couldn't find a thing to complain about, but he complained anyway.

A messenger interrupted me on a morning no different

from any other spring morning in Quest. He was one of the newer trainees. Giron, I recalled, was his name. Giron arrived as I was puzzling over the design of an incomprehensible, for the moment, Gurlenian "artifact" brought in by Zealor.

"Tribune Kranos requests the honor of your presence."

"I'll bet."

"Sir?"

"Tell the honored Tribune I will be there shortly, as soon as I get the grease off my hands."

What did Kranos want? He normally avoided me like the plague. I sighed, flipped the artifact partly out-of-time-phase to make sure no one else fiddled with it. Narcissus was getting too damned curious for his own good. He didn't have the talents, either diving or mechanical, to get himself out of the jams created by his own nosiness.

A few days earlier, he'd tried to discover the purpose of the back-row machine that assembled shield units, and if I had been any slower he would have had one planted in his shoulder. It worked on a mass-focus assembly system, made obsolete by the up-time Terran stuff which was a third the size and used less power, but it was an interesting concept, nonetheless. I'd made the mistake of not returning the time-shield, and Narcissus was trying to energize the equipment with his shoulder halfway into the focusing point.

I wiped off my hands, straightened my jumpsuit and marched up the ramps to Kranos's chambers.

Blunt as always, he had his proposition stated before I sat down on the upholstered stool across from his worktable.

"Loki, I'd like you to take a short leave of absence from Maintenance and see if you can give the Admin people a hand in designing a better personnel system. You've done wonders in Maintenance."

"Why?" That was a question I always asked too often. "I know as much about administration as this stool does."

Kranos's stern face was always smooth, and with his thick and unruly hair, it made you think he was an animated statue on loan from the Archives gallery. We didn't have much sculpture, perhaps because a people with such long life-spans didn't need as much to remind them of the past. Besides, if it were really old, no one outside the Guard really cared anyway.

The legends remained, and no one wanted to know how many warts Odinthor had. That's why the old Tribune was such an embarrassment. He kept hanging around and tarnishing his legend.

Kranos didn't blink an eye at my question. "You have a different outlook."

In the whole time I'd been in the Guard, I'd never heard of such a switch. Suggestions were offered freely in any case. "Why do you want me out of Maintenance?"

"I don't. I want you in Personnel. If you want, I'll even seal the Maintenance Hall while you're gone."

I believed him. Maybe I shouldn't have, but I did. The question was why he wanted me in Personnel, and it looked like the only way I was going to find out why was to agree. "When?"

"As soon as you want."

"Fine. How about tomorrow?"

The sooner I went through whatever the Tribunes had in mind the better.

Kranos's expression didn't change, but I got the distinct impression that he was relieved.

The next morning I was sitting on Gilmesh's padded stool, looking at Personnel tracers. None of it made any sense. I had to start asking questions. At first, even the answers didn't make sense. Finally, I commandeered Verdis, set her stool across the work table from me, and got the system explained from scratch.

Verdis had entered training a year or two before I did, and like many of the key support people, wasn't much of a diver, but as I had begun to discover, without her or Ferrin or Loragerd or a bunch of semi-divers, the Guard organization would have been hard pressed to function.

Verdis was a redhead, with shoulder-length hair verging on a shade of mahogany, black eyes, and a shortish nose. She expressed her feelings with her whole body. Now she was expressing impatience. "We have to input the exact time periods of each assignment after return. That's why divers are taught to check and verify the wrist gauntlet read-outs immediately on return."

"Doesn't that mean that a diver who doesn't report some of his assignments could build up so many bolt-holes he could never be tracked?" I couldn't resist asking.

"It also means," she replied a bit coldly, or so it seemed

to me, "that if an emergency occurred, it might be difficult to rescue them."

I thought of an objection to that, but shelved it.

The system was simple. Had to be, concerned as it was with the records of around one thousand active divers and two thousand support people. In addition, Personnel maintained the records of another five thousand inactive divers—those lost in diving or who had left the Guard. All of the records were stored in both the small Personnel computer and in the main Archives Data Banks, and were updated daily.

Five people ran Personnel. Gilmesh, Verdis, Lorren, and two trainees. The previous day's diving read-outs were dictated into the computers by one of the trainees, with the other trainee recording any changes in permanent assignments.

All in all, about four hundred time-divers were out on continued assignment at any one time. Another two hundred were involved in short or routine dives. Why so many extended dives? The law of real elapsed time comes into play. If I dived to Atlantea for ten units of holo-taking, I could not return to Query and break-out at any time except ten units after my departure. I couldn't gain time by back-timing or fore-timing and then returning to my point of departure.

Like a lot of time laws, no one knew why it worked that way. It just did. My own theory was that because the Laws of Time require a biological synchronization between objective time on Query and objective time experienced by the body, the law of elapsed time follows.

Because deep time-diving is exhausting and because of the operation of the law of elapsed time, Guards on remote assignments or extended ones are better off staying on location.

Time flows differently in various parts of the universe. Our body clocks are set by where we are born and run in tune with our home system, by and large, give or take a few time rushes.

Personally, I thought that a few divers never made it back to Query because their biological clocks got desynched and they couldn't break-out. Once or twice I'd noticed that a break-out on return seemed more difficult than usual. I attributed that difficulty to getting out of phase with the in-system time flows.

I hadn't realized how small Personnel was—even smaller than Maintenance in practical terms. While I had Narcissus, Brendan, and Elene working full time, a lot of the simple dings and dents were fixed by second- and third-year trainees. Heimdall's assistants in Assignments handled the console maintenance. Medical, Linguistics, and Archives did the repairs on their own specialized gear. Maintenance concentrated on non-specific high tech support machinery and diving related equipment, including weapons.

Maintenance had four full time personnel, Personnel had five, Assignments twenty, Medical close to two hundred. Where were all the people? The Guard headquarters staff only totaled perhaps four hundred support types, and many, like me, were really divers.

Where were the other twenty-six hundred Guards?

I asked. Verdis gave me an exasperated look. "What does that have to do with personnel tracer forms? Honestly, Loki, you can be so scatterbrained."

"Sorry, but the question just popped into my head."

"It should have popped into your head a few years ago in training. Look . . ."

As she talked, Gilmesh's old trainee sermons began to come back, and the picture made more sense. Made so much more sense I thought Verdis should be the one giving the trainee lectures.

What it boiled down to was the support functions of the Guard far outweighed the "police" functions. Query had about ten million people, roughly two thousand towns, five thousand villages, and one city. All told, Quest wasn't really a city, not with a scattered population of twenty-five thousand. The largest of the towns, Elysia, contained eighty-five hundred; the average village perhaps five hundred. So Quest had to be called a city, but only relatively.

That was part of the point. Queryans enjoyed the fruits of stolen technology. Even stolen technology has to be distributed, and roughly two thousand Guards were assigned to one-person local Guard offices to provide duplication services.

Each office had a duplicator and an independent power source. Local citizens could come in at any time and pick up a standard household item. Sounded like a big job, but explaining it was more complicated than the practice. A man might need a cooker, for example, or a synthesizer, once every five or ten years, if that. So he went to his local Guard representative, who had in his or her office mint copies of standard household equipment, plus a duplicator. Some of the bigger offices had several duplicators.

The range of such appliances was narrow. Large and small cookers and synthesizers, washers, driers, hygiene appliances; a variety of hand tools, saws, hammers, wrenches; communits; wordwriters; small handtractors; hunting weapons. There were a few other items, and that was about it.

The catch was—it was free. Any adult Queryan could request those items as needed. If someone wanted a bunch of items all the time, of course, the Domestic Affairs Force was likely to investigate, but that was another question.

Guards also often dived into cultures in search of their own personal luxury items or tools. Officially, it was frowned upon, but the hierarchy didn't seem to mind if a Guard was fully briefed and could get what he or she wanted without notice or creating cultural change.

A few hundred other divers maintained some of the remaining functions such as the weather satellites and the ecological monitoring service. "You can see that leaves the Guard spread thin," Verdis was saying.

Thin wasn't the word for it. Roughly three thousand Guards supporting the technology and culture of ten million. Didn't seem possible, and I said so.

"Maybe it's not," retorted Verdis, "but the Guard does it. Sometimes I wonder whether the Tribunes and the power-grubbers and the egotists around understand it."

Was that a dig at me?

She was flushed. I'd touched a sore spot.

"You don't think Personnel is given enough credit for managing the situation, then?" I asked, knowing full well that was what she thought.

"Loki, don't patronize me. I'll never be the hotshot diver you are, and I'll never understand why a gauntlet works. But I have to ask if you understand at all how fragile the system really is, how much depends on the Guard?"

"You're right. I don't understand." And I was mad, mad for some reason I couldn't explain, as I attacked back. "All I see is a stream of broken equipment that none of the divers, hotshot or average, understands, that none of them pays any attention to, and it all gets dumped on me to be replaced or repaired. When I get a free moment, Heimdall or Freyda or Kranos invents a mission that is designed to fry or freeze someone and assigns it to me.

"And by the time I get done with that, all the busted equipment is stacked up to the top of my bin, all waiting to be repaired for a group of would-be heroes who don't understand the difference between a screw and a bolt." I paused to catch my breath, but went on before she could interrupt.

"Now maybe I don't remember how important the Guard is. The whole planet amounts to a bunch of parasites supported by a group of glorified thieves, and that's all we are, and to puff up our jumpsuits at our own importance seems sort of funny."

Lorren was peering around the archway, mouth open as if he couldn't believe what he was hearing.

Verdis was ready to explode, mouthing strange noises, and her color had changed from what I'd call flushed to cold livid. She jumped off the stool. "You—you—"

"Hold on a unit. I didn't say the Guard wasn't vital to Query. Sitting here and seeing how it all is held together brings it all home. To call ourselves heroes is another question. We're scavengers and worse. We pull down or change whole planetary systems and destroy peoples who might threaten our monopoly of time. We pride ourselves on slaving to pamper ten million Queryans who are handed the necessities of life on a silver platter."

Verdis had the oddest look on her face, both hands resting on the back of the stool. "How can you wear the Black? You don't even believe in the Guard. I think all you believe in is Loki, first, last, and always."

"I wish I did, Verdis. I wish I did. I don't have the answers, but neither do the Tribunes." I managed a smile. "The present structure isn't going to last forever. Have you ever noticed how we rattle around in this Tower? Either the early Guards believed in huge structures and no people or there are fewer and fewer of us every century. I'm guessing, but I'll bet it's the latter." I shrugged. Let her carry the discussion, I decided.

Verdis shook her head slightly, and her mahogany hair slipped forward over her left shoulder. She was half-leaning on the stool again. I didn't think she was quite as angry as she'd been.

"What comes next?"

"I don't know. Assignments to fewer planets, more off-planet assignments per Guard, abandoning regular surveillance in out-space or out-time sectors. Maybe changes wouldn't show in the records. Have we systematically reduced the number of high-tech cultures within our ranges in order to keep control? I don't know, but I'd like to."

"You're paranoid, Loki. You suspect everyone of the worst."

I smiled, hard as it was. "Probably, but it doesn't have much to do with Personnel. So let's skip it for now."

Verdis nodded slowly.

"Now. Have you considered a direct link of the Personnel computer to the Archives Data Banks?"

They hadn't. It wasn't surprising. I'd already gathered that little new programming had been done. I guessed that the designers, whoever they had been, had kept the system simple to ensure its continuity. I mentioned that to Verdis.

"But why?" was her reaction.

"Because simple organizations and structures last longer. A complicated computerized system with all Guard functions embodied could be handled with a fraction of the present administrative personnel."

I wouldn't have been even moderately amazed if the Tribunes had been quietly blocking too much mechanization of the Headquarters' functions, but with the records of the Tribunes' deliberations routinely sealed, who would ever know? No one, but no one, ever entered their private offices and chambers, only the public Tribunes' Halls.

If that were the case, why was Kranos asking me to look for improvements in Personnel? Did he mean simplifications? In close to two million years hadn't the simplest possible procedures already been worked out? I tried a different tack. "What's the purpose of Personnel, Verdis?"

I'd caught her off guard. "What do you mean?" She paused for a moment, licked her lips. The tip of her tongue, so pale against her tanned face and dark lips, made her seem a bit more vulnerable, but the moment passed before she was even aware it had existed. "To keep track of the Guard. To provide the information to Assignments so Heimdall can pick the best divers for the tasks at hand . . ." She stopped.

"That's all, isn't it? Just to keep tabs on who's doing what, and to provide information to the Tribunes for promotions and discipline and to Heimdall for Assignments."

Looked at critically, Personnel had two functions—to keep track of Assignment time/locales in order to allow Guards to be tracked for rescue or follow-up Assignments, and to provide the information necessary for personnel choices made by the Counselors and Tribunes. I dismissed the importance of the locator input immediately. I couldn't remember the last time cross-indexing had been necessary to rescue a diver. That meant the only necessary function was to provide information about Guards and their experiences. "Verdis, who makes the assignment reports and evaluations?"

"Heimdall," she replied with a questioning note. "He's always assigned the missions."

"No, that's not exactly what I meant. You said Personnel has records of the duties and performance of each Guard. Is that right?"

"Yes."

"All right. Who rates each Guard's performance?"

"His supervisor."

That brought up another unpleasant question. "I've been supervisor, at least in name, of Maintenance for some years, and I've never filed a report on anyone, nor have I been asked to do so. Would you find out if any information or performance ratings have been entered on Brendan or Narcissus?"

She frowned, but got off the stool and went over to the corner console. She could have used the one in front of me, but she didn't. After a unit she turned back toward me.

"There are ratings in the system. They're made in your name. Are you sure you didn't do them?"

I walked over to the console and looked at the screen display.

"Narcissus . . . assignment . . . Maintenance, supervisor (provisional), Loki . . . shows some basic mech aptitude, good working habits overshadowed by preoccupation with own reflection in polished metal . . ."

"Brendan . . . Maintenance . . . displays basic mech understanding . . . good on repairs, but overawed by apparent complexities . . ."

"Elene . . . trainee . . . Maintenance . . . moderate mech ability . . . hides it well . . ."

Damn! The evaluations sounded like something I would have scripted.

Verdis stood there with a smirk on her face. "Only you would phrase them like that."

She was right. Only problem was that I hadn't. I hadn't known that evaluations were required.

I left the black-topped screen with its evaluations displayed in the flowing silver script.

"Well?" asked Verdis. Her tone was demanding.

"Maybe I did," I muttered.

Verdis didn't seem convinced of my sincerity.

"Verdis," I asked, "if I had made a report, how would I have done it?"

"Oh, that's simple enough. You'd just come down here and key it into one of the consoles. Some of the bigger departments send us a data-bloc."

"Would I need an access code or anything?"

"No. Just your own personal code. The system won't accept more than what your position allows."

That brought a number of questions to mind, some of which I didn't want to ask. I told Verdis to clear the screen and wiped my suddenly damp forehead when she turned back to the console.

Was I losing my mind, forgetting what I was doing?

Verdis came back over to the worktable.

"I suppose the Tribunes have a separate input?"

"There's one terminal in their official spaces, I've been told."

"Do they have special codes as Tribunes? Or just their own personal codes?"

"I really don't know."

Or wouldn't say, I thought. The deeper I got into Personnel, the more confusing it got.

Heimdall or someone else had made my reports. Someone who had been careful enough not to even let me know about this aspect of the Personnel system. Someone who knew me well enough to use my own words and personal code. Someone who kept in close enough touch to make those evaluations current. But who? Why?

The alternative was to admit I was crazy. If I wasn't crazy, then why had I been exposed to Personnel where I would surely find out what was being hidden from me? Gilmesh might have kept me in the dark, but what reason would he have? Kranos pushed me into Personnel, but it wasn't his idea, and was the idea to get me into Personnel or to get Gilmesh into Domestic Affairs to find out what Frey was up to? Wheels were turning. Wheels within wheels, and my formerly clear picture of Guard operations was definitely being muddied.

I got an idea. "Verdis, I need to take a walk. Be back in a while."

I was halfway out the office before she answered. "All right, hotshot."

I was ready to incinerate her on the spot. She realized it before I turned back.

"I'm sorry, Loki."

She'd even ducked.

"No, you're not sorry. You're scared, scared that in my wild and uncontrolled anger I might turn you into a heap of black ashes on the spot." I tried to keep the tone light, but couldn't.

"Could you? You're not wearing gauntlets, you know."

That made me even angrier, somehow. "I'm not, am I? You'll have to keep guessing, keeping in mind that a wrong guess could prove rather warm." I funneled a light touch of static electricity out through my fingertips and let it crackle there.

I'd been working on electrodirection without gauntlets, and it worked. How, I didn't know. That was why I trusted the microcircuitry more than my own apparent talent.

I didn't feel like arguing about what I could and couldn't do, so I tossed the miniature lightning at the far wall and let it splatter.

As I left Verdis reconsidering her words, I wondered which part of the puzzle she belonged to. With her reactions, the pursed lips, the sarcasm, she didn't seem to be part of the Assignments crew controlled by Heimdall.

None of the divers with primarily administrative duties had too much respect for the pure divers—like Frey, for example, who did little or no work in Locator despite the fact he was the supervisor. I supposed the fact I was listed

as a provisional supervisor left Verdis with the impression
I was so bad on administrative or maintenance details that
I couldn't be trusted with a complete title. The fact that
I knew nothing about evaluations didn't help much.

When I peeked into Locator, Gilmesh was standing up,
listening to Ferrin explain some facet of a Locator trace.
They both broke off and looked at me politely as I plodded
through the archway.

"Mastered Personnel already?" flicked out Gilmesh. I
could have sworn there was an undercurrent to his voice.

"No. Had a question Verdis didn't seem to know the
answer to and my brain was wearing out under the over-
load of administrative details. I see why you keep up a
full diving schedule."

"What was the question?"

"A technical detail really. No big thing. Just needed an
excuse to walk around long enough to let my brain clear."

I was sounding dumber by the instant, and I could tell
that both Ferrin and Gilmesh were having trouble not
shaking their heads.

Poor Loki, they were thinking, another super-diver who
has difficulty thinking and walking at the same time.

"You sure?" asked Gilmesh.

I nodded.

Once again, I'd opened my mouth without thinking. The
last thing I wanted to do was ask about access codes in
front of either Ferrin or Gilmesh. If Gilmesh was making
other people's reports, I didn't want to let him know I
knew, and if he weren't, I didn't want Ferrin to know—if
he didn't already.

So I turned around and left. Let them think what they
would. Better I got zapped for incoherence and stupidity
than for inspiring or uncovering treason.

Verdis was staring at the wall when I returned, but
broke off her stare and scurried to meet me.

"Loki . . . I'm sorry." She seemed genuinely concerned.

I'd have given a good original hand-cooked meal then
and there to have learned if she'd accessed or otherwise
checked my work as a functioning Maintenance supervisor. But there was no way to do that.

I smiled.

"It's just that there are a lot of things I'd never thought
about, not in the way they all come together." Which was
certainly true enough.

I'd spent some time with Verdis at the quarterly festivals, enough to get Loragerd upset, as I recalled, but Loragerd was uncharacteristically possessive for a Queryan. Verdis had been a complete cipher then. She still was.

"Ready for something to eat?"

"I don't go out for lunch," she answered.

"You don't have a rough-edged Maintenance type fouling up your records all the time either. Let's go." I hoped she wouldn't argue.

I disliked arguing.

She didn't. "Where?"

"Demetros or Hera's. Take your pick."

"Demetros."

"Fine. I want to check the progress of Maintenance. I'll meet you there in twenty to twenty-five units. All right?"

I presumed it was from her slight nod and headed out the arch and down the ramp.

I was feeling paranoid, but becoming paranoid didn't mean that somebody wasn't out to get me. I'd left a few microsnoops lying around the Maintenance Hall, and I wanted to see what had happened in my first day away from my usual stomping grounds.

Narcissus, Elene, and Brendan were plugging away industriously and kept at it. The area was clear, and my spaces looked untouched. The bin was fuller, but that was to be expected.

Tiny as the snoops were, they were the best designs I'd been able to locate in a two-million-year range. Up-time Terran. The post-atomic Terrans left the rest of the low high-tech cultures so far behind in sneakiness it was unbelievable. What was so amusing to me was that they believed that they were totally straightforward.

The time/locale I lifted the bugs from was at the front end of my fore-time range, a dive so far out it may only be a para-time, about sixty centuries forward. Sometimes, when I walked the streets of Washington or Denvra or Landan, I could feel the time change-winds whistling around me.

There was an uncertainty about Terra that puzzled me, a conflict between what was and what might have been that almost invaded the undertime. Maybe it was the attitude of the Terrans, the fact that they held little or nothing sacred. Baldur said that none of their gods was perfect, and yet they required gods all the same.

Once, right after I got my gold-pointed star, Baldur had suggested I track one of the northern hemisphere's Terran cultures, a bunch of barbarians who built sophisticated wooden ships with hand tools.

"Why?" I'd asked.

"So you can understand how much some cultures can do with so little."

I'd understood that before I'd ever left on the tracking dive, but, just like on High Sinopol, I'd gotten too curious, and when I broke out damned near got split by a steel axe.

Those fellows on the longships swung first, worried later, even when someone appeared out of nowhere. I'd blasted the axe, of course, but didn't zap the axe-wielder. He'd wanted to know who I was, even.

So I'd told him.

That was just typical of the Terrans. But it still didn't explain the uncertainty, or the continual change-winds that swirled across Terra, and Baldur hadn't said a word when I told him, not one. He'd rubbed an eyebrow.

Change-winds usually meant the Guard, but according to Locator no one was working Terra. When I came back and pushed Baldur on it, he had brushed the question away. Sometimes, he hadn't wanted to explain or to answer my endless questions, and that had been one of those times. Either that or he hadn't had any explanation for the Terran uncertainty.

The nifty little Terran snoops indicated that no one had been in the Hall but Heimdall. He had been there momentarily with Nicodemus and another trainee to deliver some space armor.

I reset the gadgets with a magnifying waldo system. They're that small. Then I ambled through the Hall, ostensibly inspecting, but replacing them when I thought I wasn't being observed.

That completed, I planet-slid out to Demetros.

Early caveman best described the decor. The Inn comprised a series of interlocking caverns, but each chamber was holed through the cliff-side and provided a gull's-eye view of the north coast breakers.

I arrived before Verdis, despite my stop in Maintenance, and that fueled my suspicions further. Whom or what was she reporting to?

One thing after another was piling up—Heimdall wandering around with deep space armor needing repairs, Kranos fronting for someone and shuffling supervisors, Frey and his secret fiddling with sun-tunnels several seasons, years, whatever, back.

As I remembered that, I wondered if such subterranean maneuverings had always been part of the Guard and whether I'd just been blind to them.

It was early enough that most tables at Demetros were vacant. I picked one on the shadowed side of the third cavern, far enough back from the edge to be discreet.

Verdis came in, and with an emotional swing to her step that indicated she was pleased about something. The way her body indicated her feelings, I had to ask myself if she could possibly be involved in any conspiracy.

"Very discreet, Loki," she observed after she'd toured the entire Inn trying to locate me.

"Didn't some wise type say that discretion was the better part of valor?"

"Probably."

She sat down in that earthy way that said she was all there, giving her hair a sort of settling-down shake as she eased into the low stool.

Wishing I knew what to say to her, with all my new-found concerns about wheels within wheels, I kept my mouth shut and hoped she'd dive in.

I needn't have worried.

"You've never had a contract, Loki, or shared quarters with anyone—the only Guard who hasn't. How come?"

"Snooping in my records, Verdis?"

She had the decency to blush, and it was becoming, perhaps because it showed a shyness I wasn't aware she had. The sudden change of color, the redness, climbed her like a wave, and receded as quickly. If I hadn't been watching, I might have missed it.

"Are you really interested?"

"I don't know. I would like an answer."

"Never hit it off, I guess, not well enough to contract."

"I find that hard to believe. Not even short-term?"

"With my background . . ." and I found myself telling her all about my parents, with their single life-contract, totally in love and totally faithful, so far as I knew, for I didn't know how many centuries. "And with that sort of example, anything short-term seems so—I don't know— why bother with a contract if it's not for a long while?"

"You do make it difficult, don't you? Do your parents believe in a series of absolutes?"

"Probably. They don't believe in the Guard, that's for sure." I went on to spill the story of my disappointments when I'd been accepted after my Test.

"So you have to believe in the Guard and its traditions, don't you?"

That was too stiff even for the best side of my better nature. "Do you always carve up people when they unbend and reveal a bit of themselves?"

"Sorry."

She didn't sound sorry, but more like she'd uncovered a rare and unusual species, someone who believed in the ideals of the Temporal Guard, as if no one did.

All the Inns are self-service. And it was a fine time for a break from the Inquisition. I got up and strolled over to the synthesizer to pick out a grilled Atlantean fishray, whatever that was, and a beaker of firejuice. Verdis selected something from Gorratte and a dark ale from Terra.

Finally, Verdis broke the silence.

"Why do you accept all those impossible missions, especially when you and Heimdall don't get along?"

"Someone has to do them."

That wasn't totally true.

There was another long silence.

"Loki, I think we'd better get back. It's getting late."

That was it. I didn't go out to eat with Verdis for the rest of the time I was in Personnel.

I stayed there for five days, and that was too long. I didn't get any new insights, just more aspects of the same questions, and there wasn't anything I could suggest to improve the place.

Somehow, some way, something I had said had turned Verdis completely off. She was friendly, but behind the pleasantness was a definite reserve.

Gilmesh returned to his empire after the six-day period, and I went back down to Maintenance with a head full of unanswered questions, not knowing where to turn for information, feeling that all my communications with the Archives were being monitored by "them"—whoever "they" happened to be.

I settled back into my space in the Maintenance Hall with a sigh of relief, however temporary it might be.

XV

There were never any alarms, no shrieking sirens, clanging bells. The Temporal Guard proceeded at a measured pace, with few exceptions. With an eternity to work in, the Tribunes could afford the luxury of planned action.

Eternity was a relative term. Practically speaking, most Guard action was restricted to the past. I could manage time-diving not quite two million years back and about six thousand, a mere sixty centuries, forward. Odinthor was reputed to have had a range of two million years back-time and seven thousand fore-time.

I glanced around the Assignments Hall. Besides Frey, Sammis and Nicodemus were sitting in the low stools on the platform around Heimdall's console.

"Let's get on with it," groused Heimdall from the archway.

Frey damped the slow-glass panels, darkening the room. A full-length holo flashed onto the wall screen. Simple real-time star plate. I studied it and couldn't see anything remarkable.

"Sammis was scouting the fringes and came across this," Heimdall said as he climbed back into his high stool.

Sammis was sitting against the back wall, his mouth set, expressionless.

I waited.

"Typical star plate," observed Heimdall. "What's important is what's not there."

He flicked a switch on the controls and another holo appeared beside the first one. They seemed similar, virtually the same shot, but there were differences.

"Midway down, on the right," cut in Frey, trying to be helpful, but sounding officious.

As it penetrated, I gasped.

In the first holo, what Frey had called our attention to was a dark splotch, a nebula, dust cloud, some light-absorbing phenomenon. In the second holo, the splotch was replaced by a brilliant star cluster.

"You're implying that an entire cluster burned out in less than three thousand years. .Is that so strange?" I couldn't see what all the fuss was about.

Heimdall shut off his grin, glancing at Sammis. I noticed that Sammis's normally animated features were blank. I didn't see Wryan around either.

"This next series shows a three-century span condensed into a few units. In getting these shots, Sammis lost Wryan."

Heimdall may have said more, but I missed it.

Wryan and Sammis? The long-contract pair? The legend? Broken by some catastrophe? Didn't seem possible, not after all the time I'd spent with them. Wryan knew too much to be dead.

I looked back at Sammis. Poor bastard, I thought.

"Loki?" Heimdall's raspy voice brought me back to the wall screen.

Heimdall didn't seem to care about Sammis, Wryan, just whatever was about to be displayed.

I nodded sharply, throttling my anger. One day, one day, Heimdall would get his.

The first two holos disappeared, to be replaced by a third. The globular cluster was still there, but dimmer. A pin-point star, or so it seemed, flashed bright-white, followed by another, and another, the chain leaping from sun to sun so quickly it looked like a white flame were racing through the cluster.

As abruptly, the line of exploding suns halted. Deep in the center of the mass of live, dead, and dying stars, a white glow appeared, pulsing.

The entire cluster erupted in brilliance and faded into a black smudge.

"Sammis and Wryan made the fore-time holo first, then went real time into the cluster. Beyond the Guard's current fringe, you know," said Heimdall. "Cautious. Came out in deep space near a G-type star. But within two units of break-out, a warship fried Wryan. Sammis duck-dodged, made a few more shots as backup, and reported in."

Heimdall undamped the slow-glass and pointed to the table across from him. "There's what he got on the ships."

The hard-copy holos were laid out for me.

For all my fiddling around back- and fore-time, I'd never seen anything resembling them. Shark ships, shining black in the space between systems, were caught in the act of destruction, destroying crippled ships of their own fleet, smaller ships of another type, blasting an empty moon. There were others—one frame of a purple planet under a normal yellow sun; a frame of a linked series of orbit fortresses, deserted, pitted and holed; a frame of a planet with a molten surface circled by an ancient and cratered moon. Destruction, fire—that was the theme.

For a long time I sat at the table. No one said anything, not even Heimdall. I knew it was going to be messy, and long. I got up and walked out of Assignments as the silence drew itself out.

As I walked down the ramp to Maintenance, for the first time I was face to face with an assignment that was genocide, pure and simple.

The shark people were something else. Destroying an entire cluster, frying any loose suited bodies floating around, turning on their own crippled ships, melting down planetary surfaces. Charming bunch. And I hadn't even made their acquaintance yet.

I was a coward, and ready to admit it. If there was an easy way to get the job done, I'd try it. Dead heroes were just that—dead.

I cornered Brendan as soon as I got back into Maintenance. "I've been drafted as a hero. Going to take twenty, thirty days, if not longer. You've got it."

I left him standing there flat-footed. He'd keep things running. I didn't have any doubts about that.

The next step was to round up the equipment I needed. After lining it all up in the Guard's equipment room, I walked out of the Tower and slid home to the Aerie. The next morning was early enough for a reluctant hero.

As I sat behind the permaglass, watching the sun set, everything seemed sort of empty, meaningless. Was I going to be assigned more and more difficult missions, year after year, until I was either dead or resigned from active diving? What was the purpose of it all?

I sipped the firejuice and watched the night fall. In the end, I decided that the questions were just a way of telling myself I was scared, more of the unknown than the sharks.

For all the fuss and furor of the afternoon before, only Sammis was at the Travel Hall the next morning as I suited up. He didn't say a word. But it was funny how he was always around, and on good terms with everyone.

From the instant of mind-chill with the departure from the Tower, I was tense. Wryan was the first Immortal I'd known closely who had gotten zapped, and the holo shots Sammis had brought back had conveyed all too starkly the sheer destructiveness of the culture I was tracking.

I had planned to back-time to the limit of my range, a good two million years back, and work forward; calculating that it would reduce the risk factor. When a diver reached range limit, it felt like the paths and time branches were all curling back with a searing red-fire edging.

I stopped as soon as I began to sense the curl, checked the time register, and my blood chilled. The read-out registered at a touch over a million, half of what my spinning mind insisted it should.

The rest of the equipment registered normal. I passed it off as a peculiarity of the cluster and began my sliding around undertime looking for a likely shark-people planet.

Dull—that was one word for it. Tiresome was another. Careful was the third. Close to a hundred thousand systems in an unexplored cluster, and I was trying to find the one that would erupt into mayhem a million-plus years fore-time of my search.

I kept track of my progress and got past sixty days without finding anything.

It took work to be a coward. The rest of them all had the feeling they were invulnerable, but being Immortal has nothing to do with that. I was the one being called upon to stick my neck out, and I didn't like what I was finding.

First, there wasn't *any* intelligent life on any of the planets I checked. Second, I was blocked from going deeper in the back-time at half my normal range. I could usually glide to a million and a half, struggle past two million. In the shark cluster, I could barely get past a million years back-time, and that was with full effort.

I had hunches, but I kept them inside. Maybe my whole approach was stupid, but I was scared. The more I looked, the more the pieces didn't add up.

Item: A star cluster presumably destroyed by an intelligent race.

Item: An intelligent race which destroys all other life on sight, and injured members of its own species.

Item: A cluster in which time-diving is difficult.

Item: A cluster which has large numbers of inhabitable planets with no intelligent life—a million years before the destructive species presumably emerges.

The last item bothered me, really bothered me. All inhabitable planets, with exceptions too rare to consider, develop at least semi-intelligent life.

For that reason alone, the surveillance boundaries of the Guard were limited to one sector of the galaxy. A substantial part of a galaxy is too much even for Immortals with the equivalent of instant travel. We forgot how big the universe was. I kept at it, though, and skip-scanned through one thousand-plus systems in ninety days, feeling proud until I realized it amounted to about one percent of the cluster.

I spent another thirty-seven days skip-scanning before something clicked.

It was a plain, seven-planet system, normal G-type sun, hard core inner planets, with two small gas giants further out. The life-detector showed the same low readings I'd been worrying about, but I sensed something different.

Planet number three had an aura, and I slid in, following the feel, the shading of time toward the ancient. The Tower of Immortals on Quest had that feeling, like the pyramids on Terra, and the Sacred Forge of the Goblins on Heaven IV.

Planet three had that tinge, faintly.

After tracing my strange feel to its strongest point, I set my own holopak for instant exposure and made a flash-through. I repaired to my staging planet to study what the holo showed.

The one frame I'd taken was stark enough, and ugly enough. The years of erosion, wind, rain, fires, and time itself had only blunted the edges of the black fortress. The structure was a good kilo on a side, if not more, and nearly as high.

Black it was, so deep a black that there was light in the space between stars by comparison, black enough to swallow light. And old. That black monstrosity dripped years. The Tower of Immortals was built yesterday compared to the black fort.

I sat down on a grassy knoll of my rest planet and studied the frame again. Other details now stood out, like the laser which was sweeping toward the holo center, or the absolute smoothness of the plain.

I shivered. Big, strong Temporal Guards who could leap centuries with a single dive weren't supposed to shiver. I did.

What sort of mechanism was it that could last millennia and track and attack an object that appeared in real-time for only milliunits?

The first contact, strictly with an artifact, and it was hostile.

I forced myself to keep concentrating on the holo frame. The regularity of the distant hills behind the fortress, virtually all the same level, was another disturbing note. Sharks, shark people, staging base, sterile planets, weapons—they all ran through my mind. The sharks had been there longer than Sammis or Heimdall figured.

With a deep breath, I slipped through the mind-chill of the time-tension and headed back to the planet of the black fortress. I stayed in the undertime beneath the structure, grasping for a link, a direction. In a funny way, all created objects in the universe have time links, shadow paths, branches linking them with their creators.

The black fort, staging base, whatever it was, had a thready link further back-time. I couldn't follow it because I was near the end of my own back-time range, but I grabbed a damned good feel for the direction, and I slid along the directional I'd picked up, keyed and ready for anything.

I could pick up the deadliness of the second contact from well beyond the system's geographical confines, a dark feel stronger than the Tower of Immortals.

I decided to call the shark planet Lyste, for reasons unclear even to me. Except that the Sertians have a god of destruction with the same name.

I set the holopak and made a flash-through of the system's fourth planet, the one that reeked of age and shark, and slid back to my bubble tent to survey the holo frame. The single frame displayed a perfectly cultivated row crop of some sort, not a single straggle of grass or weed showing. The second flash-through was aimed through what I figured from the undertime was a small city.

The holopak came up with two frames. The machinery was simple enough—late fossil fuel, but sophisticated, in an organic way. All I could pick out was a cart, apparently fueled by a stack of "logs" that seemed to be individual plants. Couldn't pick out any other overt machines. The "people" looked healthy, strong, and purposeful.

Semi-humanoid was as good a description as any— smooth black skin, hairless, scaleless, short and stocky pair of legs, upright carriage, two arms ending in a hand. That was all in the first holo frame.

The second holo frame had a detailed head-on picture of a "shark." I'd lingered a fraction of a unit to get that second frame, and that could have been a mistake.

The pedestrian marching down the street had seen me, recognized a threat, and turned in the space of less than a half unit. The reason the head-on shot was so clear was that he/she/it had been caught in the act of firing a hand-held dart gun. The dart was caught by the holo emerging from the end of the gun, and I had no difficulty in mistaking its barbed and hostile intent. As I sat on the grassy knoll, I shuddered. What was I getting into?

It was no fluke—they all had microunit reflexes.

Fine. I'd found the home planet, maybe. Now what?

I took another nap after I found myself shaking. Was sleep a way to escape? I didn't care, and when I woke maybe fifty units later, I munched my way through dried ration sticks, before considering my options.

I couldn't very well eliminate their progenitors. I was at the back-time limit of my range and, short of busting the planet, there wasn't any alternative.

Finally it jumped out of the pictures and pasted me between the eyes. Lyste was an old, old planet, probably gutted of easily mined minerals, fossilized hydrocarbons gone, and populated by a very direct and aggressive species.

I studied the holos more closely. In the next to the last one, I located what could be the object I was searching for. I climbed to my feet, tightened my equipment belt, reloaded the holopak, and slid back to Lyste for a closer shot of what appeared to be a black formation.

At the edge of break-out, I hesitated. Seemed stupid, but I had the feeling that something was waiting.

I got the holo frame, shot a second, and as I did, sensed an enormous surge of energy directed toward me. I tried to push it away and dive undertime at the same instant. I threw up my arm as I penetrated undertime—not quickly enough. When my forearm shattered, I thought I screamed, but I couldn't hear anything in the undertime.

I didn't remember the dive back fore-time to Quest, just breaking-out in the Travel Hall and watching the glow-stones come up to my face.

Next thing I knew, I was propped up in the Infirmary with a regenerator covering one side and a mass of tubes hooked into me.

"Loki?" asked a voice.

Focusing was difficult, even though it was the second time I'd ended up like that, and it was a while before I decided the voice belonged to someone I knew.

"Loragerd?" I croaked. My throat felt like I'd been swallowing sand.

I couldn't hear the response, if there was one, couldn't see the formless faces, and fell, twisting through the nightmare country into a dark pit filled with shiny black shark people who swirled and gobbled and chomped, mostly on me, but on each other when they got tired of tasting me.

Later, and I had no idea how much later, I woke up to find a young Guard sitting across the room.

"Good morning, or is it good afternoon?" I asked.

He seemed surprised. "Morning, sir," he stammered.

"Loki," I corrected him.

"Yes, sir."

"So what's happened?" I asked, as if nothing in the world had gone wrong.

Immortals were like that, recovering quickly. I was weak, but I'd recover fully, no doubt about that.

"Tribune Freyda should answer that, sir."

He left, presumably to run down the honored Tribune. Freyda arrived shortly. "All right, super hero, you've left us on blasts and bolts—"

"Did you leave me much choice?" I interrupted.

I was still sore about the situation, but she went on as if I hadn't said a thing.

"From your instruments, we figured you went back a million years, but the energy drain on the equipment shows two million. Locator pinned the spot, but no one can get anywhere close, and Eranas gave strict orders that no break-outs were to be tried until you were in shape to report."

She glared at me. "You realize that no one could have pulled you out if you hadn't staggered back under your own power?"

"Not till now." I grinned, but it felt lopsided.

"What's more, you couldn't possibly have survived the energy blast that your equipment says you took, but basically all your system damage was limited to your arm and some shock."

I had the feeling Freyda would have gone on and on, but I had to know. "Did the last holo frames come through?"

Freyda handed them over, as if she had been waiting for an explanation from me. I could feel my right arm shaking as I reached out. The left was in a cast, but felt like it was all there. That told me the regeneration had taken.

I spread the three frames across my lap. I was propped part way up and I could see them without straining.

The third shot literally showed raw energy and my forearm exploding in blood under the pressure. But the wave of energy, laser blast, particle beam, stopped cold at the forearm, and that shouldn't happen. Blood and gore could wait. Shots one and two showed what I had been looking for, and afraid of finding. The installation, though more eroded, apparently deserted, matched the ancient fortress on the deserted planet, down to the flat plain in front of the towering black walls. The evidence, while not absolutely positive, was enough for me. The same culture built both.

The sharks on Lyste were avoiding the black fortress on their own planet, which indicated that the automatic defenses might not be terribly discriminating about who or what it zapped.

Freyda sat through my studies in silence, finally clearing her throat. "Unless you have objections, I would recommend an immediate sterilization of that planet."

"Whose murder or suicide?" I asked as brightly as possible with my sandy throat.

She looked at me, with the cold look that demanded an answer because she was Tribune. And who the Hell was I, anyway?

"Who can dive that far back? And if they don't, how are they going to get into real time without getting potted? I've found traces on more than one planet; so how do we know they're confined to just one point?"

Freyda digested my objections. "See what you mean. We'll wait until you're on your feet. Hycretis says ten days or so. Twenty until you're up to full speed."

"Twenty-five," I countered. I wasn't going back into that cluster until I was fully healed. Those people were *mean*.

In the days that followed, Heimdall, Freyda, and Odinthor kept traipsing into the Infirmary. I was a novelty. Very few seriously wounded divers got back. Guards avoided injury or were totalled.

They all agreed. A back-time sterilization was necessary, and an effective one at that. The question was how. Heimdall opted for genetic poisoning. Freyda wanted to nova the sun.

Odinthor wanted to send the whole Temporal Guard back with thunderbolts. "Do the Guard some good! Shake up these softies! Give 'em real field experience, that's what I say!" the old warrior insisted.

He conveniently forgot that he and I were the only ones with the time-diving range to get there or that he'd had to be led.

I didn't say much, preferring to listen, surprising for me. I wondered how many planets were inhabited by sharks, especially considering the two identical ancient forts.

Neither Loragerd nor Verdis came to see me, which surprised me in one way, but not in another, although I couldn't say why.

Hycretis booted me out of the Infirmary within six or seven days and told me to take it easy.

Brendan had done well in my absence, and outside of one or two ticklish jobs he'd left for me, Maintenance was current. Baldur hadn't been indispensable and, it appeared, neither was I. That must have pleased Heimdall no end.

Practically, however, the time came when I couldn't put off the resumption of my shark assignment.

"Fit as a thunderstorm, fire and flash, ready to go . . ." was Hycretis's assessment.

Another trainee had been stationed at the Travel Hall to wait for me and was obviously instructed not to let me get away. He came tearing up as I stowed some of my equipment into my chest.

"Sir, the Tribunes request your presence."

"Now?"

I gathered all the holo frames and marched up to the public chamber of the Tribunes. Evidently, the trainee had scurried up before me. Freyda, Kranos, and Eranas were waiting.

"We would be most interested in your report, Loki," Eranas began.

I understood just how interested when Heimdall and Sammis arrived. I presented everything I had, not taking sides for or against destroying the sharks. I didn't have to, because if I didn't agree the Guard didn't have any way to proceed.

"I say destruction," Heimdall summed up his position. Sammis didn't offer an opinion.

"Loki," asked Freyda from the low table where the three Tribunes sat, "have you any observations?"

"Think they were once like us," I offered, "perhaps even related to or descended from the mythical forerunners. Now they rely on machines, but perhaps because time diving is so difficult."

I went on, avoiding the real question, pointing out that time-travel had led to a totally self-centered and ruthless race, one that destroyed others on sight, and one with little respect for their own wounded or disabled.

"May be," noted Kranos, "but that is not the question. Question is what you think we ought to do about it."

I consoled myself with the thought that I had given the sharks more chances than Heimdall or Freyda would have. But in the end, my verdict was the same.

"Destruction."

From there the discussion went into technical possibilities, none of which was workable.

I cut the debate and worthless solutions short. "Adaptation of the sun-tunnel."

Heimdall, the lover of destruction, got the idea right off. "Some sort of multiple linkage?"

I nodded, and everyone patted each other on the back and kept their distance from me.

I walked out while they talked, heading down the ramps to Maintenance. My idea was simple enough. Most destruction is just a matter of applying power in the right spots. The star cluster was tightly packed, with the density approaching, if not exceeding, that of galactic center.

I intended to plant linked sun-tunnels across cluster center, particularly in suns that seemed unstable, and by funneling energy flows, attempt to nova cluster center stars. From there, the process would feed on itself.

The whole process took Narcissus, Brendan, Elene, and me almost two seasons. And while the four of us worked, Heimdall and Freyda worried.

Near the end of that period, I went back to the cluster and collected real-time star shots to feed into the data banks. The Archives came up with a pattern for successive linkages that was supposed to guarantee destruction.

I had made a few adjustments to the pattern. I intended to touch off the stars of both Lyste and Lead Nine directly, which I thought would cut the risks considerably.

When the time came, I was sure I wanted to go through with it. The sharks deserved it, I thought, as much as anyone did, and the idea that such a predatory culture might survive to escape their cluster and infest our galaxy proper wasn't attractive. Neither was the thought that I was going to torch a cluster a million-plus years ahead of its normal destruction—if that destruction had been indeed normal.

All told, I had to set up seventeen linkages, meaning thirty-four dives within a hundred and fifty unit period. Actually, two links and four dives, those for Lyste and Lead Nine, could be done outside the time parameters.

The last night before I left on my mission of fire, I sat in front of the permaglass in the Aerie and stared at the winter ice on Seneschal and the shadows between the peaks.

Morning came, and I dived deep to Azure. Once there, I took a nap before girding myself for the thirty-four dives that were to follow.

I did it. It was that simple. Thirty-four dives in time, dropping thirty-four time-protected packages into thirty-four suns. Then I strapped myself into deep-space armor, picked up a suitable holopak, and fore-timed a thousand years to see if my efforts had resulted in the required destruction.

They had.

A few white dwarves peered out from the swirling nebula composed of the remnants of the once-glittering cluster.

I ran back and picked up frames showing the pulse of destruction, the stellar winds pushing out ahead of the front of fire. What the recordings didn't show was the howling winds of time-change that echoed through the undertime and the anguish as planetary sentiences were snuffed out. While some of the sharks could have escaped in their time and space cruisers, I *knew* none had, just as I *knew* I could bend energy away from me.

When I hit the Travel Hall, one person was waiting. Heimdall. "Congratulations, Loki! Magnificent job!"

I knew the moaning change-winds had preceded me.

I nodded curtly, but said nothing. Right ... magnificent job. I had destroyed a hundred thousand systems a million years ahead of schedule and snuffed out who knew how many intelligent beings because I had no other way of dealing with the sharks. Magnificent, right?

I had to bite my tongue until the blood ran to keep from blasting Heimdall on the spot.

No one else was there to welcome back the god of destruction, the lord of fire. They knew me, knew me all too well, as I was coming to know myself.

I strolled through the corridors of the Tower, still fully equipped, wrist-gauntlets and all, taking it all in. Where I walked, Guards shrank, eased away as if I wore the very flames I had kindled, and perhaps I did.

Massive as it was, the Tower seemed small and tawdry in those moments, insignificant against the night skies I had left units before.

As I headed for the South Portal, even the visitors turned away. Since there was nothing to be accomplished by returning to Maintenance immediately—who would talk to me?—I spent the next ten-day at the Aerie and on the empty places of the high Bardwalls, watching the eagles, the clean lines of the knife-ice peaks, and the winding shadows of the clefts below.

XVI

The seasons passed. I kept to myself in Maintenance when I wasn't stalking thunderstorms in the passes of the Bardwalls or bending lasers into light sculptures around the Aerie.

Once in a great while, Loragerd and I got together, but the spontaneity we enjoyed as younger Guards had remained in the past, and we drifted apart on the gentle waves of the present. Heimdall assigned me missions, and Brendan, Narcissus, and Elene did most of the day-to-day work, while I dug into more theory from the Archives, and some history on the side.

If some idiot decided that core-tapping was all right and miscalculated, and pieces of real estate went flying all over creation, messing up orbits and incidentally ripping up any time-diver who was caught unaware, that was one thing. It may have been a tragedy, a disaster, but the planetary culture did it to themselves.

If the Guard saw a situation like that developing, the Tribunes tried to head it off. But the Guard could fail. That happened when Eranas was tracking the Nepturian Civil War.

The Centaurs said nay to the Queen of Semos. She got her back up and responded with the entire Fire Cavalry. A group of Centaurs dropped a hell-blaster down the core-tap rather than give in. I thought it was a pretty drastic response, but who was I to say, particularly after destroying an entire cluster to wipe out a few time-traveling sharks?

Gurlenis was another question.

Giron had fetched me up to Assignments for Heimdall. Heimdall never came down for me himself, which was just as well for both of us.

"Sammis thought you might like an easy assignment, for once," Heimdall announced.

I wondered what the catch was. I seldom saw any assignment that was easy.

"No catch, none whatsoever," persisted the Counselor with the long black hair. "Data is on the end console."

"Assignment?" I asked before heading over to the console.

"Holo update before a cultural change."

That translated into getting holo frames of a time/locale just before the Guard meddled. I asked myself what the Gurlenians had done to merit the Tribunes' decision to alter their culture, but didn't vocalize the question. Instead, I walked over to the stool in front of the indicated console and keyed in.

Gurlenis was an Arm planet, orange sun, low hills bronzed with grass, symmetrical cities built with a green glass that held the light for hours past sunset.

Heavy transport was conducted with a sub-surface induction rail network or by solar wind-powered craft that skimmed the shallow seas. The people who built it all were bipeds, covered with a fine bronze-green fur that streamed behind them in the continuing and gentle winds. The reason for the mission, and the cultural alteration, was one publication by a scholar.

The Archives evaluated the contents and predicted that the probability of the Gurlenians developing time-diving abilities approached unity, given further development. In short, the Gurlenians would challenge the Guard's monopoly of Time.

A Guard named Zealor had been assigned the alteration. All I had to do was record the last moments of the existing culture, the moment of passage, and the results.

I made sure I had the nav coordinates down before I left Assignments. Heimdall didn't look up.

Zealor had already left to start his work. So I headed straight for Special Stores to pick up the recording equipment.

Halcyon was the Assistant Supervisor at Special Stores, and I thought Athene relied more on her than any of the earlier assistants. Like Loragerd, she'd been a trainee with me, but she'd never developed much beyond rote time-diving. She could dive anywhere she'd been taken, but couldn't strike out on her own, even with detailed instructions.

I guessed Baldur had gotten to all of us in that group of trainees, though I would have been hard-pressed to explain it. Halcyon had taken special care to upgrade the equipment they supplied, and that was important, not so much to me, but to the others. Anyway, Athene was lucky to have Halcyon handling the day-to-day stuff for her.

Halcyon was waiting. "Nicodemus said you'd be the one, and that you'd be in a hurry." She handed me a set of what looked like goggles. "Try these."

The gadgets had a thin cable which led to a belt pack. I struggled to make the goggles fit, but with them in place, I couldn't see.

"Silly," she murmured. "You wear them above your eyes."

Halcyon had long, fine blond hair, green eyes so dark they verged on black, and clear tanned skin. Her voice tended to break slightly when she was amused, and she giggled, even after all those years.

"Why?" I asked as I wrestled the goggles onto my forehead.

"Simplest spacing to get an eyewitness view, I'd bet."

I strapped on the belt-pack, smiled at Halcyon, and headed for the Travel Hall and Gurlenis to make the last record there might be of an entire world culture before Zealor reoriented it.

I strapped on gauntlets and equipment, not that I thought I'd need them, and dived to Gurlenis. I didn't follow time-paths, but skipped branches and intuited my way to the destination. Break-out on Gurlenis found me hovering over bronzed hills bathed with light from the orange sun. Late afternoon, I guessed, and the read-outs confirmed that local season was late summer.

Picking a low hill above the nearest city, I made sure the holo "goggles" were in place and glided down to the hilltop, panning the valley as I did, and ending with a view of the green glass city at the other end of the grassy lands that filled the valley.

From outside the tall evergreens that edged the city, I could see that the place was a town, rather than a city, and laid out in a definite plan.

The first close-up I caught with the holo showed three youngsters playing on a triangular grass court of some sort. On each corner of the playing surface stood a tall pole with a balanced crossbar, and three metallic rings of varying sizes. Apparently the idea was to throw an oblong object through one of the rings in some predetermined order. I watched.

The smallest youngster, and I guessed he or she or it was young because of the size differential and an air, a feeling, that I associated with growing up, moved toward one of the corner standards in a hop-step-step-step-hop pattern. The other two tried to block the advance by anticipating where the patterned zigzig would lead and setting themselves in a blocking stature. No physical contact took place, and it was more like a dance.

A couple of body lengths out from the corner standard, the one carrying the oblong made a double hop and tossed it toward the standard. I thought the crossbar swung before the toss was completed. The vanes fluttered, but there was no wind.

The oblong tumbled through the middle ring and was recovered by the tallest, who began moving toward the corner away from me in another stylized pattern, more of a hop-hop-step-hop-step.

The game, if that was what it was, seemed strangely non-competitive, but I wondered about that crossbar moving without wind. I kept the holo going until the tape contained a representative section of the game.

I slipped undertime toward the more heavily structured center of the town. All the Gurlenians I saw and caught on the holo radiated an impression of purposefulness, but the town was quiet, much quieter than I expected, even considering the attitude of gentleness I had begun to associate with the bronze-furred Gurlenians.

The town stood on a low plateau and from the gradual slope down and into the cropped and cultivated spaces below, it was obvious that the Gurlenians planned their environment carefully. The town center was linked and intertwined with grassy paths. The more heavily traveled routes were paved with a soft green pebbled pavement that gave underfoot.

Even as I watched and recorded, kept cranking away, I noticed that the number of Gurlenians out and about was shrinking. Strange, I thought, because with their wide

eyes and lithe bearing, I would have suspected them to be
a nocturnal race.

I flicked in and out of the undertime, flashing through
the corners of the city, trying to pinpoint activity. As I
slid from place to place, something began to nag at me.

As I stopped to holo a scene of the Gurlenians filing
into a central structure, I recognized the feeling, or rather
the absence of a feeling. Fear—the Gurlenians didn't
demonstrate any signs of it.

In most cultures, somewhere, someplace, there is an
aura of fear. But not on Gurlenis. Most races are at least
subliminally aware of being studied or looked at—and
react. Either the Gurlenians weren't aware or it didn't
bother them.

I shelved that analysis as I began to take stock of the
number of graceful souls gliding into the building I was
observing. My first thought was a government or town
meeting. My second was a religious observance, but I
wasn't sure either fit.

Curiosity cornered the lion. I ducked undertime and
slid into the temple. Fuzzy as it was in the undertime, I
didn't want to break-out inside a wall or a heat-source.
Those hurt. I located an open space away from the assem-
bling group and broke-out, ready to dive, if necessary.

Face-to-face with me was a Gurlenian, an older one
with white-streaked and flowing body hair and a mantle
of age wrapped around his very being. The old Gurlenian
looked at me, not at all surprised, bowed slightly, made
some cryptic gesture in the air with a single sweeping
motion, and waited. After that gesture, I received a feeling
of peacefulness, and that was the only way I could describe it.

I nodded back, and slid undertime into a darker corner
of the meeting hall where I kept the holo tape running.

Row after row of Gurlenians were seated on wide and
flat cushions, all equally spaced. The entire hall was dead
silent, yet filled with the same feeling of peace I had
received from the old Gurlenian.

Why was I the one with the holopak? Sammis thought
I'd like an easy assignment, and Heimdall had given it to
me. Why?

I didn't have time for more reflection, because the
cold wind of time-change blew, creeping up my spine like
the paralysis that followed the sting of a rocksucker.

My head began to spin, and like a picture seen through falling water in the twilight, the temple melted around me. The building evaporated in mist, and the Gurlenians, dressed only in golden, fine-flowing hair, who had been seated within body lengths of me instants before became smoke, and then less than the memory of smoke. They were gone.

The chill of the time-change-winds howled past me and barked their way down the trail to the future, leaving me standing on a rocky outcrop. I gazed out over sparsely vegetated hills and wild grasses. A few scraggly bushes had replaced the cultured and trimmed conifers. With the abrupt drop in temperature, I shivered. Some animal howled in the distance.

No more Gurlenians. They were gone, for good, and I could feel it. That wasn't quite it. Rather, they and their sense of peace had never been, and Gurlenis was now a wild planet.

I touched the stud on the belt-pack to stop the holos, lifted the goggles, and dropped them into a belt pouch.

I slid back to the Travel Hall. It was deserted. I stowed my equipment in my own chest, including the holo equipment. I figured to return it the next morning, except for the holo frames themselves.

The Tower itself was empty, except for the trainee watch staff, and I could hear my steps echoing in the silence as I climbed the ramps.

The Assignments Hall was dark except for the small light at the main console, being used by the figure in Heimdall's stool.

"Sammis, what are you—"

"Told Heimdall I'd wait for you to return. How did it go?"

"Fine, if you care for that sort of thing."

I didn't care much what I said. Sammis wasn't likely to repeat it.

He smiled, I'd have to have said sadly, if I were forced to analyze it, and answered, "Sometimes, that's the way it goes."

I dropped the holo tapes, said good night, and left, wondering about Sammis—why was he there? But I was too depressed to think it over.

I slid straight out to the Aerie, where it was still light. There I sat on the edge of my cliff, warmed by my glow-

stone floor, sipped firejuice, and saw the eagles circle, far
from the Tower, far from Quest.

The impact of the eradication of the Gurlenians wasn't
going to vanish, no matter how long I stared out the permaglass of the Aerie at the eagles of night, no matter
how many busted pieces of equipment I fixed, no matter
how much I learned about mechanical theory in an effort
to avoid reality.

And how many others had we wiped clean from the
slate of time? I knew about those that had impinged on
me—Gurlenis, the shark cluster, and a few others like
Ydris. But how many had there been?

The Archives Data Banks had the information, I was
certain. But the results of my last attempt to access historical data, when the entire Guard knew I was trying to
find Baldur, indicated that the Tribunes or Heimdall, or
someone, was following my every move. After all those
years? Probably, I decided. Patience had to be a virtue
learned by the powers that were of an Immortal society.

Real analytical thinking had always been difficult for
me, unlike Ferrin or Sammis. If I were Ferrin and wanted
to find out information without broadcasting my interest,
how would I go about it? That was the question. How did
the Tribunes know who accessed data? The last time,
they'd simply asked for copies of the requests off my personal code.

As I'd discovered in my brief time in Personnel, not
many cross checks were used. As a matter of fact, Heimdall or someone else was still making Maintenance personnel ratings in my name. The simplistic answer was not
to use my own code, but another Guard's. The next question was whose and how to get it.

I tilted my stool back, letting my thoughts ferment, and
watched the eagles soar in the twilight. They flew with
such little effort, a flap here or there, riding the thermals.

Ask someone? Nope, had to be sneaky. How about
microsnoops?

Where? Suppose I planted one focused on each console
screen used by a Guard whose code I wanted? If I obtained ten codes, or at the fewest, the codes of four or
five individuals whose request for trend data might not
seem strange, I thought I could obscure what I was after.
I had enough microsnoops in my collection. All I had to
do was check them out, plant them, and collect the data.

The next afternoon, I rounded up ten snoops from the bottom of my Maintenance locker, fitted them with wider angle lenses, and gave them a thorough check-out. Since I couldn't back- or fore-time on Query itself, I had two choices—either to mosey into each of the areas over the coming days and place them in broad daylight, so to speak, or use the undertime to flash-through during periods when the spaces were empty.

The first alternative, while superficially attractive—no cloak and dagger sliding around in the dark of night—had a few drawbacks. How was I going to plant a snoop on or near someone's personal screen while he happened to be using it?

Number two didn't appear much better. If anyone were naturally suspicious, and a lot of people seemed to be, wouldn't they have hidden remote sensing devices to monitor their work areas?

When I'd joined the Guard, I never would have considered that the honorable Counselors and Tribunes might have snoops in their Halls. After my experiences, I wondered how they could avoid it, since they had to know that the strongest divers could slide undertime within the Tower itself.

I sat there on my high-backed stool, ignoring the day's pile of repairs, including the ones I hadn't made, trying to come up with another alternative. I didn't. If anything at all went wrong while I attempted to place snoops during working hours, I'd be caught red-handed, and then some. On the other hand, with a flash-through night slide, I might end up as a picture on a holo screen, but I wouldn't be caught immediately—just the next morning. That wasn't any help. What if I didn't look like me? That was an idea worth pursuing. In the dimmer light after hours, a general suggestion of someone else might well do the trick.

That conclusion led to another series of questions, but in the end only one pseudo-identity made much sense, because he was roughly my size and his mannerisms were easily counterfeited, especially his outfit.

Nightmail is easily procured, even black nightmail, from the deep storerooms. At one time many of the Guards used it. While I couldn't obtain a light saber, I could duplicate its silhouette and exterior appearance easily enough with materials right at my own workbench. A dark cloak, a big black chain, black high boots, a

swagger, and who would know I wasn't Frey? That left
one screen key to get, Frey's own in Locator/Domestic
Affairs. I would have to use the direct approach there.

The night I picked, the planting went as smoothly as a
dive to Haskill. Flick undertime, then out, place the snoop,
ruffle through papers and drawers, clink the nightmail,
and disappear.

I got snoops into Heimdall's console, and those of
Nicodemus, Ferrin, Tyron, Verdis, and even the one
Odinthor used infrequently, planting the last one in Spe-
cial Stores for good measure.

I slid away from the Tower wearing the outfit and
tucked it away in an abandoned section of an orbit weather
station. I didn't want to fore- or back-time because it would
show on the locator console if I was being monitored.
My Queryan locale couldn't have been followed unit by
unit. In a few days, I'd need the outfit to recover all my
snoops.

I could have tried the type that broadcast, but with
all the energy flows around the Tower, I wasn't sure how
they'd work, and I'd need special equipment to receive the
data and store it. The self-contained types were less likely
to be detected, easier to operate, and had no overt ties
to me. The ones I placed looked like rivets, raised plates,
that sort of technical stuff.

The morning after I planted the snoops, my ears were
wide open, alert to any change of pulse around the Tower,
but nothing seemed to have changed. No one was wandering around asking, "Did you hear that someone was
snooping around the Tower last night?"

In some ways, it was an anticlimax. I buried myself
back in the little world of Maintenance, worried about
divers' gear, fixed warm-suits, power packs, stunners,
gauntlets, and the usual dents and dings. A good ten-day
passed before I could plant a snoop on Frey's console,
and I practically had to pick an argument with him to
do it.

On that morning, I loitered my way past his archway,
and if anyone had asked me why I was on that side of the
Square and not in Maintenance, I'd have been hard-
pressed for an answer that made sense. I always had
trouble coming up with out-and-out lies.

Frey was in, toying with his black light saber, obviously
bored. His boredom could be laid at Tyron's arch. Tyron

couldn't dive worth a damn and made up for it by doing both his work and Frey's.

Frey was the chief constable of Query by virtue of being the Supervisor of the Guard's Domestic Affairs/Locator branch, a cut and dried operation, no discretion, few and absolute rules under the Code.

I ambled in. "Got an instant?"

"Infinity and some." He flipped back as he sheathed the light saber and sat up straight on the work stool.

"Why don't we put trainees into Domestic Affairs earlier in training? They'd understand how the system works better and the real role of the Guard would be clearer."

He leaned forward and put both elbows on the table, crowding me back and away from the console screen.

"Loki, the system's worked fine for umpteen hundred centuries. Let's not meddle with a good thing."

"We lose a lot of trainees who opt out for the Admin obligation."

"No guts," snorted Frey.

I circled around to the other side of his table and leaned against a heavy wooden case with no apparent function. "At ten trainees a year or less, we're not exactly burning up this corner of the galaxy. Or replacing the giants of the past, like Odinthor or Ragnorak."

Frey laughed. "With Guards like you, Loki, who needs the past? But then, with more Guards like you, the future wouldn't have a past."

He chuckled so thoroughly I felt like shoving his light saber straight down his throat. I didn't, instead slipping between him and his console screen as he reared back and continued howling over his joke.

It wasn't that funny, but I smiled and slapped the snoop in place. "Anyway, think about it, would you?" I asked.

"I'll talk it over with Heimdall."

He'd talk anything over with Heimdall if it involved thought or words of more than two syllables.

The days drifted by quietly, like the eye of a storm on Faffnir. I knew a storm was swirling around, unseen, but the more certain I was that something had to happen, the less actually did.

After a couple of ten-days, I recovered my deep-spaced costume imitation of Frey and picked up all my snoops. With all the dodging I had done to get the one into Frey's console, I decided against deviousness and slid in and retrieved it along with the others.

The next day, as I inspected the snoops, I discovered that not one had been damaged, tampered with, or even touched. Such miraculous good fortune alerted my cautionary feelings. Either I was way off base, or I was missing something. What could I have missed?

With no answer apparent, I began to run out the tape scans from the snoops, a chore tedious enough to keep me occupied for a while since I had to study each frame under the magnifiers of the miniwaldo setup.

In the end, though, I identified the personal codes for Frey, Heimdall, Nicodemus, Verdis, Gilmesh, Athene, Loragerd, Ferrin, and a few trainees like Giron and Devindra. The biggest problem wasn't getting the codes, but figuring out which code belonged to whom.

I'd placed all the snoops with decent focus on the console screens, but they were so small the peripheral scan was non-existent. I knew the code, but not necessarily the user.

Some were simple enough. HML-10 had to be Heimdall, and FRY-27 had to be Frey. But who was XXF-13? And which Tribune was TRB-02?

Another problem occurred to me. Did the Archives, or Quellin, the Archivist, track the personal code to the user's console? If so, I'd be a sitting duck using my own console. How could that be concealed? If I went up to the Archives, the cubicles were secluded enough for privacy. That would have to do.

Midday had come and gone before I finished figuring out the codes. I was hungry. Brendan caught me as I left for refreshment.

"What do you need?"

"I'm having trouble with that generator, and the schematics all check. Won't run. Could you take a look?"

"Be right there."

Brendan trotted back to his table while I stuffed the personal code list into my thigh pocket.

He was waiting, brightly expecting me to put it all to rights. All he needed was more confidence. "You can see. I've replaced all the fused circuits, rerouted the control lines, matched all of it. But it doesn't work."

From the first glance nothing seemed wrong, and I could understand his frustration. If all the circuits were correct, and I assumed for the moment that they were, what could be wrong?

I began to laugh. "Brendan, think about it. What's the first thing you do when you repair a generator?"

"Remove the . . ." He blushed.

"I didn't mean to laugh, but you went to all this work. And you thought you'd made some terrible and intricate mistake. You didn't. Just reconnect the intake field and see what happens."

The generator worked. Brendan was torn between embarrassment and pride. Embarrassment because he'd forgotten a simple step, pride because he'd basically built the generator back up from scratch, and he'd done it right.

"Good job," I told him. "Take a break, and for Time's sake, don't make a big deal about the intake field. We've all done it one time or another."

I thought about it after he'd left and I was alone in my spaces. You could go through the most complicated procedures and forget the simplest and most vital things. Why did I want to find critical turning points of other cultures? Did the answer lie in high-tech cultures that might impinge on Query? The more I knew, the less I knew.

That night, in my high and secure Aerie, as I watched the canyons and the eagles, everything seemed so small. I could walk the air between the peaks, catch thunderbolts from the skies without gauntlets, and stalk the storms. But I felt cramped.

After the years as the nominal Maintenance supervisor, some unknown Guard or Counselor was making my Personnel evaluations for me with my own personal code, and I hadn't said a thing, just let it be. Heimdall was slowly building his personally loyal army of thugs, and even after they'd tried to kill me on Hell, I hadn't done a damned thing. But Patrice had told me I knew all I needed to know. I didn't think I did know enough. Why?

For some reason, I'd been shuttled to Personnel. Why didn't anyone want me to know about the Personnel evaluation system?

I'd been sent to record a holo of a gentle world culture's death. Without a background briefing. Why? Had Sammis had anything to do with it? On the other hand, I'd spent almost an objective year in tracking and destroying the shark cluster, and been given a totally free hand.

Was the Guard winding down, like the mechanical toy I thought it was? Or was I seeing what I wanted to see?

I went to sleep without coming up with any answers. Morning's arrival didn't provide them either. Deciding that more information was needed, and hating myself for thinking so, I ate and slid to the Tower.

Baseline data came first, and I spent a portion of the morning, after I'd organized Brendan, Elene, and Narcissus, in one of the shielded booths in Archives.

I plugged in Nicodemus's code for the question. "Has the number of trainees per century increased or decreased in the past million years?"

"Increased." The figures followed. Summed up, the Archives data indicated that prior to one million A.T. the average number of trainees per century completing the first two years of training was three hundred. The current moving average was five hundred and thirty.

I tried another tack. "Has the time-diving ability of the average trainee decreased over the same period?"

"Negative . . . subjective analysis of performance reports indicates substantial improvement."

I'd spent thirty-plus years figuring the Guard was on the way out, and the damned data banks were saying the opposite. I had assumed that the business of tearing down high-tech cultures was to eliminate challenges to an ever-weakening Query. If the Guard and Query were getting stronger, why the increased destruction? Or was data being falsified or entered incorrectly?

I asked another question. "What is the current number of active Temporal Guards?"

The Guard including trainees numbered 2,156, with approximately one million current and former living Guards.

"One million!" I couldn't believe that.

"Where are they?"

998,000 resided on Query. Statistical probabilities indicated that 2,000 existed elsewhere.

A bunch of things were beginning to nag at me. I was convinced the numbers didn't match. An average of four hundred new Guards a century over a million years totalled four million. Guards were supposedly Immortal. And what happened to three million Guards and former Guards? I was dumb enough to ask that one.

"Former inquiry included trainees. Fifty percent of all

trainees do not complete. Guard mortality/disappearance averages fifty percent."

There it was, all tied up neat and nice. Trouble was, I didn't believe a single figure. I canceled out, asked for a total erasure, and walked back down to Maintenance.

The Guard was bigger than it used to be? Why did we all rattle around in the Tower? What evidence did I have? When I had started in the Tower in Maintenance, there had been Baldur and Glammis. Now I was there, with Brendan, Elene, and Narcissus, and we were slated for one of the current trainees, a girl by the name of Dercia.

I slammed my fist on the worktable so hard the slap echoed off the walls. Both Brendan and Narcissus were there before I knew it.

"Are you all right?"

I grinned, hard as it was. "Nothing. Just amazed at my own stupidity."

They exchanged looks. "If there's anything we can do," said Brendan, "just let us know."

They were gone. I vaguely wondered what had passed between the two of them, but it had been good-natured, and I let it pass.

I'd tried to pass on Baldur's understanding and appreciation of the mechanical basis of cultures, but wasn't sure I'd gotten it across to Brendan, Narcissus, Elene, or the trainees I'd lectured. Compared to old silken-tongue Heimdall or smooth Gilmesh, my halting lectures were probably as dry as centuries-old dust.

Sammis had to have some answers. Time to look him up, if I could find him. Strangely, he was in the first place I looked, in the corner of the Assignments Hall. Why he spent so much time there I couldn't understand. He and Heimdall had little enough in common, but Heimdall did seem to listen when Sammis made a suggestion.

"Loratini's, Loki?" he asked before I could open my mouth.

Back we went to Loratini's, the Inn overlooking the Falls. Sammis started by picking out his food, even before we sat down at one of the individual balcony tables. I followed his example.

Finally, I asked my question, the first of many, I hoped. "How big was the Guard when it started?"

"Wasn't around then," he said with a half-smile, and noting my expression, went on, "but say I had been, just for speculation, I'd guess there were about one thousand in the original Guard and about twice that a million years ago. 'Course, in the first Guard, less than two hundred were divers, and even a million years ago, not everyone in the Tower was a diver."

"Do you think divers today have different abilities than the older divers?"

"Hard to say. Take you and me. You can dive a bit farther fore- and back-time than me. Not much, though. Big differences are that you can dive to and from about every different environment ever found, that you can carry a Hell of a load, and that you have some control of energy flows."

"Does it make that much of a difference?"

"Is a warrior who strides the thunderstorms and carries the fires of Hell more dangerous than a mere time-visitor?"

"But why?"

Sammis snorted. "A little knowledge is dangerous, Loki, and about how things work, you've got as little as anybody. Wait until you've got a few centuries under your belt."

"Ummm . . . ah," I began, tongue tied around itself, trying to straighten out the other questions I'd wanted to ask while I had the chance.

"Enjoy your lunch, Loki. In your business, there's time enough to ask the questions later. You may never understand us, anyway."

His eyes twinkled as he spoke. Sammis wouldn't say anything else, and when I was finished, he went wherever he was headed.

The next day wasn't any better, nor the day after. Sammis, Patrice, everyone seemed to think I was dense for not seeing what was obvious, but I saw plenty—from Heimdall's schemes to the toppling of intelligent cultures that were no threat, to Freyda's ambitiousness, to Frey's incompetence. What was I missing?

On the third day after my meal with Sammis, with no more ideas than before, I headed back to Archives.

I was getting too nervous, I knew, but I tucked a stunner into my jumpsuit. Thunderbolts were too permanent. I had decided exactly what I wanted, and that was a printout of twenty cultures within the last million years that could be shifted up to high-tech or cultures which had been high-tech and reduced by the Guard's meddling. To that, I added the criterion of possible development of inter-stellar travel in some form or another.

The Data Banks balked at the additional stipulation, ending up with some garbage that scripted, "no basis for evaluating particular isolated technological phenomena."

That might make it harder for me to go ahead with my half-formed plans to end the monopoly on the stars, but I got the list of time/cultures, plus a smaller list of low-tech planets that offered long-shot possibilities and empty planets suitable for colonization. The three lists should cover all the bases.

Twenty-plus cultures that should be out among the stars, and weren't. Ten that had been pulled out of time or star travel by the Guard. And the precedent I might have set in destroying an entire cluster. As I saw it, the trends were becoming critical.

I just didn't know what it all meant, whether I was being pushed or imagining it all and overreacting. How could I know? Was it all in my mind?

XVII

Thinking about the best way to throw a monkey wrench in the machine led me to study the aftereffects. I didn't want to get caught in the act—or afterwards.

That was why the Guard had such a hold on Query. Domestic Affairs/Locator could track down any Queryan through the locator tags planted in our shoulders at birth. The exact composition of the tags was a secret closely held by the Tribunes.

Not that I intended to let that stop me. I had the necessary equipment, and the lack of interest in things mechanical among most Guards had to work in my favor. Who would consider a mechanical solution, or understand as I worked one out? Except for a few, most of the present Guard was composed of fumble-fingers. The few who weren't were mine, like Brendan, Narcissus, and Elene. Through it all and despite the abysmal level of technical understanding in the Guard, Maintenance was holding up its end, with all of Heimdall's efforts to pour repairs on us.

To deal with the locator system, however, I needed an analysis of a functioning tag. That was the priority, and I got down to it. Setting up the heavy equipment scanner to pick up my own locator tag was the hard part, but I managed it by shorting out the safety access circuit and removing one wall from the inspection chamber. Then I had to design a special shield to screen everything but the square of my shoulder blade where the tag was imbedded.

Why didn't I get the parameters from the Locator section?

The locator consoles are sealed, automatic, and the

parameters are limited to the Tribunes. While Locator can track the signals and follow any Queryan, the composition of the signals is secret.

Why didn't I take a blank tag from the maternity ward and analyze it? I did, and found out that the signal was a twisted helix, so to speak, and combined the basic temporal locator signal with the individual aura and sent it back in a scrambled pattern. The combination was set at random by the master locator computer by remote after the implantation at birth, and once set, remained set forever. That immutability worked in my favor, provided no one found out what I was doing.

Repair facilities, even ones like the Guards', with the sophisticated air and light scrubbers, with superclean technology, microcircuit duplicators, and the rest, have an atmosphere of grubbiness that no amount of cleaning can totally remove. In the Maintenance Hall, it wasn't so apparent at first, but after years I became aware of it, more of a feeling associated with technology than anything.

A light meter would tell me that the Hall was as clean as Assignments, but the floor-to-ceiling slow-glass panels seemed dimmer. The rows and rows of equipment that I had reorganized, some of it under time protection and unused for centuries, added to the impression of raw mechanical power.

I tried to picture a time when the Guard had employed all the equipment, but failed. Some of the bulkier pieces dated to cultures no longer accessible, a few back to the time of the Frost Giant/Twilight War. I caught myself from lapsing into belief in the legend which Wryan and Sammis had said was untrue. According to them, the equipment had been gathered, but never used. According to the myth, that had been the first, last, and only pitched battle fought by the Guard. I found it hard to understand how they could all coast through twenty thousand centuries on the memory of one war, particularly when it hadn't been all that glorious.

I shuddered at the self-deception embodied in that legend and looked back over the Hall. During the rearrangement, I had obtained the access keys to all the equipment. Heimdall, like most Guards, failed to appreciate the power of the past and the strength of technology. I cut off the dreams and self-congratulations, knowing I was only postponing sticking myself under the modified analyzer because it was going to hurt.

With a deep breath, I pushed my not quite totally shielded shoulder under the beam head and jabbed the stud. After I wiped the blood from my chin and slapped some heal-paste on the lip I had bitten through, I checked the analyzer data. There was enough, for which I was glad. I wasn't certain I could have gotten through it another time. I managed to smear some more of the paste on the burned shoulder and to cover the burn with a sterile field dressing in order to slip my jumpsuit back on. I knew the wound was sterile, but the pain marched across my shoulder like a shark army might have. Sitting down on the operator's stool, I put the circuitry back in its normal patterns, although I doubted anyone would have understood the reasons for the change.

I kept thinking of the Guard as an enormous clock, designed for eternity, but ever so slowly wearing down, missing an instant here, counting two units instead of one there, while the clockmaker's children and grandchildren kept oiling and polishing it, afraid to tinker or replace any of the millions of fine pieces within. I knew the Archives said the Guard was on the upswing, but I couldn't believe that data either.

I debated leaving for the Aerie to let my shoulder recover, but decided not to wait and fed the data tapes into the master analyzer. The console screen was blank for what seemed like forever, though it was only several units before a complicated formula appeared. I tucked the tape cubes into my belt and pulled my heavy red cloak over my jumpsuit.

I strode up the ramps to the South Portal, hoping I could leave quietly as usual.

For some reason—Heimdall's displeasure with me, my own introspectiveness, or my reputation for not suffering technological idiots—few of the Guards struck up conversations with me within the Tower itself. I suspected a combination of awe and fear.

I was the only Guard in centuries to fight a Counselor, go to Hell, and return. Heimdall, on the other hand, had demonstrated that he had the power to attempt murder for insubordination and get away with it.

For whatever reason, few casual conversations were struck up with either of us when the other was around.

Many of the younger Guards would talk to me only at the Inns.

Heimdall led both a lonely public and private life, growing tighter-faced and more brooding with each year. The born-again Glammis found him too cold and had turned away, finally leaving the Guard.

In that late afternoon, as I walked through the echoing and nearly empty corridors, glancing at the holos of past glories standing out from the main walls, feeling the warmth and light of the slow-glass panels from a thousand suns, I wanted the silence, trying not to strain or bite my lip at the pain from my shoulder.

"Loki?" called a light voice. Verdis had left Personnel for the day, apparently, and was waiting by the South Portal.

She tossed her mahogany hair back over her shoulder. Usually she expressed her feelings with her entire body, but now her eyes were filled with concern. The rest of her body might as well have not been there, and that bothered me.

"Hera's Inn?" she asked.

I wanted to go somewhere like I wanted a quick dive through a black hole, but Verdis was up to something, and my gut instincts told me that refusal could cause more trouble than I was prepared for at the moment.

I nodded to Verdis, signifying my assent, and slid, not to the Inn, but to the Aerie. There a quarter of the way around Query, the sun was still high, and the light glittered off the ice on Seneschal.

I staggered over to the cellular regenerator I had swiped from the Infirmary storeroom, lost as it had been behind three rows of time-protected supplies that hadn't been touched in centuries.

Underneath the light of the damped slow-glass, I stripped off my jumpsuit, peeled off the pressure dressing, and collapsed under the regenerator. I set the timer for five units, and when the bell sounded I sat up.

I put on another lighter dressing and changed from the black jumpsuit to a red one. Maybe it had been a stupid thing to use an equipment analyzer, but a standard tissue analyzer wouldn't have been equipped with the necessary memory. More important, all the medical analyzers were monitored by the Tribunes.

I washed my face, spent another few units taking care

of bodily necessities, and arrived at Hera's Inn to face Verdis's scowl.

"Bodily necessities," I explained sheepishly.

"Bad manners," she retorted while accepting the explanation.

Inns were peculiar to Guard and Queryan life. In the first place, the doors were time-twisted, which limited entry to better than average planet-sliders or divers. The decor was best described as technological sword and sorcery, with holos and displays from the more spectacular planets visited by the Guard.

Hera had been a fair diver, but had retired into a quieter way of life, if the hustle and bustle of running an Inn could be termed quieter. She was plump, the closest thing to a fat diver or ex-diver I'd ever seen, with brassy blond hair she swore—and could she swear—was natural.

Her Inn was done in wood, real wood and mostly polished cedar from a place called Lebanon on Terra. Must have taken a good-sized forest, just from the expanse of the Inn, and a lot of divers to bring it all back. Either that or a few planks and the biggest synthesizer I'd heard of. With her connections, either alternative was possible. The floors were blue glowstone, also rare, and the illumination was provided by light-torches from Olympus.

Inns wouldn't have been possible without a sharing based on a sense of honor. Hera or any Innkeeper left a list of items she needed on a tablet by the door. Guards brought them back as they saw fit. Haphazard as it was, it worked. The Inns not favored perished or were taken over by more congenial proprietors.

Power was free, basically photovoltaic, and Hera's synthesizers would turn raw organics into a duplication of the master dishes in the files.

Verdis had already claimed a corner booth, which was a misnomer because all booths at Hera's were designed as corner booths. I sat down gingerly to insure I didn't hit my tender shoulder.

Verdis offered a smile that didn't quite make it. She cleared her throat before she began. "Loki, you've spent years now, since you were in Hell, aloof from everyone."

I couldn't say much to that. So I stared at the glass of Atlantean Firesong that Verdis held.

"For all your power and fame, you distrust the very people you work for. They distrust you. You bury yourself and the fire that springs from you in that cavern with your machines. When you do emerge, Odinthor and the Tribunes shake. All the younger Guards worship the glowstones you walk on, and if you deign to favor them with a word, they feel honored."

"And that means?"

"You could run the Guard, Loki, and yet you do whatever Heimdall or Frey or Freyda suggests. I wonder if they didn't go beyond the call of duty to plant the shark cluster on you."

I had thought about being Tribune, but for all the talk of running the Guard, I was fiftyish, looking twenty, and the Tribunes had tens of centuries of experience. The Counselors did too. Heimdall would not step down, nor would Odinthor, and Freyda of the cool voice and fires within certainly would not. I was not up to murder for ambition. At that, I laughed aloud.

"Loki?" asked Verdis, not understanding.

Loki, the man who destroyed a hundred thousand suns and a million years of life; the man who watched Zealor wipe out a gentle people at the behest of the Tribunes; the man who booby-trapped the gauntlet on Heimdall—good old thunderbolt-throwing, storm-stalking, fire-breathing Loki was the Guard who couldn't kill the greatest tyrants in Time because he knew them personally.

I looked at the planks above Verdis's head.

"Loki, can't you hear?" Her eyes were hard.

"Hear? What do you mean?"

As she pointed to the back room, the singing became clear.

> "Who's the Guard that fired the stars and sank the
> sharks?
> Who's the Guard that wired the gloves and gave
> them sparks?
> Who's the Guard that went to Hell and almost died?
> Who's the Guard that told no truths and never lied?
> Loki! Loki! That's who, the Immortal guard for me
> and you.
>
> "Who's the Guard that tamed the techs and stole the
> sun?
> Who's the Guard that faced the Tribs and made
> them run?

Who's the Guard that stood on air without a wing?
Who's the Guard that lives for life, the Guard we
 sing?
Loki! Loki! That's who, the Immortal Guard for me
 and you."

There was more, but I lost it in studying Verdis. I wondered if she'd composed the damned song—awful lyrics
and all—just to put more pressure on me.

I hadn't realized how many young Guards there were
who could sing, and they turned that doggerel into a solid
drinking song.

What was the purpose of it all? Had Verdis arranged the
whole scene, song and all, to suck me into some sort of
conspiracy? If so, how had she managed to persuade all
the younger Guards to participate? But what could she
want with me? Why the idea of my running the Guard? She
knew I wouldn't listen to anyone if I took over. As if I
wanted to. Who the Hell wanted to run a funeral procession? The way things were headed, that's all it would be,
one way or another. "Just what are you asking?"

There was a long silence between us, though the Inn was
filled with noise as the trainees and young Guards in the
adjoining room launched into another round of song.
Thankfully, it was a ditty about a seamier side of Odinthor's past.

"Loki, few of the really good divers know how important
the Guard is to Query. I'm not talking about temporal
meddling. I'm talking about supplies. The duplicators, the
equipment bank, the simplified mechanical basis of Query
make it easy to support, but what happens if anything goes
wrong?"

Verdis should have been a political agitator. Her eyes
flashed as she threw the questions at me, demanding that
I believe what she had to say.

Oh, she was right in a way, but was the situation all that
pressing? "You know I'm not terribly sympathetic to the
Tribunes," I responded, "nor Heimdall, but what could go
wrong? Query is an incredibly fruitful planet, so fruitful no
one knows how we evolved here or if we did. Ten million
people are scattered over two major continents and the
islands and geared to a simple life supported by a few
machines with low power requirements.

"If the Guard went out of existence tomorrow and never

brought another item back, it would be centuries before the system fell apart, if ever, unless the diving ability totally disappeared."

Verdis opened her mouth, then shut it, paused as if to catalogue the arguments filed behind her smooth forehead and dark red hair. "You admit, though, that the present course of the Guard will eventually lead to the downfall of Query?"

I wasn't about to admit to anything. For all I knew, while I doubted it, Verdis could be out to entrap me for Heimdall. I began to wish I'd never agreed to come. The stabbing pain in my shoulder was steadily getting worse, and the dressing I'd crudely slapped over it felt soaked through. I was not certain I was thinking clearly. "No. The present Guard policy might lead to the downfall of the Guard, which is a different question."

The second half of that statement, which I intended to keep to myself, was that the continued course of the Guard would pull down a lot of cultures whether or not the Guard structure went eventually or not.

"Are *you* supporting the Tribunes?"

"As you may know, I am supporting Loki, past, present, and future."

Someone had told me that, and I played the quote back, hoping it hadn't been Verdis. If she had been the one, she didn't comment.

I got up slowly and walked over to the synthesizer, hoping something to eat would clear my head. The Xerxian scampig looked good. I pushed the stud and waited for the machine to deliver. Verdis followed me over and selected something. I didn't see what.

A swig of firejuice and several bites of the scampig improved my stability. Verdis sat back down, finished a mouthful, then started in as if she hadn't left off. "Someone, or a number of someones, have been asking the Archives questions about critical turning points in any number of cultures which rivaled or could rival Query."

"So?" I asked with a sinking feeling in the pit of my stomach.

"We don't know who it is, but the fact that *someone* is asking that sort of question is ominous."

I leaned back into the padding behind me, trying to focus on Verdis, but the pain of contact seared my shoulder like a flame, and I missed some of what she said.

". . . may mean that since Query has so much inertia and so many Queryans outside the Guard are like sheep, that this group wants to set up a man on a white horse—"

"A what?"

"Man on a white horse. Great Black Father to take over in a period of crisis. Whoever it is doesn't want to wait centuries for a real crisis and may be searching for a crisis to create."

"Seems pretty far-fetched to me," I commented.

"Doesn't to the Tribunes."

That hit me like a flash of deep space cold. "Why do you say that?"

"Personnel has been asked to devise and issue priority codes to the Guard for the historical data banks, with a system so that no one, not even a Tribune, can use someone else's code."

I shook my head, not for the reason Verdis thought, of course. Someone was monitoring the Data Banks and my innocently programmed requests. I was glad I already had what I needed.

"We're afraid that one way or another this power game between Guard X and the Tribunes will bring down the whole Guard structure." Verdis had that intent look in her eyes again.

"Isn't that overreacting? I mean, the Guard has survived centuries of power plots."

"We don't think so. Not this time."

"Who's we, and why are you so convinced this time?"

"Dive again?" she asked.

"You keep talking about 'us.' And you keep avoiding my questions. You still haven't answered what you want from me. You haven't said why you think this rumored plotter, who could merely be a student of history, could do what no one else could do, and you haven't identified your mysterious group that's so involved with tracking down this rumored schemer."

As she cocked her head to think up an answer she hoped I'd accept, I had another thought. Was the whole meal a gimmick to see if I'd reveal anything?

"I'd rather not say more, not right now. A number of us are concerned. As for what we want from you, it's simple enough. You keep your word, and we want your word, that you won't meddle in the domestic affairs of the Guard or Query."

I had to laugh, and that surprised Verdis more than anything I could have said. "Verdis, does that mean I should promise your vague conspiracy that I won't try and set myself up as High Tribune? You make me sick. As if I wanted to become emperor of this time-flying gopher hole!" I wanted out of the Inn, then and there. "Or does it mean I should stand idly by as you and your company take over the Guard?"

"Loki, that's not what I meant at all!" Her protest was pretty loud at that. "You plod on in your own world, buried in Maintenance, oblivious to everything. Eranas is making noises about stepping down, and Heimdall is bluntly suggesting he ought to be selected to replace Eranas. Everyone wonders who is staking out past history, and why, and what really happened to Baldur, and in the meantime, Heimdall has gained a few more loyal followers. Frey is given more responsibility he can't handle, and Tyron covers for him. And you don't pay any attention at all."

I wished I'd left earlier. I could tell Verdis I cared, and blow myself out of the water, because what I intended wasn't what she wanted. Or I could say I didn't care and be lumped with the Guard establishment she'd so lovingly described. Like so many times before, I said nothing.

The songfest in the other room had degenerated into assorted conversations. Phrases drifted through the archway as I looked down at the remnants of my scampig and Verdis looked at me.

". . . Guard'll last forever . . . Loki for Tribune . . . never happen . . . not with the bitch goddess . . . fly Kyra . . . sheep, and they'll never care . . . who'll do the dirty work? . . ."

"Put that way," I said finally, because I had to get out of the Inn, "I guess I don't pay attention. But maybe I ought to. Maybe I ought to."

I pulled myself together and walked out into the antechamber. I jumped back to the Aerie. Every morsel of strength I had left was what it took to get undressed and sprawled under the regenerator.

XVIII

One night under the regenerator was enough to start my shoulder well on the way to healing and to remove the pain, though I was more than a little stiff when the morning sun floated into the Aerie.

The burn twinged when I moved quickly, but I was in a hurry in getting cleaned up and dressed. Heimdall was always punctual, and I wanted to be in the Maintenance Hall before he arrived at the Tower.

The Tower was deserted, except for the duty trainees, when I slid in and trotted down the ramps.

The production equipment I had set up in the corner didn't take more than a few units to ready. Shortly after I fed in the parameter formula, little black boxes, each with a locator tag and a power cell within, began popping out the other end of the system into a time-shielded bin.

The shielding might have been an unnecessary precaution, but I had warped the plastic edges into the back-time easily enough, and with all the rumors being circulated I figured it might save me a bit of grief. Who wanted Locator to register a thousand "Lokis" in Maintenance?

After the first units dropped into the bin, I took one and ducked behind one of the older machines for a quick time-dive back to Abelard. I dropped off the little black box there, stuffed it under the roots of some plant, and dived back to Query.

As I broke-out in the Maintenance Hall, I checked around, but saw no one. If my black gadget worked as designed, it should already have been registering my "presence" on Abelard.

Then I began my regular work by assigning the repairs which had been brought down by the duty trainees. Brendan arrived within units and carted off his share. I carried Narcissus's to his space, and Brendan came back and delivered Elene's.

Before he got out of sight, I gestured. "Would you start to work on setting up what Dercia will need? No hurry, but I'm leaving it up to you. Unless you run into something strange."

"Be happy to."

Brendan could be a real pleasure to work with, probably would end up a better Maintenance supervisor than I had ever been.

As I ran through the routine jobs I'd assigned myself, the equipment in the rows behind me continued to produce black boxes.

I needed access to a locator terminal, preferably when no one knew what I was doing. Terminals existed in three places—the Personnel Hall, under the scrutiny of Gilmesh and Ferrin; the Tribunes' spaces which were guarded full-time; and the Locator section, which had a full-time duty staff.

With all the concerns Verdis had mentioned, especially that bit about the Tribunes' interest, I wasn't too interested in a repeat of my imitation of Frey and the nighttime follies. While no Guard or Tribune would ever get me back on Hell, skulking around after hours would create more problems than it would solve.

Paradoxically, my success in Maintenance had denied me the one legitimate access to a locator terminal I used to have. When the Tribunes had made me the nominal supervisor of Maintenance, my name had been lifted from the emergency divers watch list. That particular watch list had been Ferrin's innovation to assure a first-class diver was always on call, but supervisors were exempted. Somehow, I had to get myself into rescue work, at least occasionally.

I turned off the phony tag producer and covered the bin, setting out to corner Ferrin. He was still in charge of the watch list, despite being in Personnel. He was also struggling along by himself at the moment I walked in.

After pleasantries, I hit him. "Look, you script-pusher. First I've gotten tied into support and administration. I never get anything routine or moderately interesting in the

way of diving missions, just killers when Heimdall cooks
up something designed to fry or freeze me."

Ferrin didn't even flinch. "What does that have to do
with Personnel?"

"The only diversion I ever got was occasionally rescuing
someone. Now I can't do that."

"Loki, with your responsibilities—"

"Ferrin, my responsibilities are nil. You and everyone
else know it. At least let me be listed as an occasional fill-
in."

"I don't know."

"Then ask Kranos, or Freyda, or Eranas. Ask someone."

Ferrin said he'd see what he could do, and I went back
to Maintenance and started producing more black boxes.
By the end of the ten-day I had over a thousand stashed
behind a time-protected wall in the Aerie and had disas-
sembled the equipment.

Days passed, and I was about ready to take another
whack at Ferrin when another trainee showed up late one
afternoon with a polite request from Ferrin, asking if I
would stand in for Sammis that evening in Locator.

That bothered me, but I couldn't say why. Sammis rarely
if ever missed a duty, even after Wryan's death at the
hands of the sharks. The stand-by diver, unfortunately,
doesn't have a console, and I couldn't get near one.

Duty was uneventful, as it usually was, and by the time
I left, I was tied in knots. A run across the training fields
before I slid back to the Aerie helped calm me down.

The false locator tags were still stacked up behind the
phony wall, waiting until I could verify if they worked.

As the time dragged out, what Verdis would do was
another question I didn't really want to think about. So I
didn't.

I didn't escape that easily.

Several days after my stand-by in Locator/Domestic
Affairs, she showed up in Maintenance after Brendan,
Narcissus, and Elene had left. I was closing up.

"You've been thinking and thinking, and avoiding me.
Why?"

"I've been trying to make up for all the thinking I
missed growing up."

"So it's a laughing matter now?"

"No, but I'm not one for snap decisions that might overturn two million years of traditions. Besides, you haven't exactly let me know what you have in mind."

And she, or they, hadn't—nothing more than asking me to stay out of the way. I didn't believe it for a moment. There was more involved, much more, but I was a lousy snoop. Not one sign of what was going on had surfaced anywhere.

"Loki, caution doesn't fit your image," Verdis suggested gently.

That was another way of saying that my courage had deserted me.

"Have I ever shown I was a coward? Where was your courageous group when I was shark-hunting at the end of time?"

She didn't bother with an answer, turned away, and left.

One of the things that nagged at me was that lack of certainty. I had flash-slid through most of the Tower, avoiding the Tribunes' spaces, time and time again, sometimes late at night, and had never found a trace of anything. Neither had the microsnoops I had redeployed around the Tower.

I couldn't say I was surprised. Verdis and her group, if there was a group, could meet anywhere on Query and be only a slide away from the Tower.

Days passed, but Verdis didn't come back, didn't press me, and that bothered me as much as being pressed. I waited for another stand-by duty in Locator, and finally got it—again, because Sammis had requested time off.

The night was an uneventful one, starting out just like the first duty I'd taken from Sammis, until close to midnight.

A figure suddenly appeared on the public slide stage, a woman who started screaming.

Helton, one of the two console operators, got up and headed across the stage toward her. I slipped into his seat and accessed my own locator code. The console began scripting all the past locales. I wasn't interested in verifying the whole mess, but looked to see if my present location on Query and the phony tag I'd dropped on Abelard both registered. They both did. I blanked the console and hurried over to Helton and the distressed woman.

She was pouring out her tale of woe—one of those screwy, and very rare cases. The woman's first contract-mate, and father of her ten-year-old daughter, had slid into her quarters, grabbed the daughter and threatened to kill himself and the child unless she renewed the lapsed contract. She refused, and the father disappeared with the daughter.

"He's crazy. I couldn't ever renew—not with him. He'll kill her—I know he will—he's not all there," she gasped out between sobs.

"What's her name, your daughter's name? Her personal code?" Helton pursued.

I stood there looking sympathetic and helpful. Wasn't much I could do until they'd come up with some sort of location.

"Regine," the mother stammered. "RGE-66-MC." The MC was standard meaning Minor Child and would be replaced with a color code once she matured.

Giron was on the other console and plugged the codes into the Locator system. "Undertime, Lestral, near the top of Sequin Falls!" he announced.

"Looks like he means it," commented Helton sotto voce.

I leaned over Giron's shoulder to scan the coordinates and dived right from the spot. I knew where I was headed. I'd been there before. Most Queryans have been. The Falls are quite a scenic attraction; they drop straight down for kilos into the Lestral Trench.

The water of the Sequin Falls is black, coal black and cold, if not freezing. The chunks of ice that dot the waters bob like stars on that black expanse and fall like meteors to the Trench below. They glow with a light of their own because of the ice worms and glittering microorganisms that are so common on Lestral.

Any delay on my part was out of the question, regardless of whether I needed a warm-suit or not. The father wasn't a diver and had gone for real-time Lestral, and he was ready to break-out at any instant.

With the coordinates in mind, I was undertime, and instead of following the time-lines, I was crossing, vaulting, trying to minimize even the minute crossover delay from the undertime to the "now."

For all that, lucky was the word. The father had thrown Regine into the water near the brink, and the conditions helped me locate her even from the undertime, because bodies glow like the ice against the black water.

She was heading over the edge by the time I located her, but from there it was straightforward. Sounded matter-of-fact, but to break-out in water cascading vertically, thrashing me around, while trying to grasp a small child in the space of less than a unit and dive safely undertime as we both dropped toward the biggest pile of sharp rocks on the planet was not an average dive, or a typical rescue.

I lost Regine in the cold water, and it took three quick undertime slides before I got a grip on her, and just as I touched her arm, a chunk of something stabbed me in the shoulder. I kept hold of her nightrobe, but I had to have a firm grip on flesh to carry her undertime.

I grabbed with my other hand. My feet somersaulted over my head, but my left hand closed over her wrist, and I dived, wrenching her out of time.

We got back to the Tower Infirmary before Helton or the mother had left the Domestic Affairs section, I figured.

Regine was bright blue, but breathing. The medical tech stripped her out of the nightrobe and wrapped her into a thermal quilt. She had a small gash above one eye, and a line of blood was dribbling down her cheek. Her damp hair was plastered back above her ears in a blond wave. She might have come to my waist if she stretched.

The tech turned on me, insisting on a quick check. "Hell of a bruise across your shoulders."

"Ice, I think."

"Let's take a better look."

She pushed me into the nearest diagnostic booth. Nothing showed but the bruise, and the tech left me to my own devices.

I wrapped myself in a quilt. I was still a light blue shade from the chill, but I wanted to see Regine. She had seemed so somber.

As I caught sight of her from the archway, I decided against joking. She was sitting on the edge of a bed, her color close to normal. The Guard tech was wheeling away the diagnostic equipment.

My entry rated a glare from the tech, but she didn't try to throw me out.

"I'm Loki. How do you feel?"

"Wet. Where's my mother?"

"She'll be here in a moment."

Regine's lips had a faint bluish tinge, but the thermal quilt had restored most of her body heat.

Standing there made me feel awkward, but I shifted from foot to foot for several units—waiting. Regine ignored me.

Finally, I drew up the quilt around me and went back through the archway to recover my jumpsuit. I finished wringing it out and slipped it on. The fabric dried quickly; so it was only damp.

I was leaving the Infirmary to check back in with Locator when the mother arrived with Freyda and Helton.

"Loki?" asked Freyda, the Tribune.

"None other," I said with a forced smile. "Now if you will excuse me, I need to report back to Locator."

She nodded. The mother said nothing.

As I walked toward the exit portal to cross the Square, I could hear Freyda's voice.

". . . the only one on Quest who could have saved your daughter . . ."

Probably I didn't have to, but I finished the remaining few units of the stand-by duty before sliding back to the Aerie for a solid night's sleep.

Sleep didn't come immediately, because I'd had one of those after-the-fact realizations, something I should have thought about earlier. I had gone to elaborate lengths to manufacture over a thousand phony locator tags, to get legitimate access to a locator console, gone over Sequin Falls to save a child who wouldn't talk to me. And I'd approached the whole question backwards, as usual.

Why not get rid of the tag?

How was I going to remove a tag embedded in my shoulder blade? Have a surgeon cut it out, of course.

With that thought, I fell asleep, sound enough not to be troubled with dreams or fears.

Once I got into Maintenance the next morning, I turned my concentration to finding a surgeon who could do the job under a local anaesthetic. I wanted to be able to watch.

Archives had some data along those lines, but I did want to show some care. I traipsed up to the study cubes and used Giron's code to ask about medical progress levels.

In the meantime, Terra, late early atomic, at the fringe of my fore-time range, seemed the best place.

Before I dived fore-time to Terra, I absconded with some medical equipment from the back rooms of the In-firmary. I also rigged a miniature laser which would cut the tiny chunk of metal clear of my shoulder. Rather in-volved technically, but as foolproof as I could make it. I added to that a simple locator which would point directly to the tag. Redundant, but I wanted to avoid any possible mistakes.

With the gadgets in hand, and after wheedling a language refresher out of the duty trainee late in the afternoon, when Loragerd and the regular Linguistics staff had left, I departed for Terra.

I could feel the moan of the change-winds around me, not the violent shudders and twists that ripped through the undertime when the Guard meddled, but the little tugs, the fleeting flashes that weren't quite there—except they were.

Terra equaled change. I wondered about the source of that flowing change, and while I couldn't have said I knew the reason, I would have bet that some of the "missing" Guards could have been found scattered around Terra, stirring up the gentler time changes by their very presence.

Most Guards wouldn't have picked up the little indicators, the blurring around the edges of each entry or exit from undertime, but the signs were there.

I knew what I wanted, preferably a small health-care facility isolated from any other with no one else around.

Despite the penchant of the Terrans to label every building and structure, and to number those they didn't label, I had difficulty locating a medical facility, taking roughly a hundred slides before I found what seemed to fit the bill.

The sign read, roughly translated, "Dr. Odd-Affection, clan (family?) practice."

The front room of the structure was filled with hydrocarbon replicas of plants, and empty. I had hoped so, because I had chosen the late time of local day for that reason.

Dr. Odd-Affection looked older than I was and was surprised to see me in his office. That may have been because the front door was locked. "Did you have an appointment, Mr. . . . ?"

"Loki," I supplied, before answering his question. "You will not have any patients for the next few units, and I need your skill. I am willing to pay handsomely for it. No, there is nothing illegal about it, and I would do it myself, but the location involved means that I cannot."

The good doctor looked more puzzled than intrigued.

"I can pay you with any of these." I flashed a diamond, a flat gold bar, and a small eternasteel scalpel.

His eyes widened most at the scalpel, perhaps because

of the glow, and he struggled with his tongue. "What . . . how?"

"Simple. There is a small metal plate on the flat of my shoulder blade. I need it removed. This device would remove it virtually painlessly, but I cannot expose the bone."

"In my office? It's not sterile enough."

I handed him the spray container and the scalpel-laser. "That will sterilize and numb the area instantly." I thrust the miniature locator at him. "This will point directly to the metal square."

The doctor seemed a bit glassy-eyed as I tapped the end of the surgical laser.

"That will cut the plate clear. Then sew me up and bandage it loosely. You will never see me again."

I put two of the diamonds on his desk, plus the gold bar. "You can also have the scalpel and the local anaesthesia."

I could see the conflict by the workings of his face, but I guessed that he finally decided that anyone who appeared out of thin air and wanted to be cut open was crazy enough to listen to.

"Why?" he demanded.

"Because I was tagged with this tracer plate while I was unable to resist, and I'd like a bit of privacy."

"But I can't do it here," he protested.

"Where?"

He told me, and it didn't make much sense. Something about a hospital and his license and the government. I supposed I could have gone elsewhere, but he seemed so conscientious that I decided to solve the problem for him.

A squarish machine with a keyboard rested on a table next to the wall. I gestured at it and fused it into junk.

"But you want me to cut you open while you're awake." He paused. "And I'm not sure you're not some sort of criminal."

Took me a while, but in the end, the combination of rhetoric and thunderbolts convinced him.

He was a bit unnerved when I insisted on an arrangement of mirrors to watch him, but I figured he couldn't be too bad because he didn't seem to be motivated primarily by greed.

Even with the anaesthesia, it hurt. Dr. Odd-Affection wanted to immobilize it, but I requested stitches and a temporary sling. I was diving straight back to the Aerie and the tissue regenerator, locator tag in my pocket.

I placed all the diamonds, gold, and medical equipment on his surgical table, hoping the good doctor could put it to use.

I staggered along the time-paths and broke-out in the Aerie. My legs were shaking, and recovery was top priority.

There wasn't much I could do for the next few days except recover. Recover and think. I was not about to put my nose back in the Tower until I was totally well. Who knew what was brewing?

I feel asleep.

The next day, as I lay there on my stomach under the regenerator, staring at the clouds that obscured the canyons below, I tried to take stock.

Item: I had 1,000 plus phony locator tags stored behind the wall not two body lengths away.

Item: I wasn't going to need them.

Item: Verdis and company were unhappy with the present Guard structure.

Item: Contrary to what I had thought, the numbers of Guards were increasing, and so was the amount of high-tech destruction.

Item: Eranas was the last of the old Tribunes and was talking about stepping down.

Item: One "group" was trying to keep me in the dark and hiding facts from me.

Item: Another was maneuvering me enough to expose me to those same facts.

Item: Sammis had told me to wait.

Item: Verdis wasn't going to.

Item: Heimdall would be the next Tribune.

Conclusion: I was going to have to do something.

I wasn't sure what, but Sammis to the contrary, the present state of Guard stability seemed to be coming to an end.

The questions were more numerous than the possible answers.

Verdis and her allies were pressing. Heimdall was building a private army, and Freyda had some plan of her own.

One conclusion was simple. If the Guard survived in its present form, Heimdall would be calling the shots.

I didn't want that, whatever else happened, but back-time tampering with Query itself wasn't possible. At the same time, tampering with other cultures to create rival high-tech cultures wouldn't work if I tried it on a piecemeal basis. All Heimdall and Freyda had to do was send back unquestioning young divers or their disciples to undo what I had done and we'd end up with a time war that would make the Frost Giant/Twilight War seem insignificant by comparison.

On the other hand, if I grabbed the rocksucker by the tentacles and eliminated Heimdall, the structure would sooner or later create another, or Freyda might follow through—not with the same intentions, but to make the Galaxy safe for Query.

Plus, I didn't have the resources for an extended war. Hell, I didn't know exactly what I wanted to do, or if I wanted to do it. So far, all I had managed was to set it up to be able to disappear without a trace, like Baldur, if he had, and I had doubts about that.

Even with the tissue regenerator, two days passed before I was totally healed. I wasn't setting foot in the Tower until I was ready for anything.

Three mornings after the ministrations of Dr. Odd-Affection, I planet-slid to the Tower and popped out of the undertime right in front of the South Portal.

I walked into the Tower wearing the mesh armor I'd gotten so long before from Sinopol under my jumpsuit, gauntlets, and a stunner strapped under my forearm, ready to drop undertime at the slightest provocation.

I trotted down the ramps to the Maintenance Hall, nodding to the few trainees I passed and prepared for anything.

The only surprise was the empty bin by my space and the note Brendan had left.

Not sure we did it as quickly, but decided you didn't need to come back to it all.

                                          B—

I had to smile. Brendan would do fine. Narcissus would do an adequate job, too, if anything happened to Brendan. If. If I carried through my mad scheme, I needed a few props. Both could be fabricated elsewhere, but I'd needed information from the Archives.

So I went back to Archives and a shielded booth and keyed in my request, asking for a hard copy. "Galactic Sectoral star chart, normal space, centered on Query."

The second query was shorter for the Data Banks to script out. "Field theory . . . enabling equations for FTL drive . . . with universal math key addendum."

I stopped back in Maintenance to leave a note on Brendan's console, telling him I was under the weather, but that I hoped to be back as soon as possible.

Following that, I marched up the ramps and across the Tower to the Travel Hall, where I picked up my personal equipment chest and slid it and myself back to the Aerie.

My next step was to confuse the issue.

I began pulling the phony locator tags out from their hiding places, time-diving straight from the Aerie, and placing them on planets scattered both fore- and back-time, but making sure I avoided the systems listed on my print-out of possible high-tech cultures.

By objective nightfall at the Aerie, I'd dumped several hundred "Lokis" throughout the Guard's corner of creation. I unloaded the rest into the Lestral Trench.

I tumbled into my furs for some sleep, but sleep didn't come.

In a short-lived culture, decisions had to be made in a hurry. You never would have the time, might never live to see the consequences of a wrong action. On Query it was different. At the back of my mind, the thought kept recurring: you can always wait and see what happens.

The thoughts merged with dreams, but I was up with the dawn and time-diving clear to Sertis before the sun broke with the horizon.

I'd been there dozens of times before on routine procurements, but this was different.

Three or four establishments turned me down cold.

"Copy that on metal? No."

"That's out of my line. Try . . ."

Despite the fact that I was no longer tied into the Locator system, I had the feeling that Heimdall's blood-seekers wouldn't have too much trouble tracing me through Sertis, not with the signs I was leaving. Every metal-working shop and jeweler on the planet would have heard about the red-haired fellow with the accent who wanted a screwball map copied on one side of a metal plate with funny squiggles on the other.

All I needed was one basic plate. I could duplicate from that.

After more than a dozen false starts, I found a woman who dealt in exotic metals and engraving and who promised the copy within a ten-day local. I left a substantial deposit and the promise of a more exorbitant payment.

Needless to say, I merely time-dived ahead and picked it up. I studied the result carefully, but as far as I could see, she'd copied both the map and the equations exactly. No doubt that a trained astrogator or astronomer could pick out the starred system without difficulty. The starred system was Query. But however I could have described it, Query's system was clearly emphasized.

I was back in the Tower by nearly normal working time, even so, and had managed to duplicate more than thirty of the plates on a thin eternasteel by midday. Packing them into a light carrying case was no problem.

The thought of leaving caught me. Ferrin or Heimdall would have planned it down to the last unit and realized it sooner. But why skip before I had to? That amounted to leaving a signpost announcing my hostile intentions.

I regeared mentally, tucked the star-plates and case into the big bottom drawer under my work bench, and dragged a repair job into position. A simple one, which gave me a chance to think.

What a circular path I had been treading! First, I had decided to confuse the locator system by duplicating my personal locator tag signal and strewing it all over the Galaxy. Then I had reversed tracks and had Dr. Odd-Affection remove the tag. In the meantime, I was wearing the removed tag on a chain with a miniature power cell while I was on Query to insure that the Tribunes did not know I had removed it.

I had gotten the information necessary to use outside cultural pressure on Query, but I hadn't done anything because I figured it would start a time-war if Heimdall weren't removed. Then I'd temporized by saying to myself that Heimdall would only be replaced by someone like him.

Sooner or later, and probably sooner, I was going to have to make up my mind. What was I going to do? And how?

As I struggled over the questions, and automatically knocked off the gauntlet repair in front of me, Verdis glided in with the warmth of a blizzard and smiled. "I'm glad you're still here." Her smile wasn't genuine because her black eyes weren't smiling with her mouth.

She twisted her body to flip her heavy red hair back over her shoulders.

"So am I, I guess," I answered, smiling a phony smile to match hers.

"Have you heard the rumors?"

"Rumors?"

"Facts, actually," admitted Verdis. "Frey's been charged with 'High Treason.' "

"What?" I was afraid of what was coming next.

"The Tribunes placed snoops around the Tower. They have frames of Frey rifling desks and recovering snoops of his own. He swears it's a plot, that he's been framed."

"When did this get out?"

"Last night. Hearing is set for late this afternoon. Heimdall is demanding that Freyda not sit on the Tribunal. It's a mess." With that, her smile became real.

"You're pleased," I noted.

"Not displeased, but I never thought Frey had the brains to think up something like that."

I decided to muddy the waters. "He doesn't. Nor the mechanical talent to handle snoops."

"Sounding awfully certain, Loki."

I shrugged. "I've no great love for Frey, but he's either telling the truth or someone else is in it with him."

Verdis pursed her lips. "Could be, could be. And who might that be?"

"Verdis, I'm scarcely up on intrigue. As you so pointedly reminded me at our last meeting, I bury myself away from reality. You already know the answer. You just want me to answer for you. Count me out, thank you."

She shook her head. "Loki, you amaze me. The biggest scandal in centuries—one of the Guard caught plotting, and you want out." She glared and mimicked my voice. "Count me out. It's getting a bit complicated. Yes, count me out, Verdis."

I chuckled. Her imitation was good. "Young lady, just what do you want me to do? Go up before the Tribunes and make a declaration? 'I have no basis for my statement, honored Tribunes, except I *do* know Frey is a mechanical

idiot and incapable of higher thought. So he either didn't
do what you've charged him with or he's someone's dupe.'
Is that what you want, Verdis?"

She stamped her foot on the glowstone flooring. "Loki,
you're impossible! I don't know whether you practice
density or if it comes naturally. If you can think that all
up, everyone already has. Who handles almost all the
microcircuitry? You do! And Heimdall and his goon
squad will be down shortly to take you into protective
custody, at least as soon as he takes over Domestic Affairs
because Frey has been relieved of duty. And good luck,
because you're either the culprit or Heimdall's way of
getting out of the mess he's made. I suppose you'll sit here
and wait, like always."

She turned and marched toward the ramps.

I figured it would take Heimdall a little longer to act
on his conclusion than Verdis, but I wasn't pleased.

I left the repairs stacked around the work table and
pulled out the copy of my cultural meddling print-out.

My request had been coded in increasing order of difficulty, that was, which changes could have been made more
quickly, followed by those which would take more time
and more time-dives.

The diving was bound to become more difficult than
directed by the Data Banks information because I intended
to point the finger of Time at the Guard and at Query,
which would require additional dives and improvisations
to put the blame where it belonged.

Brendan came flying in. "Loki! Get out of here! Heimdall's headed down the ramp with the Strike Force."

"Thanks." I meant it. "Now get out of here before they
drag you in as a scapegoat."

Brendan got out.

Fight now or later? My gut said now. Common sense
said later. After all the planning and all the information-
gathering, I was still getting pushed around, rushed.

I jammed the print-out into my jumpsuit, grabbed the
plates from the bottom drawer and slid straight undertime
from the Maintenance Hall to the Aerie.

Concealing my ability to do that was secondary at that
stage.

Standing in the Aerie, I surveyed my small nest, from the
permaglass to the stores of destruction, the power cells,
the equipment I had gathered over the seasons.

I had been considering action for years, putting it off, planning and replanning in my dreams, but I was down to a decision point, with Heimdall close behind. I could sneak out into the stars or strike out at what the Guard had become with Heimdall.

Maybe Heimdall was more the Guard than I was, but it mattered little at this point.

I had wondered why he didn't arrange my death when I was unconscious after nearly losing my arm in the shark mission. I concluded it wouldn't have done to have the wounded hero die mysteriously after braving and surmounting the perils of the past, particularly when there was a good chance the sharks would get me anyway if I tried to complete the mission.

Heimdall must have figured he had it both ways. If I didn't return, he was well rid of me. If I refused to go, my image would have been tarnished enough to remove my influence.

I shook myself. The time for dreaming and speculation was past.

As I contemplated the wild scheme I had hatched, I changed from the black Guard jumpsuit into something else, glancing down at the river and the deep canyons from time to time as I did.

With a start, I realized I had changed into a totally red outfit. That fit.

I would challenge the fires of Time, perhaps whatever gods of Time might be, and red was my color. Red for the fires that burned within.

XIX

The name at the top of my list was Altara IV, supposedly the planet where the time-changes would be the easiest to make.

Wrist gauntlets in place, eternasteel tablets in the carrying case slung under my shoulder, I squared myself for the first of the time-dives with which I would wrench Query's history into a different mold.

I slipped into the undertime with scarcely a ripple, hardly aware of the mind-chill.

The back-time for which I was diving contained a turning point. All histories have them, a place where an "almost" culture might have emerged. Given a push at the right times, or a mailed fist on the opposition, the prognosis for events leading to high-tech development was favorable.

On Altara IV a bronze age evolution on the small island continent had been wiped out by the invasion of a barbaric bunch of ax-wielders who outnumbered the lizard people of the island ten to one and who never bothered to settle on the island continent, but continued their wanderings into oblivion.

My first break-out was to locate the barbarian encampment, and after three scans through likely twilights, I found campfires scattered around the sand bars and the twisting land bridge that led over the horizon to the land I had chosen to protect.

With a skip-flick-flick-flick through the undertime, I centered on the narrowest segment of the unstable rock and sand that composed the causeway.

The destruction was simple enough. I tossed the small anti-matter capsule toward the land bridge below and departed undertime. The sand erupted; the fire spewed heavenward; and the waters rushed into the new channel that would block the island continent from the mainland.

And I flamed into view over the camps of the ax-wielders.

And in the twilight the god of fire appeared to his people, and from thence to their enemies. The lightnings were his cloak, and the sparks dropped like the rains of winter, and the enemies of his people knew him not, for the god of fire had long been absent from his place.

The multitudes of the enemy did not bow down, nor did they cover their eyes, nor show any sign of respect.

And the god of fire was angered, and his lightnings, they rained upon the unbelievers, and few were spared.

Their screams spread upon the night and were not heard, for they had not believed. They had seen and had not seen; they had been shown god and did not worship.

The night was as day, and the lightnings struck the land as the hammers of the smith pound upon the forge, and there was heat, and many of the waters bubbled and seethed.

And the people of the island, the chosen ones, kneeled upon hard rocks and marveled, and were amazed. By the hammers of the god were they astounded, and they worshiped, and then, then did the god of fire put aside his lightnings and depart.

With a shiver, I slid undertime along the chill wind of the time-change I had created, riding the creaking surges forward.

A city shimmered wth lights, beckoning through the time-tension barrier.

I answered the call and broke-out.

The city section I saw first was squalid even in the night, gas lights throwing shadows across low stone huts.

I skip-slid into the following day and toward the harbor, looking for a warship, certain of finding one.

Not one, but a squadron, a small fleet, powered by some

steam-fire system, attested to by the smokestacks. Crude metal plating and gun ports proclaimed they were intended for combat.

The god of time and fire arose from his slumbers, and in the twilight of that evening gathered his thunderbolts that the ships of that king, and the pride of that people, be brought down to the fishes of the sea, and along with the vessels, also the soldiers and sailors who defied the god of time by their blasphemies.

For no harbor was yet safe from the god of fire, and no city escaped his judgment; and his judgment was, and it was that the warships of the sea should be no longer. And raised he his mighty arm and collected the flames of the sun and the lightnings of the storms and once more, as he had in the past, made the night as day, and brighter than the noontime it was as the fires fell from the heavens unto the ships and the waters. And the ships were no more.

The people were sore afraid and remembered the tales of old and the prophecies they had mocked, and they prostrated themselves before their god and prayed for his forgiveness.

Unto them who prayed was their god merciful and upon the black rock by the waters which still seethed gave unto his people his holy tablet, and departed then the god of fire upon the lightnings and the fires.

Where one fleet sailed must have sailed another, if not several, and I began a quick slide search of Altara IV.

In my haste, I was not strictly impartial, searching only for warships of apparently different origin.

And unto the enemies of his people visited also the god of fire and rained upon their vessels also the fires of the sun and the lightnings of the storms. And those vessels also perished.

The change-winds around Altara IV moaned more loudly as history changed into para-history and para-history

became history, and as I rode those winds further fore-
time.

I whisked through local centuries in an instant to break
from the undertime into objective time. Differences were
evident, with canals, intensive cultivation, and the lines of
what might have been quick-transit systems all visible
from my commanding view. Those were not what I
needed.

I slid undertime and scanned the planet, hunting for the
energy concentrations that must have existed. They did.

Three powerplants were ideally spaced, and I girded
myself for the next step.

*For in their pride, his people had builded themselves
towers to store the fires of the sun and to trap the lightnings of the storms, and to have each do their bidding.*

*And they said, we are like the god of our fathers,
mastering the fires of the sun and the lightnings of the
storms, and flying like the eagles.*

*But the god of fire was displeased, and in the space of
an instant hurled down the towers of power, and they were
stone and dust.*

*Yet the people were still proud, and in their pride, dared
their god and the heavens, and, behold, crossed the skies
faster than eagles, and their craft of the air made the sun
stand motionless in its course.*

*And a craft of the air approached the god of fire even
as he had toppled the towers, and flew nigh unto the god
and turned not.*

*The almighty one drew unto himself, and from the
thunderbolts of the storm made first a signal; so might all
the peoples of the earth know his displeasure, and the red
of his fires surpassed the green of the sky.*

*And those who had forgotten recalled again the tales of
their god, and trembled, and were fearful.*

*Another sign displayed the god, and yet another, for to
warn that flier who had dared the heavens after the fashion
of his fellows and challenged the god of fire.*

*At last fled the defiant one, but the lord of fire suffered
not that his servant should escape, and he gathered unto
him his flames greater than the sun of the noon, and cast
down the flier who fled.*

*Many feared, yet saw not; because the people did fear
and did see, but understood not what they saw, the god
went to the high place of his peoples where gathered the
most mighty, and so cast it down, making the hills like the
plains, flat and smooth as finest ice, and in the center of
that holy place, left there the last of his holy tablets that
his people might read, and reading, might learn what was
to lie before them.*

And he was pleased.

Departing in a column of flame, I rode the screaming,
wrenching change-winds for para-instants before racing
ahead, back to Query, back to my Aerie.

I shuddered, but I could not feel for those who had
suffered—not and still redress the balance.

Standing over the cliffs, my Aerie seemed poised over
the canyon of destruction, but I knew it was all illusion.

My power packs were dead, and I replaced them.

My supply of miniature antimatter bombs was depleted,
and I restocked.

One gauntlet was fused, and the skin beneath red and
tender, but I willed it to heal, and it did.

I looked around my Aerie, my weapons' storeroom,
cluttered and jumbled with implements of destruction,
before setting out for the second wrench I would make in
the machinery of time.

I replaced the eternasteel tablets with their message, star
chart, and formula in my carrying case and pulled on another gauntlet over my healed right wrist.

Three swigs of firejuice, a battle ration cube, and I was
prepared to dive. Already I could sense the change-winds
in the back distance over the curve of time, blowing toward the "now" of Query, and I knew I had much to do
before they arrived with their messages.

After a stint as the Lord of Destruction I would become
the Lord of Creation, before I donned the mantle of the
Lord of Destruction once again.

I time-dived and slid down the black branches into the
back-time, three hundred centuries or so, and out to
Heaven IV.

Heaven IV was not on the print-out I had gotten from
the Data Banks. That alone might have kept Freyda,

Eranas, Kranos, and Heimdall buffeting in the change-winds, even if they had gotten a copy of the list.

I forced my way down the back-time-paths toward the planet of the angels, with a specific aim in mind—an angel nursery.

Although the term nursery sounded formal, it wasn't, because the place was more of a sheltered cliff on one of the tallest peaks I'd ever seen, but overlooking, as always, the goblins' Hell smoldering far below under the dark clouds and seething heat.

For the god of time and fire had come unto the place called Heaven, to take his due from the angels and from that mount where the children were gathered.

Yet a single angel protested and raised his lance against the god of fire, and that angel was no more, for against the thunderbolts of the god he could not prevail.

And from that place called Heaven the god of fire departed, time and time again, carrying the children, two by two, to a far planet, until gathered there were two score and more.

And to guard them, against the cold and against danger, further provided were they with angels to succor them, for they grieved and their hearts were heavy, and they were alone.

The planet on which I had placed those uprooted angels had a slightly heavier gravity than Heaven IV, and the atmosphere was thinner. Intelligent life had not yet evolved, but the biosystems were compatible.

Statistically, a long-shot, but I *knew* it would work out. That is the business of gods.

Flying would not work well, except for short distances, and more metal meant a tech culture.

That I did not intend to leave to chance. I slid fore-time on the first murmur of the second change-wind I had blown into our stuffy corner of the galaxy.

Twenty centuries up were towns, small cities, and beasts of burden, fields, fires—enough for a first appearance.

I lit up the sky at twilight over the square of a town,

cast a few thunderbolts into the town center, and deposited a tablet.

After repeating the performance over a more distant village, I then departed up the line.

I did not expect much more from the change-wind, but the murmurs were louder as I rode forward, peering from the undertime at the changing surface of the planet.

At fifty centuries fore-time from the objective time of the transplant, I found ships upon the shallow oceans, and laden power wagons upon roads.

And the fallen angels had prospered, but in their prosperity had disregarded the words of their god and had taken up new ways, and sailed the seas in ships of metal and turned the soil with metal beasts, and had in truth forgotten their god.

Yet he laughed, and his laughter shook the forests, and drew thunder from the skies.

And the fallen angels stopped, and they listened, for they feared, for the sound was strange unto them.

But the strangeness of that laughter did not turn them; they listened and did not hear.

And their god was angered, and in his anger cast his thunderbolts upon the highways and upon the wagons that traveled them and upon the seas and the ships that sailed thereon, and put his mark upon the very stones of the hills ere he departed.

He waited in the shadows of time unbeknownst, and bided his time until the millennium had come.

For again, the people who had been angels had forsaken their god and were proud in their handiworks and in their contrivances, and raised their wings against their god.

The god of fire strode across the heavens and flattened the cities, and struck the ships from the seas, even those which were mighty, and picked the ships of the air from the skies, and twisted the iron ways into forms that confounded their makers.

All that and more did the god of fire, who laughed at what he had wrought.

For lo, the fallen angels did not cower, nor were they ashamed, nor were they filled with fear, but instead shook their wings against the sky and against the fires.

And they seized the eternal tablets of the god and were filled with wrath, and in their hearts they plotted and directed their ways against the very stars.

The winds of change wailed, and reached into the space beyond the firmament and behind the time and twisted both and brought chill and the cold that was beyond chill onto the gales that reached even unto the home of the god of fire.

XX

"So now you're a god?"

I realized it was Sammis I had tied up in the slope chair and linked with a unit chain to the Aerie itself. He probably could have escaped, but had waited.

I shook my head. The stillness was deafening, and it seemed like I was two different people. Maybe a poor way to explain and it didn't excuse anything. Just easier, I guessed, to destroy and remold world cultures while letting the god-side of me take the blame.

"Hardly, just doing what's necessary."

"Eagle crap!" he snorted. "I saw the look on your face when you surprised me. You came in here like the God of Fire. Wryan would call it psychotic dissociation or some such."

I swigged some firejuice and finished off two battle-ration cubes. One was a full day's nourishment, but diving like I'd been doing was *work*.

The change-winds were blowing.

"Really much easier to manipulate poor unsuspecting sapiences than face the real problem, isn't it, God Loki?"

Sammis or not, I could have punched him. He was right, at least about it being easier to deal with out-time cultures, and I might as well face it. I'd have to sooner or later.

"I didn't notice you doing much about it, great original Tribune."

"You may be right," he sighed. "That's a problem we all have, those of us who are sane, Wyran says. Life is too easy to face the hard decisions, and so we plan and watch and wait and hope, and are the compliant victims of the schemers and the madmen. I'd hoped you were different, especially after your head-on confrontations with Heimdall."

I was ready to go and was replacing my power cells, another burnt-out gauntlet, packing up more eternasteel tablets, and finishing off the firejuice in the beaker.

"What do you mean?"

"You're strong enough to take on the entire Guard in a single battle, I sometimes think, and win, and yet you never raised your voice after you came back from Hell, never said a word."

"And neither did anyone else," I reminded him. Hell, they had all hung back and wanted me to do their fighting for them.

I swung on the carrying case.

"How will you stop Heimdall? He'll undo everything you do."

I halted, caught in mid-stride, but both riddles were crystal clear, oh so clear, and with them, the response to Sammis's questions.

Sammis insisted I was a god. So did most of the Guard, both those who supported me and those who opposed me. And with that lineup, I had assumed the choice was simple—either you're a god or you're not. *I* knew I wasn't, not in terms of my own definition of a god. But the definitions weren't the real question, and I'd been hung up on definitions, just like everyone else.

Without even understanding, Sammis had flamed right to the point. "Who" wasn't the question. Nor "what," but rather "how." Like "how are you going to deal with what you are?" Like "how will you stop Heimdall?"

That second "how" I could answer. Now. The other would come, had to come, and soon. But first—Heimdall.

"Actions speak louder than words. Or definitions, Sammis."

"Wait!"

His voice was lost as I slid across the skies of Query to the Tower, glittering as it rose from the Square to challenge the noon sun.

Heimdall could not undo what I had done without his tools, his sources of information. Without them, he could not locate the turning points, nor give temporal turning points to the Guards he would send to undo what I had done and would yet do.

I ducked under the edge of time and broke-out in Assignments, flaming, lightnings gathered to my chest, but only Giron stood at the main Assignments console, his mouth opening wide at my appearance.

"Out!" I ordered him, for I did not wish him harm.

Without fanfare, I unleashed my energies across the consoles to leave fused metal, twisted plastic and acrid smoke as witnesses to my visit.

Assignments was the beginning, only the start, for the information remained in the Data Banks.

Below the deepest depths of the Tower foundations, levels below the Maintenance Hall, locked in behind walls that would halt a battle cruiser, were the memory banks, the lattice crystals that held the information amassed through millennia.

I bypassed the walls, breaking-out inside the sterile confines, skip-sliding down the dim rows of lattices, flinging lightnings before me and dropping antimatter cubes behind. With a final toss at the core, I ducked fully under-time and slid into the sunlit sky above the Tower.

Though the muffled sounds of explosions rumbled through the ground and the Tower trembled, the massive, buried, and time-protected walls surrounding the physical data storage area held firm. The Data Banks themselves had not been so lucky, I knew.

More as a gesture than anything, I gathered more power from the air around me and flung a last thunderbolt at the steps in front of the South Portal and scored the glowstones with a line of black fire that would live within the glowstones for eons.

I turned my attention to the past I must create anew. I needed to choose from the possibilities left on my list, for the moments of hard decision would be coming sooner than I had anticipated.

Heimdall and his cohorts would be grouping already, and the schemer would be plotting any way he could to stop my efforts.

Mighty gods had deceived themselves, and I was only a man, whatever immortality, whatever weapons of the gods I might bear, whatever delusions it might take to remake a small corner of the galaxy. To myself, I would have to answer, not for what I might be called, or for the names I refused, but for what I had done and would yet do.

Along the way, I had a score to settle, somewhat indirectly, which might cloud the change-winds more.

I time-dived from the sunlight and sky above the Tower toward Gurlennis, back until, flicking in and out, back and forth, I could sense another link to Query, a figure breaking-out into the sky above nomads' tents, where gentle wanderers camped—or at least those ancestors of the green-bronzed philosopher I had met in a para-time instant, an instant that was not and would not ever be, yet would.

To break into another's past time-line was a feat thought impossible, but determined as I was to do it, I broke and bent the fabric of those instants to my will.

And the purple of the night was sundered into fragments, and each fragment was a song, and the peoples of that time bowed and prostrated themselves then before the song; for not only was there music in the heavens, but fire.

For the god of fire, he who was called Loki, raised his arm against the other, who was called Zealor.

And Zealor called upon Loki and begged of him mercy, and asked that his days not be numbered; but Loki the god of fire was not dissuaded, and turned the lightnings of fire and the powers of time against Zealor, and Zealor was no more.

The wanderers who beheld the fires that exceeded the stars saw, and covered their eyes, and were filled with awe.

He who was called Loki laughed, and the sound of his laughter brought waves to still lakes, and caused the leaves of the trees to tremble. When he had laughed and lowered his hand, behold, where once there had been a mount was a holy place, and thereupon the god of fire placed his holy writ for this chosen people, lest they forget.

As I dropped back undertime, shivering, the die was cast. After having killed my own, knowingly and deliberately, no matter how noble the reason, the time of denying my own responsibilities, my own failures to take stock, had passed, and passed forever.

Sertis, good old stable, always mid-tech Sertis, was next, and the revolution of fire would strike the unexpected to fan the no-longer-gentle winds of time-change into the hurricane of time.

The king-emperors of Sertis had ruled because they controlled the water, and thus, the minds and power of Sertis. Water enough existed, but it was locked into the polar caps and the plateau glaciers.

I headed for the fiftieth century before my own birth.

The god of fire appeared and struck his lances upon the ice that had been, that had crowned the far poles, and the ice and snow were no more, but became as boiling water, and broke their boundaries and sundered the mountains that confined them.

Pillars of fire and soot were there, also, of red and of black, and when the ruler of the place called Sertis felt his throne quake, asked that ruler of his generals the cause.

And they knew not, save that the fires of Hell had appeared at the far poles, and that the ice had departed, and the water had come.

Then, the soldiers of the armies were afraid, and heeded not their commanders, nor the voice of their ruler.

And when the priests appeared before the assembled peoples, neither were they heard, but were offered by the peoples as sacrifices to the god of fire; and the god listened and left unto them his holy book that his will might be done.

The winds of time-change screamed as I crossed them on my time-vault back to Query.

Would I exist when I was done? Had I become as a god with no beginning and no end?

From the undertime the planet Query would be shaken, twisted, bent like a leaf in a tempest, assaulted by the change winds out of time. For each wind from the pasts I had altered would create its own winds, and the second winds would blow unto the third winds, and no man or god would know his place while blew the wild winds of time.

In and out of time, solid as I approached, stood my Aerie, as stood the Tower of Immortals.

"And now?" asked Sammis as I broke-out and began to replenish my stores of destruction.

"The rest will come, Sammis. The rest will come."

I noticed he was free of the chain. He had been waiting for me, and he was waiting for me to speak again.

"By the way," I asked, "how and why did you and Wryan fake her death? Little lapse of tense there, old god. Were you the one who provided all the behind the scenes assistance? And why?"

In retrospect, all of it seemed so clear. Only Sammis could have maneuvered so cleverly. Sammis gently provided suggestions, and all the Guard listened. Stupid of me not to have seen it. Wryan planned, and Sammis executed, even that first test to determine my capabilities. I saw not just what Sammis was, for he was Sammis Olon, but the others—my parents, and Baldur.

Why had it taken so long for me to see the obvious? How my parents had stayed on Query long enough to give me what I needed. Or how and why Baldur had left for Terra to create legends and to shape all the differing Terran cultures with facets of our own, and with his insistence on the importance of understanding technology. Or how—the list was long, too long.

"It wasn't that hard, Loki," answered Sammis, who stood there nearly forgotten, "not with all the distractions you provided. Wryan and I were ready to leave earlier, probably would have, except when you came along we kept hoping—"

Sammis wasn't that pure, and I cut him off. "How many did you test? Over how many years? How many were too scared to dive again? Old god, don't dwell too much on idealism! What kind of will does it take to follow the same course for centuries upon centuries? What kind of power is that?"

All the time I was talking, I was replenishing and watching the man I had finally accepted as Sammis Olon.

Time, subjectively and objectively, was short, and I girded myself for another dive, another series.

"Goodbye, old god. Where's Wryan?"

"Where she's always been, grand-great-grandson and young god. She and I wish you the best. If you can accept yourself, no more, no less, you'll make it."

That stopped me. Great-great-grandson?

"Great-great-grandson?"

"You know, Loki, you kept suppressing the things you didn't want to know. That's the brute strength of youth, but the same thing that will keep you from greatness—if you let it."

He smiled, then went on. "Your mother is Wryan's and my great-granddaughter, and if you were told it once, you were told it a hundred times."

As he said it, the memories were there—"great-granddaughter of Sammis Olon," the stories of the Guard—and other remembrances: looking up at someone crying, seeing a look that might have been fear on a face looming above me.

As I remembered, felt the memories toppling into place, I could hear the change-winds howling down toward the Now like night eagles swooping in for the kill.

"Your saving grace," continued Sammis implacably, "has been your willingness to undergo punishment for your mistakes. Accept yourself and keep that willingness, and it may be enough to protect us all—all of us, mortals, Immortals, and you."

Sammis delivered the words quietly, as if he were stating well-known facts or established truths.

"Where's Wryan?" I was grasping at straws.

"We'll be watching. It's a wide universe. Treat it kindly."

He vanished as I watched. He was diving to Wryan.

I shook my head to clear it. Duty, if I could call it that, would be to finish what I started before the change winds unleashed their all-too-long-thwarted fury on Query.

I could not meddle with other cultures as devastatingly as I had on Sertis, on Altara IV, or the offshoot of Heaven IV. Time was short, its noose tightening.

I had eleven tablets left. I intended to deposit each on a different planet, each in one of the time/locales identified by the sundered Data Banks as promising for a high-tech development, knowing that my very appearance in a cloud of flame would spur something.

Midgard was first, close-time, and I dropped the tablet on the ceremonial steps of the Asgard, thunderbolting the statue of the Serpent as I did.

The other nine were a blur, and when I struggled across the bucking black time-paths to the last, Weindre, and forced my way into the Technarchial Center to deposit the last eternasteel tablet, I could hear the creaks in the warp of reality while still undertime.

As another last gesture, I etched the black thunderbolt

across the front of the Technarchate's Fountain of Power and placed the tablet under it.

For better or worse, the Guards' corner of the galaxy would not be the same. And no one would undo what I had done.

Hell and Timefire! No Guard, no God, but Loki, could tread the paths of time in those instants against the wild change-winds. And next would I assure none would so tread after the winds passed and the worlds settled into their new histories.

Some things I could not have avoided, no matter how I pretended, and some matters were not to be handled by stealth. Nor would I have had the appellation "coward" stand in the memory of those who cared.

I broke-out in Assignments.

Heimdall was absent.

"Loki!"

Nicodemus reached for a stunner.

I knocked it clear of his hand with a trickle of fire from the gauntlets. Not exactly, for I looked at my wrists, and the gauntlets were fused metal circling my lower forearms, mere metal decorations. I knew I no longer neeeded them, but I left them in place.

"Where's Heimdall?"

"Tribunes' spaces," answered Nicodemus.

Before, always before, I had avoided the Tribunes' spaces, but power blocks or no, I did not intend to do so then, and I did not, smashing through the physical and para-time barriers as if they did not exist, hurling myself into the center of the once-sacred Tower.

Heimdall, Eranas, Freyda, and Kranos stood around a black crystal table, waiting.

"Greetings, fallen gods, and Heimdall, whom I shall call false god for the sake of convenience."

"Proud of yourself, Loki?" That was Kranos. He'd never understand.

"The sons of the father's sons." That was Freyda.

"Why?" demanded Eranas, in anguish, face twisted. He would never understand either.

Heimdall didn't bother with words. He just pointed and fired. His aim was good, but it didn't matter. I let the energy sheet around me.

I walked toward him, around the black crystal table,

and he leveled another thunderbolt from his gauntlets at me. I gathered the energy to me and kept walking.

I heard Freyda mutter, "Without gauntlets," and she was gone undertime. No matter, she would accept what came, not being one to fight the inevitable.

Heimdall backed away.

Kranos unfroze, jumped at me, so slowly he seemed poised in midair. I dropped under him and snapped his legs like toothpicks, broke his back with two hands. He fell in a heap and was as still as death.

Eranas stood motionless, the blackness growing in his eyes, as I moved step by step toward Heimdall, who retreated step by step until his back was against the time-protected wall.

Heimdall, the honorable, the Counselor, the Guard who would be Tribune, turned the full power of his gauntlets upon me. And though I could feel the power sheeting around me, it was as nothing, and I took another step.

As both gauntlets separately had failed to destroy me, he linked them together and blasted the thunderbolts of Hell toward my face. They flared past me as if they were no more than smoke, and in the slowness of that Now, I took another step toward the false god who would have been king of a battered galaxy. The universe has no gods, and while some have the power of gods, those who thought they were indeed were mad. As I had been mad.

He lifted his hands to strike me, and with two fingers I crushed his wrist into powder.

Heimdall, the once-mighty, the schemer, the demi-god who would have ruled gods and lifted himself, gasped once, gasped twice, squared his shoulders, and dropped his arms.

"Do your worst, with your hands dripping blood and fire! Do your worst and feel righteous in your slaughter!"

I broke his neck with a single blow.

Silence.

I took in the black room, the crystal table of time, for that was what it was, a tool of the Tribunes sheltered and used in secret.

I stared at the black crystal, willed it to shatter, and it did, the falling shards themselves exploding into dust that was no more.

Eranas, the failed, who looked and would not see, who saw and would not act, stood rooted in his own private forever Now, his vision locked into a universe that soon would never have been, blackness creeping over his soul.

He, too, would die when the change-winds whistled around the Tower and stirred the silent dust of time, for his mind could not bear the weight of its own past.

Some things I had to finish, and I slid straight for Freyda's mountain hideaway, the one overlooking Quest that had been in her family for millennia.

As I broke out of the undertime, the invincibility broke also, and I was scared, or sore afraid, as my former god-side might have said. I was sore afraid, for the changes I had wrought could have been far beyond my own conception. How small that conception was just began to dawn.

Freyda was sitting on the hidden balcony, watching a hawk circle over the valley in the afternoon sun, sitting a bit too upright to be at as much ease as she meant to convey. She acknowledged my entry without turning, staring at the city below, still wearing her Tribune's black, star and all.

"I assume that's you, Loki—god of fire, god of destruction and madness."

"You expected me."

"Sooner or later. I was one of the few who didn't underestimate you. Gods take longer to grow up."

I didn't correct her assessment of me as a god. For Freyda, in some ways, things were simple. Either I was a god, or I wasn't. And I'd unconsciously accepted her frame of reference, until Sammis's questions, while somehow knowing it wasn't correct and fighting the simplistic definition.

But now the definitions didn't matter. The actions, my actions, mattered.

"Why didn't you stop me then?"

"Ten years ago it was too late to stop you. Your mother said it was too late to stop you when you were born. You don't think people didn't try? They just started too late—after you were born. The entire Guard couldn't have destroyed you after you returned from Hell. Sammis was convinced you went only as a penance. One way or another, with your birth, the Guard we knew was doomed."

It might have been—only I hadn't known it. After all, up until a season before, I hadn't understood most of what I was doing. I told Freyda that.

"Loki, don't you see? It didn't matter. If the Tribunes had strangled you at birth, the guilt would have rotted us from within, at least those of us who counted. If you had let yourself die on Hell, or if we had, no Guard would have ever trusted the Tribunes or Counselors again. And what about you, the real you? Have you ever really been forced to do what you didn't agree to?"

"I'm sure I have," I answered, but Freyda didn't go on.

The sun flashed through her hair, and the effect as she turned was the instant impression of silver, of age before her time, which disappeared even as I noted it.

"Sit down, young god. Sit down and watch the end of our era and the beginning of yours."

I sat.

"What's the insistence on the god business?" I protested. "I'm no god." I knew how she thought, but I had to try.

"Oh, not in the theological sense, but with your powers of mind over matter, in practical terms it doesn't make much difference. You throw thunderbolts without bothering to use microcircuits, walk on air and water, heal yourself and probably others, destroy with a glance, go when and where you please regardless of the barriers raised against you, and you cast down and raise up whole planets and cultures."

Her dark eyes pinned me where I sat.

"Now. You define a god for me," she finished.

What could I say that she would accept? Yes, I could do all that she described, all that she listed and more. But I was certainly not all-knowing, nor all-understanding, nor even all-powerful.

"Then, I guess you'll have to call me a god."

Her attitude made one decision, or sealed it for me. Living legends, particularly those reputed to be gods, never live up to their image. Now, I would have to follow, in my own way, the example of my parents, of Baldur, of Wryan, and strike out from Query, always treading the tight time-path of accepting my power along with my own limitations.

Freyda turned full-face to me. "How does it feel to destroy the oldest institution in galactic history, Loki? Does it make you feel grand?"

That was the first real bitterness I'd heard from Freyda.

I shook my head, not caring if Freyda believed me or not, thinking more of Verdis, Loragerd, Narcissus, and the

others who still believed in the shining destiny of a new
Guard rising from the ashes of the old.

The systems I had unshackled would not be put back in
the ancient bottle of temporal restraint cast so long ago by
the Triumvirate. I had seen to that. Yes, I had seen to that.

Freyda, the last of the Tribunes, sat on the balcony of
her retreat in the hills overlooking Quest and pointed to
the City of Immortals.

"Can't you feel it?"

I glanced at Freyda, seated in her sculpted chair and
gazing out at Quest from her protected terrace. So crisp
she was, every white-blond hair in place, golden skin
smoother than glowstone, black eyes glittering.

"Can't you feel it?"

The change-winds were boiling just under the horizon
of Now, their black chill building.

I nodded, and in that instant when the winds of time-
change struck, everything went out of focus, from Freyda,
the firs framing the view of Quest, to the Tower of Immortals rising from the central Square. And the wind of
time howled; the icicles marched up my spine as I stood in
the sun, the golden sun that hid behind the clouds that
were not there; the very ground trembled; and black
cracks in the fabric of the instant splintered across the sky.

The histories, the might-have-beens, the was and the
were, the is and the are, warred upon each other. Through
the black windows of time hung in front of us, battles
never fought were fought, all at once, all together, and
the new turning points of history and para-history, of
space and para-space, were hammered out in the fires of
para-time.

Freyda sat, her face frozen, for she did not see the
windows of the brand-new past opening into the new
Now.

In one window, and I called it that, for what else could
I call a vision of a past that was inscribing itself on the
present as I watched, a ship swathed in light burst over
the eastern horizon and streaked on a downward course
toward Quest.

From the central Square rose the Tower that glittered
with the muted light of a thousand suns, soaring out of the
perfect lawns and walks, out of the rows of scarlet fireflowers.

Before that first ship reached the city, the cool green

air of that instant-past Query was wrenched apart with the sounds of a second ship. That one, tubular and black, somehow shrouded in darkness in full sunlight, drove at the city from out of the west, barely clearing the Bard-walls as it plunged toward Quest.

I looked again at Freyda. She was motionless, staring at the City of Immortals, waiting to see the results of the mighty cataclysm she felt, but had no sight to watch, for the windows of time were closed to her.

She did not see, for all her looking, for all her feeling. She did not turn as the ship of light unleashed lightnings at suddenly deserted streets.

That vision did not happen in the Now, was only a picture of what had transpired in a past we never knew, but was *the* past from henceforth.

Under the light of the golden sun as it emerged from the clouds that never were, I was cold, not just from the chill of the change-winds that swept Query, for they had passed into the future, twisting and shaping it into new patterns.

No. I was cold—and not just from the winds of change.

I gazed, and beneath us on the plain that was suddenly filled with the rubble of old buildings still rose the Tower of Immortals. The remainder of Quest, a city razed around it, was jumbled humps and lumps.

Yet around that wreckage wound the ways and walks of a wide park, and fireflowers bloomed. There was order, and there was power without the arrogance of the old Guard. Query still challenged time, but not to subdue others for the mere sake of conquest.

The Tower stood, as a memorial, as did the rubble, both reminders of a past that had needed change—and that had been changed.

And while the dead, such as Heimdall, Eranas, and Kranos, were still dead, the others, Loragerd, Verdis, Narcissus, Brendan, would chart the new destiny of Query. They deserved that honor, and that challenge, and without my heavy hand.

All that I knew, and though I could not say how, I accepted that knowledge, for I was of Query, and would always be so, in whatever corner of the universe I found myself.

A question remained.

Freyda and I stood on her balcony, a balcony changed

slightly, but the same, and with the world changed around us, we were yet the same.

"Us?" I asked.

Freyda understood.

"Because you made this present, this Now, you cannot be changed. If you were, it would not be. I suppose I am unchanged because you have willed it so, young god, or because of some other quirk of time, about which we know so little. That is both a gift and a curse."

She smiled faintly, oh so faintly, and her smile said, "Goodbye."

"What will you do in your new universe, young god?"

I did not know, only understanding what I would not do. Understanding that I would not play god without accepting the burdens and the responsibilities that went with it. Understanding, too, with bittersweet certainty, that I would fail at times to meet that commitment, and that even those with the power of gods can fail.

I must make a final jump, a final slide across the skies of Query, to the Aerie, which remained, untouched. A thin layer of dust blanketed the glowstones, the empty rooms, as though I had left them long ago.

Under Seneschal, I let the afternoon wane, the twilight rise around me for my last goodbye before I ventured forth into the galaxy I remade, out from Quest, out from Query. Out following all those who had left without the trumpets of fire I summoned, out after Baldur and his Terrans, out after Ayren Bly, out after my parents, out—the list was longer than I knew, with no real need to go on.

The first star of night, the night before the dawn, appeared.

Greetings, Baldur.

Greetings, Wryan . . . wherever you are.